CHARLIE FORD MEETS SECRET AGENT MAN

CHARLIE FORD MEETS SECRET AGENT MAN

CHARLIE FORD MEETS SECRET AGENT MAN

By
J.D. Tynan

A Better Be Write Publisher
New Jersey

CHARLIE FORD MEETS
SECRET AGENT MAN

All Rights Reserved © 2006
By J.D. Tynan

No part of this book may be reproduced or transmitted in any form or by any means, graphic, electronic, or mechanical, including photocopying, recording, taping, or by any information storage retrieval system, without the permission in writing from the publisher.

A Better Be Write Publisher, LLC

For information:
A Better Be Write Publisher, LLC
1100 Buck Street, Suite 110
Millville, NJ 08332
www.abetterbewrite.com

ISBN: 0-9771971-5-8
ISBN: 978-0-9771971-5-6

Book Cover designed by Carl Cone

Printed in the United States of America

~Dedication~

To the Connecticut nannies

For the endless hours, the nights you spend awake with ill children and for the mornings you endure chaos just to make a child feel loved. In a sometimes thankless job, remember, you are making the difference in a child's life and you will never be forgotten.

~Thank You~

A special thank you to my sister, Cyndy.
The first person I told of my insane idea to write a novel. Thank you for your inspiring pep talks, your honesty, and your humor.

To my younger sister, Jenny.
Thanks for your friendship and undying optimism.

Without the lifetime love and support of these amazing women, I wouldn't be who I am today. I love you and am forever grateful that we were created in the same womb.

To Trisha.
Editor extraordinaire. Thanks for your wonderful work editing both my books!

To Janet Evanovich.
Whose website and admission of past failure gave me the courage to try.

To my husband and two children.
Thanks again for letting Mommy go for her dream! I love you too much.

To Maggie.
I know I've said this a hundred times, but thank you. I won't let you down.

www.jdtynan.com

Chapter One

The grass is always greener. Isn't that how the old adage goes? In my case, the meaning is quite literal because the next-door neighbor, Mr. Jenkins, spends his golden years fertilizing, weeding, raking, and aerating his perfectly manicured front lawn. But that's not what I'm talking about. What I'm talking about is how Rick Newman from across the street gawks at Lewis Riley every morning as the man kisses his perfect wife and waves to his two-point-five kids who play with the dog just beyond the white picket fence that lines their yard in a land we all call Suburbia.

Sure, Lewis Riley's life seems wonderful to a singleton like Rick and it wouldn't bother me so much if Lewis didn't do the same damn thing. Just this morning I caught Lewis staring out the window in envy as Rick washed and waxed his Porsche 911, his boat, his matching pair of jet-skis and then turned and kissed his one-night-stand goodbye on the front lawn. Lewis looked as if his tongue was about to fall right out of his slack-jawed mouth. It happens all the time and even I can admit that I look at Jennifer Lopez and think she must have an amazing life. After all, she gets romanced by Hollywood's sexiest hotties. Well, with the exception of the *puffy-guy*. What *was* she thinking? Anyway, she's beautiful and talented and seems genuinely nice. *And* she gets to get married whenever she wants.

The point I'm trying to make here is that I don't think anyone has ever looked at me and thought the grass was greener over at my place. Yes, I hate to say it, but I doubt that Jennifer Lopez has ever uttered the words, "That Charlie Ford has the perfect life."

I'm just feeling sorry for myself because I just dropped my toast on the tile floor. Jelly side down of all things. Hell, my morning couldn't get any worse.

Or so I thought.

"Charlie," my fabulously supportive father yelled down from his den. "Phone."

A man of few words: That is my father. Unless of course, he is preaching to me about how badly I screwed up again. Then he can monologue like the best of them.

"Hello," I mumbled into the phone.

The shrillness of her voice had me holding the phone a good six inches from my ear.

"YOU GOT FIRED!" my mother yelled from the Acapulco deck of *The Love Boat.*

I rolled my eyes so far back into my head, that I actually saw my ass from a completely new perspective.

"Mom," I started to say, but her slurred ranting continued.

"AGAIN?" she finished off; and I swear I heard her slurp down an entire frozen drink in fifteen seconds flat. "Blah, blah, blah."

I stopped listening because Rick was outside waxing his Porsche. I don't know which one I liked looking at more, the black shiny car or the tall, bronze hunk. I stared harder and plastered my nose up against the glass.

It is definitely the car.

"Mom," I had to cut her off because I feared that she might ask me to repeat what she had just said to me. "I have another call," I lied and hung up on my mom.

I'm going to hell.

The guest bathroom of my parents' house is where I showered. Then I made the bed up that they so kindly let me sleep in. I did it so *he* wouldn't have to be reminded that I was actually staying in *his* house. Again. Needless to say, this wasn't the first time I'd come home after losing my job. At least this time, my mother was in the Caribbean with her college sorority sisters; something she does every year to escape my father's lecherous appendages and her job at the hospital. My father is a surgeon. She's a neonatal nurse. They met in the emergency room and it's been love in bloom ever since. It kind of makes me nauseous sometimes.

My first order of business for the day was to walk Ruger. Ruger is my dog when he craps in the yard, and my dad's dog when he's quietly sleeping on the floor. He's half Bull Mastiff and half Rottweiler. He's black and deep chestnut brown, and he's the most magnificent creature I have ever seen. Someday I will do right by him, and I will take him away from these kooky people.

My parents live in a newer subdivision just south of Bend, Oregon. Bend offers an array of outdoor sporting events: Mt. Bachelor for skiing, a myriad of lakes for water sports and more golf courses than I can count. I have never met anyone who has ever had a problem with its clean, crisp air or towering pine trees. It's pretty amazing to live in Bend and I have done it most of my life. With the exception of the past twelve years, of course.

Mr. Hollendale, my former high-school anatomy teacher, lives three houses down and I always make time to stop and chat with him. He's the sexiest fifty-year-old I have ever seen. "Hi." I batted my eyelashes and prayed his wife wasn't home.

"Charlie Ford." He looked happy to see me, but not surprised.

Shit. My dad can't keep a secret to save his life.

"I hear you're back in town for a while." He shook his head as if I had just failed his mid-term.

I felt small all of a sudden.

"Drugs, Charlie?"

Yep. Just as I suspected. I'd been home for approximately...I glanced down at my watch and scowled...twelve whole hours and my father had already told the teacher on me.

"It's not what you think," I tried to explain, but it was like talking to a wall. Brett Hollendale is an upstanding pillar in the community and all, but surely he wanted to hear my side of the story before sending me to the guillotine. "I..."

His sideways glance at his wife pulling into the driveway had me turning to see what he was looking at.

"Mrs. Hollendale," I said through clenched teeth. I've always hated that woman. She is a big....*female dog*, to put it nicely. I smiled and turned on my heel and let Ruger goose her with his slimy snout before yanking on his chain. "Sorry," I mumbled before heading down the street.

Great. Now I felt like the entire neighborhood was watching me from their windows; afraid to come outside because the Fords' drugged-out daughter just got fired.... *again*. "Sorry, Ruger," I said to the dog and headed back home.

My father was on his way to the hospital for a late morning back surgery and I thought I could squeeze in a quick heart-to-heart before he left.

"Dad," I said from behind my bottle of Evian. "I wasn't doing drugs."

"Charlie. I think it's time you went to college."

FUUUCCKKKKK. Okay, a little background about that. When I was seventeen years old, I told my dad that I didn't want to go to college.

He said, "Fine, then join the Army."

I laughed because I thought he was joking.

He glared and I stopped laughing. In fact, I don't think I have laughed in front of him ever since.

That was my father's way of making me do something that I didn't want to do. He knew I hated following orders more than I hated the idea of going to college. And I *did* hate the idea of going to college. My grades were mediocre, I didn't get scholarships like my brothers did and I *did not* want to be a Beaver. *Yuck.* My brothers were both Ducks, but my SAT scores weren't good enough to be a Duck. Good enough to be a Beaver, but not a Duck.

Needless to say, my brothers are both over-achievers and both played football for the Pac-Ten. Josh went on to play arena football in Austria. Dave is now a doctor.

Dad likes Dave the best. Go figure.

Anyway, to make a long story short, I stood my ground, dug my toenails into my Adidas tennis shoes and said, "Fine. Where do I sign up?"

My father's eyeballs actually protruded past the confines of their sockets. I had never seen anything like it before in my life.

I joined the Army a week after I graduated from high school, and here I was twelve-years later, having the same discussion.

"Dad," I warned. "We've been through this before. You can't *make* me go to college."

"Charlie," his head shook in contempt. "You have to grow up eventually."

And eventually I plan to. But not until I'm thirty and I still have three more months until that is going to happen.

"I'll get another job," I said with confidence. After all, I worked for a wonderful agency that had taken wonderful care of me for the past three and a half years. They hadn't let me down yet.

Later that day after my father left, still shaking his head at me for not listening to him, I called Parker Rooney at the agency that often places me.

"What do you mean, '*No?*'" I practically shouted into the phone. "Parker, I wasn't stoned."

"Then why did you tell Mr. Ludlow that?" he asked very skeptically; knowing that no one in their right mind would yell that out as an explanation as to why they had sideswiped another car. It just didn't make sense. Hell, it still didn't make sense to me. But I did it just the same.

It all happened two days ago, in Greenwich, Connecticut. I was taking the twins to see the newest Pooh movie on the big screen and I was driving the fabulous BMW X5—one of those wonderfully posh new SUVs, with leather seats, a retractable sunroof and a DVD to keep the kids happy on long trips.

I loved working for the Ludlow family. I had my own private wing in their mansion. I flew with them to St. Martin for a weekend of fun just because the weatherman said it was going to rain in Greenwich and Mrs. Ludlow hated getting her hair wet...and the twins? Oh those little boys were the apples of my eye.

Okay, so they were little hellions, but I was making good progress. I had only been with the family for three months and it usually took me about four months to break the kids' spirits and get them to behave appropriately. I was on the cusp. I was so close, but then it happened. The defining moment of my life, in which I saw my life flash before my eyes and I really, really thought I was going to die. (I'm kind of a drama queen.)

The car I sideswiped belonged to a very nice old woman, and although she wasn't in the car when it happened, she did claim that she got whiplash just from watching. Now, there was a drama queen.

Mr. Ludlow was called to the hospital by an overeager young resident who wanted to make absolutely sure that the boys were all right before releasing them. I got yelled at in the hall for crashing their new SUV. I got yelled at in the cafeteria for being so stupid. And then I got yelled at that night by Mrs. Ludlow who had to get drunk (actually she gets drunk when she breaks a fingernail, so that didn't surprise me) to deal with the fact that her nanny actually had the nerve to get into an accident while her precious three-year-olds were in the back. Like I would have planned that. Shit. I wanted to see Pooh rescue Tigger just as badly as the boys did. I hate hospitals and I hate people yelling at me.

Mr. Ludlow didn't come home until really late that night, so I sang the boys a song before bed and tucked them in before crawling into my own bed.

At seven the next morning, which just happened to be yesterday, there was a note on my door instructing me to meet Mr. Ludlow at his office in Manhattan. *Yeah,* I thought. *I love the city and he's never yelled at me in his office. This will be a whole new adventure.*

I arrived at his office at precisely 10:00 A.M., thanks to the private car that came around to pick me up from the fortress in Greenwich. Dale Ludlow is the president of a highly reputable municipal-fund company and his own private band of brothers usually tailed the kids and me because yes, Ludlow thinks highly of himself and thinks he is that high and mighty. I just didn't get it. To me he was just a pot-bellied, rich ass-wipe who treated me like trailer trash.

His building takes up an entire square block on Wall Street. When I got out of the posh Lincoln Town Car, I looked up and cringed. I felt like I was being escorted to the firing squad.

Ludlow's security team was assembled in the office when I arrived. I know I have Army training and all, but what did he actually think I was going to do? Come in strapped with explosives and beg his forgiveness? I don't think so.

"Charlene." He refused to call me Charlie, even after repeated attempts to tell him that I loathed being called Charlene. "Here is your final paycheck. You will find your belongings downstairs along with a plane ticket back to Oregon."

"Uhhhh." That was my pathetic comeback line. "But..." And there was another. Wow, I was being fired...again.

Nope, not this time.

My stomach churned and adrenaline surged through my veins. "I can explain."

"You got into a car accident with my children present. I can't tolerate that."

"But it wasn't my fault."

He looked at me with the same blank stare that he always gave me.

"It was Jacob." The minute I blurted that out, I knew I was done for. In his eyes, his little devils were angels and now I had done it. "I mean...well..." I searched for any way out and the best I could come up with was, "I'd been stoned."

His brows furrowed, he made a quick divergent gesture to his thugs and I was lifted off the ground by my armpits. I was literally being dragged out of his office by two rent-a-cops. And, boy, did that ever piss me off. I managed to get one arm free and I banged on the thick glass as we passed the outer office.

"I was stoned I tell you. I'd been stoned," I screamed out again and was dragged down the hall, into the elevator and out onto Wall Street.

Yesterday was perhaps the worst day of my life. Well, I take that back, but it was close.

So, here I was today, from the *un-comfort* of my parents' living room, pleading with Parker Rooney of East Coast Nanny Inc. to place me with another family.

"The kid threw a rock at my head," I explained further. Something I had wanted to tell Mr. Ludlow, but starting any sentence with, "Your kid...." is never a good idea. Parents have this defense mechanism that shuts down their common sense when someone accuses their children of such atrocities. "I was driving and the kid threw a rock the size of his little hand right at the back of my head. Literally....I had been stoned." I said to Parker.

Okay, so it was a bad choice of words. No one except Biblical figures used that term, but it was the only thing that fit. I had been *rocked* just sounded somewhat *perverted*.

I could actually hear Parker laughing on the other end of the phone line. It sort of irritated me and had me clenching my hand into a fist, but on the other hand, it *was* somewhat amusing.

"How do you manage to get yourself into these situations? No one else I know gets stoned by the kids they watch. You're...."

"I know," I said flatly. People have called me many things in my life, but lucky is not one of them. "So, can you place me?"

"Are you sure you wouldn't rather go back to the Army. Maybe you just aren't cut out for kids."

One—I refuse to believe that, because I look forward to having my own kids when I'm thirty-four and another when I'm thirty-five. Unbeknownst to my father, I do have a plan for my life.

And, two—kids are a heck of a lot easier to deal with than a Master Chief by the name of Brick.

"Noooo," I said slowly so he fully understood my intentions. "I want you to place me again, please."

Then I just had to make my father listen. I can live the rest of my life letting him think that I'm a failure, but there's no way that I want him thinking I'm a druggie and it really, really chapped my ass that Mr. Ludlow had the nerve to call my daddy to tattle about my apparent lack of judgment. I mean really! I'm nearly thirty-years-old. What kind of crap is that?

"Greenwich again, I presume?" Parker did his thing on his computer and wrestled up a couple of potential employers. "How about older kids this time?" He knew that my checkered past mostly revolved around caring for toddlers and everyone knows that toddlers are brutal on new nannies. "Ah ha," he said.

I loved the sound of that. I could feel the world lifting off my shoulders. I deserved a peanut butter and jelly sandwich.

After inhaling a sandwich and walking Ruger again, that time with my head held high, my shoulders shrugged back with confidence and a broad smile on my face—I probably looked stoned—I went to see my father at St. Charles' Medical Center on the east side of Bend.

My father had just returned from surgery and had the same look of elation on his face that I did. He loves his job and I know he loves me, too. He just has a different way of showing it.

"Dad," I said sternly. "We need to talk."

He had already replaced his bluish-green scrubs with his long, white coat that makes him look like God. His dark hair was dappled with silver, but he had a regal air about him that warded off any implication that he was an old fart. Everyone loves my dad. He is just that kind of man, popular and alarmingly handsome. I had always loved going to the hospital as a kid and walking around with him, holding his hand and visiting his patients during rounds. For years, I thought I wanted to be just like him, and then I found out that I was allergic to the sight of blood.

I took his hand, just as I did as a child and I led him straight over to the cafeteria before he could come up with another excuse as to why we couldn't clear the air. "Coffee?" I asked, before I went to grab a cup for myself. He nodded, but was still speechless, which was surprising, because in his eyes I had screwed up big time and that was usually when I got *the speech*. When I returned with hot coffee, he was already seated. "Look, I don't know exactly what Mr. Ludlow said to you, but I was not stoned. I do not take drugs and have not ever taken drugs in my life. Hell, Dad, I've never even smoked a joint."

His big blue eyes actually softened and he leaned back in his chair. "Why would he say that then? He seemed upset that you were stoned and driving his kids around. Rightfully so, I would say."

I sipped my coffee and cleared my throat. "Remember when I got fired last spring for telling the mother that her kids filled my shoes with dog crap?"

True story.

My father's eyes lit up and I swear he almost laughed.

"Well, I got fired because I said, 'Your kids...' It didn't even matter what came after that. The point is that each time I got fired it had something to do with some snot-nosed brat pulling a dirty prank on me. I never learned to keep my mouth shut I guess, so when Mr. Ludlow wouldn't listen to me about how his kid threw a large rock at my head, I just blurted out that I had been stoned. That way I didn't have to start my sentence with, 'Your kid...' Do you see what happened?"

My father did start laughing. My God, I almost wept, and I rarely weep. His smile widened and he looked absolutely relieved. "I'm sorry, Charlie. I should have listened to you. How do you get into these situations?"

"Bad karma?" I chuckled lightly. After all, I had been murder on all my babysitters. I guess I just wanted attention because our babysitters were always ogling my perfect brothers and I swear that none of them even knew I was in the room. Most of my babysitters were neighborhood teenagers who had their sights on Dave and Josh. They never wanted to play with me. They just stuck me in front of the television and got on the phone, or snuck around in my brothers' bedrooms on the pretense of looking for my shoes, but I knew what they were doing and I knew that not one of them gave a damn about me.

I hugged my father, told him all about my new job and went back to my parents' house to pack.

When I returned home, I was still smiling when I began packing. Not that I had really unpacked; I had done some laundry, had gone through my necessities, and I tossed out what I no longer needed. Everything I owned fit perfectly into three large Army duffels and I liked it that way.

I tucked my almost-shoulder-length dark hair behind my ears and stood in front of the full-length mirror, staring into my own brown eyes and right into my soul. This time I was going to make it work. This time I wasn't going to take any crap from anyone. After all, my life was about to move ahead as planned. I had to finish what I started; and nothing—and I mean nothing—was going to blow it for me this time.

Then I turned to the side and realized that my muscle tone was dwindling. My thighs didn't have that nice defined edge to them anymore, my upper arms needed some toning, and I needed to do some serious squats to lift my sagging ass.

Chapter Two

My flight to LaGuardia took the usual five and a half hours, but then we had to wait another thirty minutes because the plane couldn't make it to the terminal from the tarmac. People were shouting and cussing because they were going to be late. I, for one, was thankful to be alive. How stupid could these people be? What if the plane had decided it couldn't make it from the sky to the runway? Heck, it could have broken down in the *sky*.

"Thank you, Lord, thank you." I finished my impromptu prayer, said a couple more Hail Marys and Our Fathers and grabbed my bag from the overhead compartment.

I was no stranger to LaGuardia International Airport. By my count, I had lost my job four times in the past two years and that meant I had visited this airport about eight times. This time, I swore would be the last.

And if, perchance, someone fires me again, I'd just fly home via JFK. Ha! I have every base covered.

A white man in a black suit wearing a chauffeur's cap was holding a white card with my name on it. Charlene, of course. "It's actually Charlie," I said when I approached the man. He didn't smile.

I took my seat in the back of the limo and immediately closed my eyes. I have a thing against sleeping while in the air. I'm afraid the plane might plummet to the ground if I'm not watching. It's sort of like backseat driving from coach.

It didn't take long to reach Greenwich, and when we pulled up to my new home my breath caught in my throat. The house was magnificent, the grounds were pristine, and I knew this was my new home, hopefully, for the next year. I was going to make it work and this time, no kid was going to ruin it for me.

"Charlene?" a nice elderly woman asked me in, I think, a French accent. A twelve-year-old girl was staring at me with a venomous glare from the woman's side. "Zis is Annabelle."

"Bella," the pre-teen sneered at the old woman who, I assumed, was her grandmother.

"Hi," I said and followed them into the house. Bella was almost as tall as me. That doesn't say much because I'm only five-seven, and her father is, after all—*a god.*

"Wow!" I've seen my share of fantastic homes in Greenwich, but this one is worthy of "The Lifestyles of the Rich and Famous."

"Is that you?" I pointed to an oil painting on the left wall of the foyer.

Bella rolled her eyes then nodded. Clearly, we had somehow started on the wrong foot.

"It's beautiful." I smiled. Compliments sometimes helped.

She scowled.

I guess not.

The grandmother, who didn't seem to speak much English because she was just pointing to various rooms, took me out the back door, past the dog's house, through the rose garden and into my own private guest house. Heaven.

"Zis is yours."

Bella opened the door for me and plopped her butt down onto my bed. *My bed.* In my own guest quarters.

Awwwwww.

"Can we go to the mall?" Bella finally spoke to me.

I looked at Grandma who had already turned around and was heading out the door. I shrugged. "So," I said, taking in my surroundings, opening and shutting my fridge, my oven, and my microwave. Then I opened and shut every cupboard, looked at the contents of the fridge again and grabbed a couple of Calistoga waters for me and my newest assignment. "Where's your dad?"

"L.A." She flipped on the TV and stared at me. "Why are you here?"

Ummmm. That was a new one. I shook my head free of cobwebs and wrinkled my eyebrows together. "What do you mean?"

"I mean," she said snottily. "Why. Are. You. Here?"

That made it so much clearer for me. "To. Be. Your. Nanny," I said in the same monotonous voice. "What. Is. The. Problem?" That not only cleared the air, it also cleared the room.

Bella slammed the door behind her and ran across the vast, plush lawn as I gawked, open-mouthed, out the window. Toddlers suddenly seemed easy.

I took some time to unpack my clothes before the phone rang. I picked it up. "Hello."

"Yah."

It was him; oh my God, I was talking to Roald Munson. "Charlene?"

"Yes." I swallowed hard. "It's actually Charlie, though. I prefer to be called Charlie and thank you so much for hiring me and thanks for the nice place to stay and just thanks."

I am such a moron.

I heard his deep booming laughter and his accent was even thicker than in the movies. He sounded like Jean-Claude Van Damme, but looked like a cross between Fabio and Arnold. Yum.

"Okay, Charlie." He rattled off some instructions about the press and about how I couldn't take Annabelle into town for a couple more days because of the whole break-up mess and if I wouldn't mind keeping an eye on the dogs so the housekeeper could take a few well-needed days off. Then he said that his mother was going back to Belgium, and that I should not let Annabelle out of my sight for even a minute and then he hung up.

Busy man, I guess.

I sighed deeply and made my way across the lawn and into the back door of the main house. It was really more like a castle. I guess he felt more comfortable in castles because, according to his E! True Hollywood Story, he mainly bounced around between southern Turkey, Hungary, and Armenia and lived in the finest of castles with his mother and his father, who was a very important diplomat.

The kitchen was already abuzz with noise. I peeked in to see Grandma helping Bella make homemade pizza. Bella glared but I ignored it. I know a lame cry for attention when I see one. I was *Queen of Evil Glares* as a teenager. It was the only way that I got my father's attention. Clearly, Bella craved attention. Especially since her mother had recently left the house in a bitter split that splashed all over the television and grocery store tabloids.

"Can I help?" I asked Bella and killed her with kindness with my perky smile. "I make a tight pizza."

Okay, *my bad*. I don't really know what *tight* means these days. I heard it on a Sprite commercial and I figured it was fitting.

Bella snorted at me and handed me some cheese to grate.

"You don't have to pretend to like me," she said snottily.

"I'm not pretending," I said. "I don't know if I like you or not. I need a few days before I can make that call." I sneered playfully at her and went to work grating the ball of mozzarella. Grandma was busy making sausage on the stove and kept her distance from the flying insults.

"You won't last two days," Bella retorted wickedly, but never bothered to look up from her chore of spreading pizza sauce on the dough.

I, on the other hand, dropped my jaw and gawked at her. "Wanna bet?"

I'm so smooth sometimes. I even amaze myself.

NOT.

I have never gotten the concept of the great comeback. Sure, I can always think of one, but it takes me a day or two before I perfect it. I once used one on my ex-boyfriend when he called me a loser. So, you can imagine two days later, me showing up at his door, saying, "Well, at least I don't fart in my sleep," didn't quite go over as planned.

Needless to say, we broke up. I hated that he called me a loser, but more importantly I hated that he actually thought I *was* a loser. He didn't know me very well.

The pizza finished baking while Grandma finished packing. She exchanged some colorful words with Bella and although I didn't understand a word that they said, I got the feeling that Grandma was warning Bella to be nice to me. Bella turned a scary shade of white and clearly, Grandma Gemma had threatened something awful; like perhaps Bella moving to Belgium with her, or cutting her off from her inheritance. Anyway, Bella was actually nice to me for about ten minutes after the old woman left. We ate pizza in silence, but then I received another evil glare and her bedroom door slammed loudly when she bolted into her room. Ugh. This was going to be fun. Especially since we had to spend the next three days in the house...together...alone. God help me.

It was my third day in the Munson/Squire household before I got my bearings and finally felt comfortable enough to walk around in my pajamas.

Gregory, the housekeeper, had just come back from a long-needed three-day weekend and was giving me the rundown that I had desperately needed two days ago. Like where they kept the dog food, who delivers the fastest pizza and why Annabelle's last name was Squire.

"King Arthur." Gregory ripped open the new bag of dog food and dumped it into its own Rubbermaid container labeled 'dog food' in the pantry. Duh. Why would they keep the dog food in the pantry with the people food when it would make so much more sense to keep it in the dog's quarters? Literally, those dogs had their own house, with running water, heat and a soft glowing nightlight.

Absurd?

I think so.

I shook my head. "King Arthur?" *What the heck did that mean?* It was common knowledge among us, *domestic technicians* for the rich and famous, that most celebrities use different last names for their kids to keep them out of the spotlight. Not that it helped much.

Gregory not so politely rolled his eyes, doing a great impression of Annabelle. "Roald's third film. He played a squire. He thought it sounded like a good name. Besides, he couldn't use his own. He keeps her pretty secluded because of the press and what's happening with his father and all."

Oh goody. The *gay* just can't keep secrets.

"His father?" I ask, trying not to sound like undercover paparazzi. "I thought his father lived in Hungary or something." What I knew about Roald Munson consisted of about forty-two minutes of E! Television.

"Actually," Gregory actually looked around at this point—as if anyone was in that fortress but us—"his father's whereabouts are unknown right now: something to do with that political coup in Armenia. He's a diplomat, you know, and I heard that he's pissed off the wrong people." He winked and put the empty Iams bag into the garbage. "Some pretty powerful people think it would be best if he never came out of hiding. It's been pretty intense around here." Gregory finished up and began clearing the dishes. "Don't tell anyone I told you that, okay? And don't let Annabelle out of your sight."

I hadn't an inkling about telling anyone, because who would I tell? I rarely speak to my perfect brothers, I have no girlfriends and the last time I had a boyfriend was almost four years ago. What can I say? I live for the kids I watch and my sights are constantly on my goal: my plan; my perfect future.

I was lonely, though.

I nodded, and then the friendly Annabelle interrupted my thoughts.

"What's your problem?" she asked snottily and yanked open the fridge. If she would just smile here and there, she might actually seem human.

"You know...." I was just about to let her have it. My blood was boiling. I had **PMS** and there was no damn chocolate around in this god-forsaken castle. I blew out a tattered breath. "Let's go to the mall."

If she hadn't been so happy to be getting out of the house, I swear she would have killed me with the bottle opener she was holding. The girl had daggers in her eyes for me and I hadn't a clue as to why.

I pulled the car out of the garage slowly and, to tell you the truth, I was a bit skittish about driving a big expensive Hummer after demolishing the side of the Ludlows' BMW. It wasn't the first time I had driven a Hummer, I did it all the time in the Army, but this Hummer was nice. Really nice and really tricked out.

I was literally shaking.

"Any day now."

Boy, I was sick of her mouth. At that point, I decided to change my life plan and have two boys instead of one of each. She had just altered my life-long dream of having a daughter.

Out of nowhere, I felt very sorry for my father.

I finally peeled my sweaty palms off the steering wheel and shifted the Hummer into drive.

The mall in Westport was where I wanted to go because J. Crew was my style. That and Banana Republic fit me to a tee. So that's where we went. I followed Post Road down through Darien and Norwalk and relived some former good and not so good nanny moments. I sure wished one of my other jobs had worked out, because that would've meant that I wouldn't be here, sitting next to the Prima Dona from hell.

Every three minutes she was checking her lip-gloss in the mirror and teasing her bangs. If she were my daughter, I wouldn't let her out of the house looking like she did. Hell, she looked like she was eighteen.

I removed her from my peripheral vision by turning my head to see if I could squeeze this monstrosity between the two Mercedes sedans just up ahead. Better to be safe than sorry. We parked at the far end of the lot, all alone. I turned off the ignition and opened my door.

"Where..." In mid sentence her blond hair flipped over her shoulder in contempt, "do you think you are going?" Her eyes narrowed at me. "Just drop me off and *go.*"

"Yeah, like that's gonna happen." I snorted with laughter and grabbed my purse. Come hell or high water I would be buying a new outfit today.

"You're such a bit..."

I could hear the words trailing out of her mouth as I slammed my door shut and the old me would have strangled her in the parking lot. I took a deep breath in. I let it out slowly and repeated that procedure as I grabbed her arm and tugged her toward the big Mecca that had been calling me since my arrival back in Greenwich. The mother ship was calling me home.

I whipped open the door at J. Crew and closed my eyes, breathing in the scents of fabulous cotton and Peruvian wool. "I'm home," I said under my breath. I didn't dare open my eyes because if she gave me her classic, 'I hate you,' eye roll one more time, I was going not only going to get fired, I was going to be incarcerated for cold blooded murder.

"Don't leave this store," I glared. "Understood?" And I was off.

I had three outfits chosen in the first ten minutes and three more waiting for me at the checkout counter. I had just lifted the last pastel green tank off my head when she knocked on the door.

"I'm going to The Gap," she said.

And then I said, "No. You. Are. Not."

Then she said, "Oh yes I am."

And then I said...again, "No. You. Are. Not." I swung open the door to my dressing room, gazing into her glare. "Look," I said sternly. "You will not be going anywhere without me, and as you can clearly see. I. Am. Not. Dressed."

That is when she took off running away from me, into the middle of the store, blonde hair fluttering dramatically in the wind. At this point, I didn't care that I was topless. My bra was one of those Victoria Secret plum-colored numbers with no seams and it did look good on my toned upper body, so I went with the rage in my belly and I raced after her. I was sure the whole debacle would be in the National Inquirer first thing in the morning. *"Naked nanny goes berserk on Roald Munson's emotionally fragile daughter in local J. Crew store."*

I could just see the headline flashing in my head as I grabbed her upper arm and flung her around to face me. "What is your problem?" I couldn't believe that I stooped to use her famous line. Heck, I invented that line when I was twelve. "Why are so damn bitchy all the time and what did I ever do to you to deserve this crap? Your father said that I'm not to let you out of my sight. Is that clear?"

Tears actually welled up in her eyes and I thought for sure she was going to break down in sobs.

"What does he care?" she blurted out before shrugging from my grasp and heading for the door. All eyes were on us and I was still topless.

Annabelle remained right out in front of the store while I changed back into my clothes, said goodbye to the purchases I had wanted to make and promised the sales girl that I would be back for those perfect jeans.

We spoke no words on the way home and the silence gave me time to realize that I knew nothing about this girl's problems. I just hadn't taken the time to evaluate her behavior because I had been so busy trying not to strangle her in her sleep.

I had a grave feeling that Annabelle and I had more in common than I could have guessed.

Chapter Three

Two days later, after more silence and many tears shed by Annabelle, her father walked through the garage door and scared the living shit out of me.

"Jesus Christ!" I climbed back into my skin that I had just jumped out of and planted my bare feet onto the cold tile of the kitchen floor. I had been sitting on the counter in my flannel boxer shorts and tank top, and had a peanut butter and jelly sandwich on route to my mouth when he entered the kitchen at 1:00 A.M.

"Sorry," he chuckled and dropped his luggage onto the counter. He wasn't as tall as I thought he would be and he looked...exhausted would be a good word. "I didn't mean to frighten you." His deep voice reverberated in my ears as my heartbeat returned to normal.

"It's okay. I just wasn't expecting you."

That and I really wasn't dressed appropriately. When I worked for other families, I always made sure that I wore my big ugly flannel grandma pajamas for occasions such as this one. After all, I was young, physically fit and, according to the last man I dated, I was *sexy* and had a great rack. Needless to say, we didn't date long. Men either call me a loser, or they look at me like a sex object and I am neither, so I don't date often.

"You must be Charlie. How's everything going?" he asked and eyeballed my sandwich like it was chocolate in the eyes of a deranged woman with chronic PMS.

"You want me to make you one?"

He actually looked at me as if I was speaking Swahili.

I blinked a couple of times and took his slight head-bob as a yes. Perhaps his former nannies weren't as considerate as I was. Heck, I didn't know what was going through his mind.

"Grape or strawberry?" I asked while rummaging through the fridge.

"Grape." He cleared his throat loudly. "Please."

Wow, he has manners too. I think I might like it here.

We talked for a bit while we ate our sandwiches and drank milk. I feel comfortable chatting with celebrities after I get to know them, use the same toilets as them, wash their laundry and pick up their kids' toys. However, I had done none of this with Roald Munson so far, so I was still at that crucial, *wanting to blush every couple of minutes*, stage of our new relationship.

"How's Annabelle doing? Has her mother called?" he asked and then handed me a paper towel.

I probably had peanut butter stuck to my chin. Great.

"She's a typical twelve year old." I cocked my eyebrow and looked into his eyes. He really has wonderful eyes. Kind of bluish-green. "And honestly, I don't know if Nicole has called or not. Annabelle and I haven't spoken much."

He shrugged his shoulders.

Clearly, everyone was going through tough times.

I said goodnight and hustled back to the guest room. I guess I could have gone out to my quarters, but I had gotten so used to the guest bed, that I decided I would spend one more night in the house. Besides, all my stuff was already unpacked up there and it was the middle of the night. As I quietly passed Annabelle's room, I could see her light on through the crack in the door and I would have had to be deaf not to hear her sobs. It broke my heart that I couldn't do anything to stop them. I had tried many times in the past couple of days to get her to open up and talk to me, but then we just ended up screaming at each other and then both of us ended up in our separate rooms.

The next morning, Roald came down, looked genuinely happy to see his daughter and for the first time since I had met her, she actually looked like she might smile. They embraced warmly. She made him some toast and tea. He kissed her head and then went into the den.

Can you say dysfunctional?

I can.

I nearly wept when I looked into her eyes. The pain of neglect filled them once again. Pain that I myself knew all about.

"Do you want to see if he wants to go to Compo with us?" I offered as an olive branch. Perhaps if Daddy Dearest was along, Annabelle might be nice to me.

She just shrugged. "He won't."

"Wanna bet?" I had high hopes. What can I say? The Army taught me to be self-confident and aim high. Or was that the Air Force motto? I always get them confused.

I cleaned up the breakfast dishes, handed Gregory the towel, told him to go take a hot bath and I entered Roald's den on the pretense of refilling his teacup.

"More hot water?" I poured some without a reply and then sat down across from him and tapped my finger on my thigh until he looked up from the latest tabloid with fire in his eyes.

"Why do you read that crap?" I asked.

He shrugged and looked at me for an explanation as to why I was in his face.

"I think it would be a nice idea if you came to the beach with Annabelle and me today. She really missed you and not having Nicole around is really affecting her."

"Oh." He looked concerned, but not as concerned as he was over what the National Enquirer had just printed about Nicole's affair with Braden Booker, her new lover and co-star in her latest box office hit. "She didn't say anything to me."

"Well, have you given her the chance?" Boy, I really needed to shut the hell up, but I didn't. "It's none of my business, but I think she's really hurting. I hear her cry at night and she's on edge and maybe she should see a therapist."

I didn't mean that last part. Therapy wouldn't benefit Annabelle much, not yet anyway. My mother had tried to get me into therapy a number of times and I always refused to go. Now I would love to go. I'm mature enough now to see that I need it.

I am still rebelling against my father's wishes because he never gave me the time of day when I was young and it's starting to mess with my life.

I'm still keeping the fact that I have already graduated from college a secret, just to keep him nagging me and I find that every time I get fired, I start craving his drawn out speeches about how my life is going nowhere. I actually look forward to them. That's just sick and wrong.

"I think she just needs you to be close to her right now. Trust me. I know what I'm talking about."

I think he actually listened to me because he smiled, said thanks and called Annabelle into his den using his intercom system.

Twenty minutes later, they emerged arm in arm. Annabelle was smiling and we headed to the beach.

I packed a picnic for them and then made myself scarce when we arrived. The beach club had always been one of my favorite places to go in Westport. There were always a multitude of half-naked men to gawk at and I loved Piña Coladas. I abstained today because for once, I felt good about my position as Bella's nanny and I was starting to make progress on her behavior, or so I thought.

"I have to go." Roald said as he approached with Bella. Boy, he was so cute. Irritating, but cute.

"No," I said because Annabelle looked so hurt. "I mean, you can't. I..." I tried to think of a good excuse to keep him there, but his cell phone never left his side. The poor girl. "I...I....twisted my ankle," I lied and lifted my ankle up, willing it to look bruised and swollen.

He did the unthinkable and lifted me up.

Shit.

He carried me to the Hummer, tossed me into the backseat and we all left. So much for my keen ability to bring them closer. I was the bad guy once again, because his attention was on me and not her.

"I'm fine," I said again, as he dropped me onto the couch. Annabelle booked it up to her room and I didn't see her for the rest of the afternoon. Roald made me a sandwich with chunky peanut butter and grape jelly and brought it to me on the couch, then he slid in beside me and we watched a couple of movies together.

It was by far the weirdest thing that has ever happened to me.

Two more days had passed and I had made a little more progress with Annabelle and her father. I made them eat dinner together every night and attempted to keep Roald's attention on his daughter by bringing her into the conversation every couple of minutes. They still had a long way to go, but they were not altogether hopeless.

The phone rang just as Gregory put their steaks down in front of them. I usually ate in the kitchen with Gregory and eavesdropped on their dinner conversations. If the conversation went dry, I would run in and say something witty about Annabelle. I was getting it done; that is until the phone rang.

"Yah." He was speaking a different language that I didn't recognize and fled to his den. He returned to the dining room and the phone rang again. "Yah." Then he was speaking English, but he was clearly not thrilled with the person on the other line.

It was Nicole.

Annabelle tensed in her seat when he finished yelling and handed her the phone. Annabelle didn't say much, and then she hung up. "Mom wants me to come for the rest of the summer."

"No." He slammed his hands onto the table. "You are going to Kenya with me."

Her eyes lit up and she ran around the table to hug her dad. It was wonderful to see, and although I know it was a ploy to get back at his cheating *soon to be* ex-wife, I was happy that Annabelle would get to see more of him. Then it hit me.

Shhhhhhhiiiiiiiitttttt. If Annabelle spent the rest of the summer in Kenya, that meant *I'd* be spending the rest of my summer in Kenya. Shit. Shit. Shit. I loathe Africa. Oh, my God.

I paled and sat down on my barstool. I wasn't even paying attention to what I was shoveling into my mouth, until I smelled the stench of Brussels sprouts. I loathe Brussels sprouts just as much as I loathe Africa.

The phone rang again. There was more shouting and I clearly heard him say that Annabelle would be accompanying him to Africa for the final month of shooting on his new action film.

Fan-friggin'-tastic.

Gregory finished the dishes, with some help from me, and then I made it upstairs to say goodnight to Bella.

"Did you hear that?" She sounded so excited. "Africa. I've never been to Africa."

"I have." I smiled because she was smiling. "It's beautiful. You will love it." I lied. I had once spent six months there during my eight years with the Army, it was overrun with giant bugs the size of my fist and wild things that yelped in the night and bugs the size of my fist, and...did I mention bugs the size of my fist? I shivered even though it was still eighty-eight degrees outside.

"You're coming, right?" She actually sounded happy about it.

"I guess so." I shrugged. "Maybe I should go find out."

She smiled and practically shoved me out of her room to find out if I would be accompanying them to Kenya. I walked downstairs, and found Roald in his den, curled up on his leather sofa, holding a picture of Nicole in one hand and a bottle of Jack Daniels in the other. Oh crud.

I turned, hoping he wouldn't see me. *Too late.*

"Come in."

Against my better judgment, I sat down on the edge of his desk and looked at him. "Are you okay?" I usually helped the children, not the parents, but he looked as if he needed a friend.

"She said it was forever."

I rolled my eyes. I wanted to slap him out of it. *Hello, this is Hollywood.* Nicole said, 'I do,' when he was the hottest thing under the sun. She had his kid, she rode his coattails to stardom and now she had broken his heart. It just wasn't right, but what had he expected? Nicole Harrison had been married three times before she married Roald. She was practically Liz Taylor.

"I'm really sorry," I said and sat down next to him. The photo he was holding was from their wedding day and even I could see that her eyes just didn't look like they said *forever.*

We talked more about Annabelle and about how she was warming up to me finally. Then he did ask me to come to Kenya and I accepted because I intended on doing whatever it took to stay employed. Besides, I had a special feeling about Annabelle.

Roald handed me the bottle of whiskey with a grin. I slammed some down and wiped my chin with the back of my hand.

Sometimes I can't believe my life.

Then he kissed me. *Oh hell, he kissed me!* Roald Munson, drunk on Jack Daniels just kissed me. Needless to say I quickly moved away from his lips and stood up.

"Uhhh." My great lines are sheer poetry. "I, uhhhh." Then I heard the pitter-patter of footsteps and a door slam violently. *Shit. Shit. Shit.*

Roald, the drunken oblivious one, just grinned and patted the couch.

I don't think so, pal.

I'm a nanny, not a geisha girl and yeah, I did like it. Who in hell wouldn't? However, I do have a strong moral objection to getting involved with any of my employers, and just because he was newly single and *a god* and well—drunk—didn't change that fact for me.

"Goodnight," I said before I left and headed right upstairs, packed my bag and slept for the first time in my quarters, alone in the dark with a knot in my stomach.

The next morning, I took Annabelle for her immunization shots. I, fortunately, didn't have to get a booster, because I had been abroad recently. We then spent a considerable amount of time at Banana Republic, J. Crew and the army surplus store on Wipple Drive. If I was going to trounce around in Kenya for a month, I wasn't about to ruin any of my shoes and I needed to get some serious supplies. Backpacks, boots and dried food in case all we were served was eyeball soup and cockroach guts. I got a canteen for Annabelle and one for me, and some other fun survival stuff that I thought she might get a kick out of.

Apparently, I was right on about the possibility of her seeing the kiss because the venom was back in her gaze and she hadn't said a word to me all day, other than to say, "I hate you," a number of times. I tried to get her to talk, I really did, but one can only take so much of those hate-filled words.

Roald left right after lunch, so I hadn't even seen him to talk about what had transpired. All he left was a note and he was off to Africa. Annabelle and I would be meeting him in a couple of days. I couldn't wait.

Not.

I called my father and mother and listened to them mope about Josh and how this was his last season with the Austrian *Glouster-cocks,* as I called them. My father had always been optimistic that Josh would someday make it to the NFL, but Josh was thirty-eight and it was time for him to retire. Then they raved about Dave's article in the Pacific Northwest Medical Review about something to do with vascular surgery and blood.

Why did I have to be a girl?

I had hoped to have a few minutes alone to talk to my dad, but his golf buddy had just arrived to take him to Sunriver for eighteen holes, so I said goodbye.

I sat down on my bed feeling as if I had the weight of the world dropped on my shoulders. Perhaps it was that I was trying too hard to fix Bella and Roald's dysfunctional relationship and that I had never tried to fix my relationship with my own father. It dawned on me that I was nearly thirty-years old and I had never told my father how I felt. That's pretty immature, even for me, the girl who refuses to grow up.

So, I took out the stationery that my mother had bought me when I was in the Army and I actually put it to good use. I wrote him a long-ass letter, telling him everything. Starting with kindergarten all the way up to the present. I told him that I cried when he decided that Josh's football game was more important than my kindergarten production of "Willy Wonka and the Chocolate Factory" that he never bothered to see. I told him about high school and how I hated being known as the Ford brothers' goofy little sister.

I told him about the Army and the hell I went through to try to fit in to a man's world. I had never told him about my special training that never panned out because it was just one more thing for him to be disappointed about. I don't think that he would have looked at the fact that I had gotten as far as I did and then quit, as a positive thing. He would have just seen the part where I threw up my hands and quit.

I hate that about my father. I really do. He knew nothing about what I had done and how close I had gotten to a dream that I never realized I had.

The Army had taught me a lot about self-control, about living my dreams, and about how I could do anything that I set out to do. As a result, I took that advice from my superiors and I was hell-bent on becoming a Special Forces Specialist. I passed the academic requirements with perfect scores. I passed the weapons training with the highest grade in my class, and then I did three weeks of *hell*. I can say right now that what I went through looked nothing like *GI Jane*. Demi Moore made it all look good, but there is nothing sexy about having your face ground into the dirt by some overly cocky jerk named Brick. There's nothing sexy about puking your guts out until you no longer can see straight, and there is nothing sexy about someone calling you the 'C' word every other minute.

What I can say is that I wanted to be a bad ass. I wanted to be affiliated with the best of the best, and I was; up until that fateful day. That day I held my head up high, thrust my arm into the air and said, "I fucking quit." It was during maneuvers that it happened, I'd been beaten to a pulp. I looked like hell, I could taste my own blood and I wanted out.

I still see no shame in it; one day I will be the best of the best and I will proudly wear a uniform but it won't be for the Rangers and it won't even be for the Army.

I finished my letter to my father about how much I loved the Army, and how I was actually thankful that he made me that ultimatum. I also went into detail about how I felt neglected and inferior my entire life and I let it all out.

I also felt somewhat inclined to send him my bachelor's degree, but since I only had another two semesters until I finished my master's degree, I wanted to wait. Actually, I wanted to see the look on his face when I told him that I had been secretly using my GI Bill to fund my education and unbeknownst to him, I am not a loser without any direction. I graduated with honors and I am nearly finished, which is why I was so hell-bent about returning to Greenwich. I set out to finish what I started, and being a nanny was the best way to finish school without having the stress of rent, utilities and partying nightly.

I actually cried when I finished the letter, which rarely happens. It felt good to come to terms with my pain and when I was through, I had a seventeen-page letter to send to him. Front and back. I tucked the letter into my purse and intended to send it, just as soon as I was on a different continent.

Annabelle finished her conversation with her grandmother, and then called her mom in Los Angeles.

Nicole Harrison was one of Hollywood's top actresses. She could select her roles and as of late, she could choose whose bed to sleep in. Just last night, I caught the tail-end of "Entertainment Tonight" and saw her gliding down the red carpet for Braden Booker's new movie preview, and I hoped that Braden Booker was using her like she had used Roald. After all, he was an up and coming actor and she was the older, more experienced actress. That would serve her right.

I stood at the door and listened as Annabelle went on and on about Kenya and all the cool things that I bought for our trip, and she made it sound like her life was perfect, which I knew was the farthest thing from the truth.

The downstairs Grandfather clock chimed twice, letting me know that it was time to go and once my heart rate returned from hyper-speed, I knocked gently on the door and then I peeked my head in.

"Go away," she shouted and tossed a large stuffed dolphin at my head.

"It's time to go." I stood firm and tossed the dolphin at her head. "Are you ready? Do you think you forgot anything?"

"Why are you talking to me? I hate you."

"Well, I happen to loooovvveee you," I said super sweetly, and pulled her into a massive bear hug and although she writhed and shrieked, I knew that she enjoyed the embrace because—well, let's just say, I remember what it was like to be twelve.

Vinny drove us to JFK airport and I had everything packed for a fun flight. I took care of all the essentials: gum, water, jerky, Snickers, tampons—just in case—and, of course, a myriad of crossword puzzles, CDs and the letter to my dad.

Bella took her seat beside me, closed her eyes, turned on her earphones, and ignored me over the Atlantic Ocean. I didn't mind because I was watching movies and shoveling peanuts into my mouth as if they were going out of style. I finished two cheesy romance novels that another passenger had lent me and then I finished a couple of crosswords before the pilot's voice broke my concentration. Half an hour later, we were safely on the ground again.

Our first stopover was in London. I had only been to England one other time, in the Army, and it always seemed so gloomy. No wonder English people are so droll. They are miserable and they have no lips—that might also have something to do with it.

I entered the gift shop, bought a couple of shot glasses because when I was here with the military we didn't really get time off to buy souvenirs.

Then I went to customer relations, bought airmail postage, and hesitantly handed over the letter to my father. It took me a good five minutes to actually get up the courage to hand it to the nice, no lipped man behind the counter, and even then I still couldn't hand it over.

Finally, Bella nudged me in the arm and said she swore she just saw Britney Spears. I could have cared less. Now if it had been Colin Firth, I would have tackled him and demanded that he talk dirty to me.

Bella looked at me, looked at the envelope, grabbed it out of my hand, and thrust it at the no-lipped man.

"Thanks." I smiled. "I needed that."

When we finally landed in Nairobi, Kenya, we learned that we had to wait a couple of hours to take a small commuter flight to the landing strip just south of where they were filming yet another version of "King Solomon's Mines."

I think that Hollywood has completely overdone the whole legend of Alan Quartermain and, furthermore, I just can't see Roald Munson playing the same character that Sean Connery once played, or for that matter Richard Chamberlain or Stewart Granger. He just didn't fit; but I'm obviously not a famous movie producer, so what do I know?

Now, Hugh Grant would make a great Alan Quartermain. Hell, he'd make a great Mr. Ford. I'd marry him and have his babies any day of the week. Okay, I digress. I was just trying to keep my mind off the flies and the scary guys with guns and the fact that my underwear was permanently stuck up my butt crack, thanks to the sweltering heat and humidity.

We holed up in a small airport terminal until our guide came to take us to the plane. It would have been nice if Roald had come to meet his daughter at the airport in a strange country. Especially since men with semi-automatics were walking around the terminal looking like something out of "Commando." It was unnerving to me and I'm an adult—

an adult with Army training, no less. I can't imagine what Bella was thinking. She hadn't let go of my hand since we landed. Perhaps she does love me after all.

I stopped for a couple of Cokes and batted my hand in front of my face to keep the flies away. I think I prefer civilization to the great big outdoors. This was not my idea of a dream vacation. A dream vacation for me would be a couple of weeks in St. Martin with a Swede, named Sven, who had hands that never quit. I really couldn't believe that I was thinking about sexy Swedes at a time like that. I was just delusional that's all. I blamed it all on the heat, of course.

Before getting out to the small plane that would take us to Kisumu, we were both patted down by said men with guns and I thought for sure Bella was going to cry. It was scary to have normal men pat my butt and thrust their hands into my crotch, but these guys seemed to be enjoying it a little too much.

The first white man that I had seen all day yelled something that sounded like hurry up, and we ran over to the decrepit plane. I stopped dead in my tracks and looked up.

"Uh uh," I muttered as I looked at the ancient piece of hardware that was supposedly going to take me over the mountains. "No freaking way," I said to the white male, who didn't look too impressed with me.

Bella grabbed my hand and begged me to come, but the rubber on my shoes seemed to have congealed with the hot tar of the asphalt. I was frozen and I had a bad feeling about this.

Another white male quickly shuffled me up the stairs.

I was in hell. The seats were too close together and the leather was ripped and torn. I took a seat next to Bella and remained silent while the rest of the passengers boarded.

Overall, I counted ten passengers and two pilots. There were no flight attendants to pass out peanuts and Bloody Marys and no pillows or blankets. Bella and I were the only two female passengers. That was a bit unsettling, but then again, what woman in her right mind would come to such a place? Don't get me wrong, I did learn to deal with dirt and grime in the Army, but I still didn't like it. No one has to like dirt, *do they?*

Bella squirmed beside me, so I took her hand in mine and patted her knee for good measure. "We'll be there soon. I'm sure of it." *I hope.*

I clenched my jaw and listened to the other passengers mumbling about nothing and then we were airborne.

Bella put her earphones to her ears, closed her eyes and laid her head on my shoulder.

I kept my eyes toward the front and did what I always do. I mentally flew the plane from coach.

After finishing my Snickers bar and half my bottle of Coke, I grabbed the crossword from my bag and had just clutched my pen in my fingers when all hell broke loose.

When I said there were ten passengers on board, I was mistaken.

There were seven passengers and three hijackers. *Holy-shit!*

Chapter Four

I once thought that I wanted to be a bad ass. I once thought I wanted to remain a member of the Army Special Forces that dealt with situations like this all the time. All I knew right then was that I just wanted my daddy. Better yet, Arnold Schwarzenegger. Where's Arnold when you need him? Okay, okay, he has the state of California to run and has no time to save my sorry ass, but who's left? Sylvester Stallone is just too old. Bruce Willis is just too beautiful. So who does that leave?

Scared does not fully embody what I was going through when I saw the first guy stand up and point a gun into the cockpit. Frightened is not a strong enough term to describe how I felt when the second butthead pointed his gun at us, the passengers, but I had Bella to think about. Bella was my number-one priority, so screaming like a girl and passing out cold on the floor was not going to be an option.

Although, come to think of it, passing out felt like the right thing to do, so I did.

After I regained consciousness, I counted the passengers and there were only five. The blood on the seats and airplane walls told the gruesome story about what had just transpired and Bella was shrieking next to me; I felt like I was going to puke and I really needed to get a handle on my allergy to the sight of blood. When I was in the Army, I handled it well by keeping smelling salts in my pockets, unbeknownst to Brick, the Master Chief from hell. Nevertheless, I was without smelling salts and there was so much blood.

The three men converged on the rest of us and shouted some not-so-nice words and although I'm not fluent in *asshole*, I'm pretty sure they told us not to move or we would die.

Okay, fine by me. I couldn't have moved if I tried.

The taller of the two white males with pistols said something to the other tall white male with an even larger pistol and I was confident that they were South African because I had seen "Lethal Weapon II" a number of times and I remember the bad guys' accents.

Where in the hell is Mel Gibson when you needed him?

I was back to that again. Going over it in my head. What would Wesley Snipes do? After all, he had been in a number of hijacked-plane movies and he always saved the day.

Bella had finally stopped crying and was silently saying a prayer in another language. I'm assuming that her grandmother had taught her well, after all, Bella had spent lots of time with her grandparents during their travels to foreign countries. I just couldn't think of a thing to say to her; not one gosh darn thing that would be of comfort.

The man behind me read my mind and whispered, "It's going to be okay," from behind Bella's chair.

He certainly wasn't going to be the hero. I had read the inscription on his briefcase and his name was Duane. What kind of name is *Duane*? It was nice of Duane to say that to Bella, but it wasn't the truth. Things were not fine. We were going to die. These were most likely terrorists and we were going to crash into that mountain up ahead. *Ahhhhh.*

Okay, I said to myself in my head, because I didn't want Duane to know that I was the only hope of getting us out of it alive. I didn't want him getting his hopes up because I was the only one on the plane with eight years of Army training in special tactics and I was the only one who could take down a man with a gun in two decisive movements. *You are losing it. Control. Control. You have to remain focused.* I did my best to regain any of the training I had learned, but this was real. So real that I could smell death, and it reeked.

I gave up on remembering any of my training and concentrated on Bella and on how scared she was. The men were sitting, chewing on *my jerky* and staring out the window at the dense jungle. I had no idea where we were and I really didn't care. It didn't matter to me at that point where I was going to die, it just mattered that I was, and I really didn't want to. The only solace that I felt was that I had sent that letter to my father and had finally said my piece. Damn, I had wanted to see the look in his eyes when he learned that I had a master's degree in criminal justice. Wouldn't that knock his socks off? A couple of tears trickled out of the corners of my eyes and I squeezed them shut to stop the rest. I was not going to cry. I was not going to be that weepy stereotype who watched her life passing before her eyes.

I squeezed them tighter, and in my mind, a montage of my life started playing and I became that sappy stereotype. I started thinking about my brothers and about how I had some serious making up to do because I had blamed them for our father's predisposition of loving them more than me. Then I thought about Ruger and about how I had promised to buy his dream place in the country with acres and acres of jackrabbits to chase, and I was so close to that dream.

I had all the money I needed in the bank. I just had to finish school and then I could take him away from my parents. I thought about my mom and about how sad she would be that she didn't get to see me get married and have kids. The tears were rolling out by this time, and when I felt a warm hand on my shoulder, I opened my eyes and looked into Duane's eyes, right through his Coke-bottle glasses.

He was a nerd incarnate. Poor man. Even his checkered shirt and un-matched bowtie reeked of geek-dom.

"Where's your purse?"

I had no idea why he was asking such a bizarre question, so I narrowed my swollen eyes and by God, I was not going to get mugged on top of everything else.

"Your purse? Where is it?" He was being quite adamant.

"Why?" I said under my breath, and kept my eyes facing forward per the asshole with the gun's request.

"Just give it to me, please."

I felt around with my feet until my toe hit my bag.

Bella stared bright-eyed and begged for me to stop moving. I kicked my purse under the seat and mentally made a note to kick the geek's ass for mugging me, if we should survive unscathed. I heard him wrestling around behind me and was certain that he was rifling right past the tampons and bottle of Midol to get to my wad of cash, which wasn't a lot; maybe just a twenty-dollar bill or two.

I hadn't heard any demands on the radio, or any cursing in awhile. My ears started popping out of nowhere, so I was certain that we were descending, hopefully onto a nice runway and not into the ocean.

I said my fair share of Hail Marys and crossed my fingers under my butt just because my hands were shaking that badly and I wanted Bella to think that I was in control. I don't know why that was so important to me, but it was. I looked over at her, gave her a small wink and a smile, and then I held her hand as we bumped around on the ground. We had a rocky landing that bloodied my nose and shattered a couple of windows because either we had hit a couple of trees, or perhaps I had screamed so loudly that they shattered from the high-pitch of my shrieks. It was hard to tell.

The assholes seemed to have survived intact, and pulled a dark-skinned gentleman out of the plane by his ankles. The man shrieked and screamed like a toddler, and I genuinely felt for him. I just hoped I had enough control not to scream when they came for me.

We waited with racing pulses and bated breath for what seemed like an eternity before assholes numbers two and three came back and held a powwow with asshole number one. There were scores of head bobbing and guttural noises made but, again, I had no clue as to what they were talking about.

Not being able to hear made me think of the bionic woman and of how I so would have liked to see her show up and save the day.

Bella squeezed my hand tighter and brought me out of my trance. Asshole number three, the tall lanky one, grabbed me by the upper arm, yanked me from my seat and said, "MOVE IT."

He could have said it nicely. I mean, where does it say that hijackers have to be assholes on top of everything else? Wasn't it bad enough that they just rerouted seven passengers to an unknown destination in what looked like the middle of hell? They didn't need to be rude on top of it all. Sheesh.

Bella was right behind me and I knew that because I could hear her sobs. They brought Duane out after her, along with one other dark-skinned gentleman, whom they took aside and immediately disposed of.

Then we were four. Four hostages, three bad guys, and then I saw the bad news. There were more bad guys with a lot more guns. Eleven—no—twelve; I could see feet beyond a red Jeep, and that made thirteen. Thirteen bad guys!

We were dead.

Duane seemed eerily calm for a dweeb. I half expected him to lie down on the ground and beg for mercy, but he didn't. He hung his head low and remained silent as they marched us into the first canvas tent.

I know canvas tents well, so I felt at home. There were a number of cots on the floor, and a couple of canteens of water. That was where they handcuffed us to a metal bar that lined the floor. Each of us had our own separate chain linked to the bar, giving us enough slack to either lie down, kneel or sit on the cold dirt floor.

Great. More dirt.

Bella finally burst into full-blown sobs once the assholes left us alone and Duane just sat, slumped over like a catatonic slug.

"We're okay," I said. At that point, I did think we were okay. They seem to be quite selective about who they were killing off, so I wondered if this was just a run of the mill kidnapping, or perhaps something I couldn't even fathom. I didn't want to speculate at that time, I just held her close and said a prayer.

Duane got down on his knees and said one with us. He was a very sweet man, and he seemed kind and gentle. "I'm Duane Johnston," he said and extended his hand. As if Duane wasn't bad enough, he had the unfortunate.... *Wait,* I had heard that name before. Why was it so familiar to me? I shook the thought, extended my hand, and shook his firmly.

"Charlie; and this is Annabelle," I said.

Then I looked around at our surroundings and tried to eavesdrop the best I could. Except, all the bad guys were speaking some native tongue and I hadn't a clue. I knew about three words in Nilo-Saharan and maybe two words in Swahili and nothing they were saying came even close.

If only they had hijacked us in Mexico. I was fluent in Spanish after all, and I really could have gone for a burrito and a margarita. I fumbled with my chain and got it untangled just enough to help Bella get comfortable on the cot.

Then I had to pee. Great, if my day hadn't been bad enough, now I was going to lose bladder control in front of *Duane*. "Ah ha," I said aloud when it finally hit me. The Rock, the Rock's name is Dwayne Johnson. I had forgotten all about The Rock. Where the hell is The Rock? I need you. I want you; you must come save us from the assholes with guns.

Okay, so I watch too many movies. I'm a nanny, what else is there to do? I could date I guess, or I could take up basket weaving, but I prefer movies. Movies with big, bad action heroes. Movies staring Roald Munson. Hell, I'd have been happy with having him there right then. Actually, to be quite honest, I would have settled for Buffy the Vampire Slayer at that point in time.

I wanted to go home.

To pee, or not to pee? That was the question. Should I just go in my pants? Should I ask Duane to turn around so I could do it right, or should I shout out to the assholes and hope that they knew what the Geneva Convention stands for?

"Hey." I really didn't want to pee where I sleep, that just reminded me of Hell-week. "Hey, you out there. I need to use the bathroom." I knew that at least three of the assholes spoke English.

One of their heads popped in. "You have two minutes."

The lanky one shuffled me from the tent. They did have a portable outhouse set up, a couple more tents and three or four red Jeeps. The main concentration of assholes seemed to be at the larger tent where I heard harsh cries and loud moans resounding. I was glad that we weren't in that tent, but then again, that could change.

I had no idea what the heck was happening, why we had been hijacked or why only the Africans had been shot execution-style. I just knew they weren't after me because I'm 'nobody' from Bend, Oregon.

Duane, I guess, could be some sort of genius computer whiz who was going to build weapons for guerillas whether he liked it or not.

Then my stomach tied into knots again. *What if they were after Bella?*

That was the most satisfying pee of my life. I felt somewhat better as the guy shackled me back onto the metal bar.

Duane seemed eerily calm again. Almost as if he was channeling some spiritual being to help him through that difficult time. His eyes remained focused on the tent opening and as it got darker and darker, he got stiller and stiller. I almost thought, at one point, that he had stopped breathing all together. Then I started staring at his chest and it continued rising and falling, just not as rapidly as mine did.

"How do you do that?" I eased up onto my elbow, thankful that Bella had finally nodded off to sleep.

He moved his gaze from the tent opening to me. "I breathe," he said, and he sounded an awful lot like my Yoga instructor.

I didn't do well in Yoga. If Yoga had been a graded class, I would have gotten an F. I just don't get the whole breathe concept. I'm a big bear. You know what I'm thinking because I have big broad movements and I scream a lot.

Duane was like a panther. Quiet and refined, but he looked ready to strike if need be. He'd be really good at Jeopardy. I bet he'd be the first to buzz-in every time. I guessed that was why he was channeling his inner strength. To be the next Jeopardy champion.

"Whatever." I really wasn't interested in becoming one with my diaphragm at that particular moment. I wanted to become one with a king-size bed with flannel sheets and a pizza—a big one, with everything. I'd even eat anchovies. I closed my eyes to ease the ache in my stomach.

To my surprise, I slept rather well on that uncomfortable cot with imminent doom hanging over us.

I didn't wake until Bella nudged me in the boob.

"What?" I said grouchily, and had flash backs of my ex-boyfriend who always woke up horny. I would have given anything to be in his bed right then. "Sorry," I mumbled as an apology and looked up at her tear-streaked face.

"I'm hungry," she confessed. The poor girl looked frail and dehydrated.

"Hey," I yelled loudly.

Duane didn't even flinch. He was an odd bird. He was still staring at that damn opening.

"The child is hungry." Not to mention the adults too, but I could wait. Bella could not. "Please," I tried again and that time, someone tossed my bag in. Thank God I packed snacks. I peeled open the last Snickers and handed it to her. She inhaled it in three bites, and then looked at me for more. She looked like Ruger at the dinner table, waiting for scraps. I opened a bag of Doritos, handed it to her and then handed a granola bar to Duane.

He shook his head and went back to his *breathing*.

I shrugged and ate it myself, saving half for him or Bella if we lived long enough to eat it.

The camp seemed to get very quiet after a short while and all I could hear was the shrieks of monkeys and the loud sound of a cricket that was either right in my ear, or burrowed into the dirt directly below my cot. Smells from the camp had stopped. I was no longer being tortured by the smell of coffee.

The heat was enough to drive me insane, so I peeled off my shirt and ripped the sleeves off it. Then it was a nice, cool tank top and I must say Duane was like no man I have ever met. He didn't even flinch while I sat there in my Victoria's Secret sexy bra and ripped the sleeves off my shirt.

His ability to not be affected by starvation and lack of plumbing was amazing.

I laid my head back down on the cot and stared at him in amazement.

He finally moved his eyeballs—just his eyeballs—over to meet my gaze. "Problem?"

"You're amazing. I've never seen anyone so calm in my entire life. Aren't you the least bit freaked out about this?"

"No," he said, and I actually believed him. "Now please be quiet."

I didn't feel like being quiet. Being quiet felt like I was just waiting for them to come into the tent, drag me out by my hair, and torture me. "What do you do for a living, Duane?"

"Computer stuff."

I narrowed my eyes on the man. He didn't sound like a computer nerd. They usually said things like *mobile motherboard ISB technician* or *intranet services specialist.* They don't say computer *stuff.*

"What kind...." I was just trying to make conversation, before we all died. If I was going to share a mass grave with this man, I wanted to know what he did for a living and where he was from. Sheesh.

"Shhhh," he shushed me. He had some nerve.

Bella was still asleep which was a good thing, because the minute one of the assholes' blonde head popped into the tent, Duane struck with lightning speed and snapped his neck like a twig. It made the most god-awful sound, and then the man's dead body dropped to the dirt.

Duane had somehow gotten out of his restraints and pulled the man's body into the tent.

"Holy hell," I shouted breathlessly, and backed up as far as I could away from Duane. "Wh-Wh-Why'd ya do that?" I never even knew I had a stutter until that moment in which I looked at the dead guy and tried to speak. Thank God, there was no blood.

Bella woke up and screamed bloody murder at the sight of a dead man lying next to her.

Duane quickly shushed her and gave us both an evil glare.

"Who are you?" I demanded and he winked.

That was it. He winked.

He grabbed my nail file and he managed to get both Bella and me free of our chains, before he stuck his head out of the tent.

It suddenly made sense that he wanted my purse. The man was MacGyver.

Duane looked left, looked right and I finished cleaning out the pockets of the dead guy. All I found was a pack of cigarettes, a lighter, a bunch of African coins and a couple of Tums, but no food. Damn. At least we could get our calcium for the day.

Duane grabbed my hand, I grabbed Bella's and we were out the door of the tent and under the cover of a canopy of tall trees. I could tell that elephants and giraffes had had their way with these trees, which meant that we were all about to get the poor man's version of an African Safari. Yippee.

Duane got us safely behind some trees before running back to the camp for a few short minutes.

My sense of survival in the big bad jungle couldn't have come at a better time. Besides the fact that I was shocked that computer nerd had saved our asses, I wasn't entirely sure that computer nerd wouldn't do the same thing to us. The way my luck was, he had saved us just so he could chop us up in the jungle and eat our organs to keep *himself* alive.

I blame my wild imagination on people ignoring me as a child.

I couldn't hear anything at that point, and I decided that it was just as dangerous to be with a man who could kill with just his own two hands, so we took off running as fast as my size eights could carry me. My heart pounded in my chest and the burning in my thighs was just another reminder that I wasn't in the best shape of my life. I still had the speed, but I was paying the price. *Bella was being dragged through the brush by her frenzied nanny.* Thank God, the paparazzi weren't around.

Duane soon caught up to us. I don't know how he did it, but the man had like super powers or something. I rather hoped he was Clark Kent for a moment, but I feared that he was a serial killer. I even had names picked out for him in case the FBI ever found our bodies—the Serengeti Strangler or the Savanna Stalker.

His jaunt through the African plains didn't even disturb his breathing. He returned with a couple of handguns, three canteens of water and blood on his hands. "Why are you running from me?"

"Duh." I felt my eyes roll back and I think I said that aloud, and then I did the usual and passed out in the weeds.

When I woke up, I was staring down at Duane's ass. Literally. I was atop his shoulder getting jostled and bounced as he ran through the tall brush. Good thing was that when I puked, I managed not to get any vomit on his Dockers. Considerate of me, wasn't it?

"Fuck," he shouted and dropped me like a hot potato to the jungle floor. "What the fuck?"

I puked again, but not much came out; just the Tums that I had eaten. "Nice," I said as I stood up and brushed the dirt from my butt with dignity. "There's a kid present. Would you mind keeping the cussing to a minimum?"

To my amazement, his glasses had been tossed to the ground, his hair ruffled from its perfect nerd-like state and he tossed his checkered shirt to the ground, leaving him in a very tight, not-so-white tee-shirt. Nerd-boy was ripped.

He took two aggressive steps towards me.

I peeled my eyes off his torso and glared into his eyes, "Who are you?"

He didn't say anything, but turned, mumbled under his breath, something to the effect of, "*stupid broad,*" and then started walking faster.

Bella and I could barely keep up, but after debating with my inner instincts, I quickly decided that he was our only shot at survival. We couldn't possibly survive out there on our own, without food, water, and a gun to keep the wild things from feasting on our meaty bodies.

Great. I preferred Duane the Yoga enthusiast. I had no idea who I was dealing with here, but I had no choice in the matter.

"Did you grab a phone? A walkie-talkie, a radio? Anything?" I finally caught up to him.

"Look, lady..."

Now I'm a lady. Great.

He looked me up and down, scowled, and then continued walking.

"I'm talking to you." I grabbed the back of his arm.

Okay, bad move.

He tossed me to the ground before I even knew what hit me. I mean, I know I have some moves of my own, but this guy was quick. His forearm was pressed tightly against the under side of my chin, pressing my head into the dirt. His body was poised on top of me and if I had been quicker, I would have nailed him right in the cajones. Except that I wasn't quicker, so I got him hard in the hip.

He didn't even flinch. He *was* Superman.

He pressed harder with his forearm and glared fiercely. "Charlie, is it?"

I nodded the best I could under the circumstances.

"Don't piss me off." Then he let me go.

I got up, dusted myself off and followed him, silently, holding Bella's hand.

"Asshole," I said under my breath and got no response from the man. I suppose I shouldn't have said that because I had just witnessed him snap a man's neck and I'm sure he was just biding his time until he could do the same to me, but I was pissed off and when I'm angry I tend to cuss—a lot!

At dusk, we stopped and found a quiet place under a tall tree. I had seen my fair share of beautiful animals, but to tell the truth, they really aren't that beautiful when they are up close and personal. In fact, even little innocent gophers looked like they could rip my throat open with one bite.

Duane had obviously done this before and as I watched him make Bella a bed with big tree branches and leaves, I actually thought he might be a nice guy. He made a fire and he was wonderful with her. Not so much with me, but he was good with her. With me, he had no patience. It was as if I had done something to him in another life and he hadn't forgiven me yet. He barked orders at me, gave me that sinister stare, and demanded that I go catch something to eat for dinner.

He had a gun in his hand at the time, so I didn't argue. I hesitantly took off in search of Bugs Bunny and when I found him, I shot him in the ass. "Sorry, Bugs. We're hungry." I grabbed the white fury bunny by the legs and carried it out away from my body, so the blood wouldn't drip on my new Banana Republic capris. I did have the worst luck in the world. I had finally found a pair of pants that actually fit perfectly and they were certainly going to be ruined when a stampede of elephants kill me.

The sky was darkening more and more every second and I still was having a hard time believing what had happened. What did I ever do to deserve the wrath of God? I've never done drugs. I've only slept with three men in my entire life. I go to church every couple of years. I obeyed my parents even when I thought they were nuts, and I eat my vegetables. Why, God? Why?

I was back in the blink of an eye and, if I do say so myself, Duane was surprised and that amused me to the point of conceit. I held the bloody dead bunny in front of him and Bella started shrieking wildly.

He consoled her and ridiculed me for not being more sensitive. I couldn't win with this guy and I could care less.

Except I do care, I thought as I tossed and turned in the dirt. I do care that men think highly of me. Just one more good reason to see a therapist.

I'm constantly trying to win the approval of any man I meet. I'm also highly competitive and that never goes over well with the opposite sex. Perhaps I'm just too much woman for any man to handle. *Yeah, right.*

Even then, I was staring across the fire at him telling Bella a goodnight story and I was jealous. I was actually jealous that this buffoon was spending time with Bella and not paying attention to me. Boy, my issues run deeper than I ever imagined.

"Goodnight," I yelled across the fire. Then I rolled over and closed my eyes.

When I woke up in the middle of the night because I was chilled, Duane was sitting vigil over the fire and he gave me a quick nod of acknowledgement when our gazes locked.

"Sleep well?"

"No," I snapped and stretched the kink out of my back. "Do you want to sleep now? I could watch the fire."

He narrowed his eyes. Now that's the Duane I knew and loathed. "Can you stay awake?"

He looked as if he didn't trust me. Little did he know; I once stayed up for over seventy-two hours straight. I wasn't about to divulge anything about myself at this point because I was still unsure as to which side he was on. He was most likely just another bad guy that I would eventually have to escape from, but for the time being, I just enjoyed the company.

"I can do it," I stammered and got to my feet, picked up the other gun and held it firmly in my grasp before lowering myself onto the tree stump beside him. He looked at me with a tight jaw. "What did I ever do to you?" I said out of pure spite and because I was cranky. PMS hits me at the worst times. "Go to sleep. You look exhausted." There I was, doing my mommy imitation and I do it well.

He shook his head with a smirk and curled up next to the fire. It wasn't long before we stopped staring at each other and he closed his eyes.

I remained awake because I had to and because I had just survived a day from hell on a plane with men with guns, and I wasn't about to be eaten by Simba while I slept.

Bella actually looked peaceful as she slept and I wondered if her father would fire me for this little adventure. Surely, Roald wouldn't blame me for getting on a plane with hijackers. Then again, stranger things have happened to me. I am the world's unluckiest woman.

I shuddered and stared at the fire. I heard coyotes in the distance and I'm no Marlin Perkins, but I know a jackal when I hear one. I heard the high-pitched squeal of some poor animal caught by what sounded like a panther and that had me thinking about Duane again. His black hair was short, but was still shaggy enough to lightly touch the tops of his ears. He wasn't handsome by the usual standards, but something about his eyes weakened my knees. It was probably fear. After all, those sensations do get confused from time to time, especially for me.

His arms were taut, yet relaxed while he slept and every so often, his mouth would twitch upward in the hint of a smile.

He popped one eye open and looked directly at me. That thing on his face was most certainly a smile. Okay, it was more of a salacious grin.

"Stop staring at me while I sleep." He closed his eye again. "It's creepy."

I laughed quietly, which felt good because I needed to have a little levity brought into the situation that I found myself in. Bella and I were miles from nowhere in the middle of Africa with a scary guy, no food, and three tampons. If I started my period now, I would be humiliated by tomorrow afternoon. Great! My life couldn't get much worse.

I stopped staring at Duane because it wasn't helping my resolve to remain awake. Every time I looked at him or Bella, I just felt that much sleepier.

I heard a rustling in the woods and I wondered if perhaps the other bad guys had followed us. That would certainly make my life worse. I hoped it wasn't so, but I didn't take a chance; I whipped around and squeezed off a shot at the dark figure in the tall grass.

The gunshot brought Duane to his feet, gun drawn. He looked wide-eyed at me.

I was numb. I either had just killed a bad guy, or Big Foot. I motioned to Duane with my gun and he followed my line of fire right to Bambi's momma. He pulled the deer from the weeds and told me to close my eyes.

"I don't have a problem with animal blood," I said as an explanation. "It's just human blood."

"Let's not take any chances." He motioned for me to close them and I did. When I reopened them, he had the deer's neck mutilated and had a couple of pieces hanging in the fire. "Breakfast," he said, then lay down and closed his eyes.

I was fuming. No "*Thank you, Charlie, for keeping me fed.*" Ooooh, he was tremendously irritating.

The good news was that I got to witness the most amazing sunrise that I have ever seen. It was as if God had just sent me a sign that I wouldn't die that day.

Then I heard the roar of a Jeep. Duane was on his feet in no time and had Bella over his shoulder, running toward the cover of the trees. I had my gun drawn, as did he, but he looked much cooler than I did. He had this down pat. I was beginning to think that he was a crazed mercenary who lived off the land. Because most technology whizzes can't kill with a single snap, or gut an entire deer with a pocketknife, unless, of course, he had been a boy scout when he was a kid. Then again, that wouldn't explain the neck snapping ability.

Honestly, I didn't know what to think.

The Jeep roared by and when I saw that it was a government Jeep, I made as if I was going to jump out of the trees and flag them down. That's when *buffoon-man* hauled me backwards and held his hand tightly clasped across my mouth.

Call me immature; call me crazy, I don't care. I lapped his palm with my tongue, over and over again until he released me.

"Are you nuts?" He wiped his hand down my chest a couple of times. I think he was enjoying it a little too much.

"*Hello*," I said under my breath in case I had to urge to start cussing too. "We need to get home. Those men could still be after us. We need help."

"NO," he shouted and I feared for my life. He raised his gun up against my temple. I felt the cool hard steel of it against my skin. *Gulp.*

"What you need to do is shut the fuck up. Listen to me. Do what I say when I say it and follow me."

I nodded. What more could I do? I had a gun too, but I was not prepared to use it, so pointing it at him would have been futile.

We headed back to our camp. Doused our fire, ate Bambi's mom, packed up my bag and we followed Duane.

It was hours later when I looked around and felt a familiarity. I don't know a lot about Africa, but I do know what it feels like to go around in a circle.

"Excuse me." I was talking so much nicer to him since I understood his intentions fully. "Are you sure you know where you are going?"

His Evil-Eye glare was coming at me. Yep.

My mother had not taught me well. Mothers are supposed to teach their daughters that they are never ever supposed to question a man's sense of direction. That only leads to fights, screaming and cricks in backs from sleeping on couches.

I continued down the trail and stopped only when he said we could. Many times during the day, he actually gave Bella a piggyback ride, which I thought was wonderful. He also knew what kind of fruits we could eat and divvied up the water the best he could.

Bella and I remained silent because I wasn't fond of the evil glares, and he seemed more at ease when I wasn't flapping my jaws at him. Bella seemed to be doing all right under the circumstances. Hell, under the circumstances, she was doing a hell of a lot better than I was. I'd had no idea that I was so opposed to nature. No, I take that back. I'm not opposed to nature as long as I know it ends somewhere. That just seemed never-ending.

Duane got us up to a plateau high above the plains and that was where we stopped for the night. That being my second day without real food, a toilet, a shower and a clear picture of my future, I was beginning to lose it. Literally, I dropped to the dirt and wept like a child.

"Why?" I shouted at God, which I do from time to time. "Why me? I swear you are punishing me for something. Why can't I just have a normal life, without getting fired every five-months, without getting guns pointed at my temples, and without periods? What is your problem?" I shouted then collapsed into a heap of shaking bones.

Bella became the strong one. "We're going to be fine. Do you remember telling me that? We're going to get home, you can marry my dad, and I won't be mean to you anymore. I promise. I'm sorry if I've been mean. I didn't mean it," Bella said as she held my hand. I'm sure that Buffoon was plugging his ears at that point.

Back the hell up...

"What?" I almost laughed. "You want me to marry your dad?"

Her eyes filled with tears. "Isn't that why you took the job, to be with my dad?"

Absurd.

Perhaps not, perhaps, the three nannies that preceded me over the past two months were after her father's affections. Thus, the attitude I got when I arrived.

"Wow, that actually explains a lot," I said and curled an arm around her shoulder. Duane made the fire again and left us two girls to finish our heart-to-heart.

"I don't want your dad. I took this job because I love being a nanny and I have two more semesters before I finish my master's degree at UCONN. Your father has nothing to do with it."

Duane came back with three or four rodents, a peacock and some figs and dates.

"But you kissed him. I saw you kissing him before we left."

I could tell that Duane was desperately trying to keep a smile off his face. He was privy to a lot more than I wanted him to know. Not that it mattered, I was just happy that he finally tucked his gun into the waistband of his pants.

"Your father was a little drunk and upset about your mom leaving. He was just being...." I almost said it, but I held back.

"A man?" Duane finished for me and waved his hand in the air, as if prodding me to finish my sentence. "I didn't mean to eavesdrop, but I assume that's what you were going to say."

"Yes," I said smugly. "Your father was just being a man and trying to fix everything by glomming onto another woman."

Duane laughed and sat back against a large boulder. "Not all men glom."

"Ha!" I retorted.

"Ha!" He actually smiled.

Bella sat back and smiled too. "So, you don't want to marry my dad and you're still going to be my nanny after I was so mean to you."

"Bella, I've been in your shoes before and I know what it's like to want a father's attention. I don't blame you for being a bitch. I was the same way when I was a teenager. My father was so damn busy watching my perfect brothers that he didn't even see me half the time."

"So, you don't hate me?"

"Are you kidding?" I pulled her into another hug. "Bella, you remind me so much of myself at your age, it scares me. I think that if we just talk to each other from now on, that we might actually become friends. That is if you want to be friends with an old lady like me," I said playfully.

Bella and I talked some more and got comfortable around the fire. That is until he interrupted us. I looked over at him and stood up, dusted off my butt and made as if I was stretching out a kink.

"Rat or bird?" He really had the buffoon thing working for him.

"Bird," I said sharply and when he turned to pull the peacock leg from the stick, I pulled the gun from his waistband and held it up to his temple. I too have some impressive moves and I could tell that I had just taken the wind right out of his sails.

He dropped the peacock leg into the dirt and got very still. I appreciated that he was taking me seriously. The safety was on, so I knew it wouldn't accidentally blow his head off, but I did get somber for a few short minutes.

"How does it feel?" I stared at the side of his face that was tight with rage. "Don't do that...." I pushed harder with the gun and made his skin pucker right where it made contact with his temple. "Drop the stick."

He dropped it.

Bella scooted out of my way so I could back off just enough for him to stand up.

"Charlie," he said slowly, and stood up even slower with his hands raised in the air. "Put the gun down. I'm sorry for doing what I did, but I have my reasons. Please, put the gun...."

He had me on the ground on my back before I had time to flinch.

Damn I need to work on my *cat-like* reflexes. He tossed the gun aside and it was just him and me; no guns, just evil glares and tight lips.

My heart beat wildly in my chest.

"Do that again, and I will tie your hands behind your back and drag you the rest of the way."

"Fine," I shouted and actually saw spit flying from my mouth, which is not attractive in any light. "Then tell me who the hell you are and what you are doing with us." Now that he was unarmed and lying flat against me, I saw him in a completely new light. He was a man. He was *all* man, with muscles that tightened when he stirred, and he had a ripple to his abs that I haven't felt since my days rolling around with fellow men in green. Damn. I was turned on.

"Look." He lifted his chest off mine just enough for me to take a deep breath. "You just have to trust me."

Then he got off me, stood up and extended his hand.

When I refused to take it, he raked it through his hair a couple of times. Clearly, he felt a bit stressed.

"Let's eat." He grabbed up both the guns and tucked them under his feet just in case I got any wild ideas.

Chapter Five

"**Where did you** learn about guns?" Duane asked me around the fire that night.

Bella had conked off to sleep after eating a healthy portion of dirty peacock and some figs. Neither of us women-folk would eat the rodent, so Duane let us share the bird as an apology for pointing his gun at my head.

I shrugged in lieu of an explanation. I still didn't know who we were dealing with, why those guys hijacked our plane or why we were going in circles. "Around the hood," I finally lied, because it was fun and I was certain that he had been lying to me for the past two days.

His head rocked back when he laughed and I got a clear shot of his nostrils. Even on a guy like Duane, nostrils are just not sexy. Not even in the firelight. Most things are sexy in the firelight, but not Duane's nostrils. I shook my head to return to normality and fixed my gaze on his big brown eyes.

"How about you? Where did you learn all those moves?"

"The hood," he mocked, and I really didn't think it was funny.

I looked around and listened to the sounds of the night. "Do you think they might come looking for us?"

He shrugged, but I knew he was keeping something from me.

"Alright, hot shot, what's the dang deal? Are you some sort of mercenary freak, CIA, KGB, a spook, what?"

"Charlie," he said. "Has anyone ever told you that you talk too damn much?"

"No."

Actually, no one has ever said that to me. I personally don't think that I talk too much. Sure, I can't shut off my brain even for a minute, but I'm usually quite careful about what I say and when I say it. I'm usually a very guarded person when it comes to conversations with neck-breaking maniacs. He just didn't like my questions. "Are you refusing to answer the question?"

He winked again and leaned back against the rocks, closed his eyes and started snoring within minutes. I stayed awake until he changed positions, then I said, "Your turn," and I curled up with Bella and fell fast asleep.

When we woke up, I started feeling a familiar pain in my lower abdomen. Great, my period was right on time. Duane was already helping Bella eat some fruit when I snuck off into the bushes. I would have given anything for a shower, or a box of Tampax.

When I returned, Duane was putting one gun into the waistband of his Dockers and he tightly grasped the other in his palm.

He looked at me.

I looked at him and neither of us said a word.

The temperature had to be up in the mid-nineties by the time the sun was beating straight down on us. We had been walking for what seemed like miles. My hair was matted to my forehead. I reeked like body odor and Bella looked wiped out and was muttering to herself in tongues. She was clearly becoming delirious from dehydration and lack of junk food.

"We need to find clean water," I said carefully, so he wouldn't ram his gun down my throat. "We can't go on without water. It's hotter than Hades out here."

"Nice nanny talk," he groaned, and kept on going.

I stopped dead in my tracks and grabbed Bella before she keeled over.

"Let's go," he demanded, and then Bella and I sat down. I could've gone on a bit further, but I had a child to think about as well.

"Water."

"Get up." He waved his gun at both of us and although I don't think he meant it with hostile intentions, I sure took it that way. I'd had it up to my eyeballs with his shit and I was certain that he was leading us right back to where we started.

"I know what you are..." I shouted loudly and stood up. "You're a Marine."

"What makes you say that?" he asked with a chuckle as he stepped toward me.

"Because I heard that Marines were COCKSUCKERS," I screamed at the top of my lungs and glared hard.

He took three intrusive steps towards me so that we were toe to toe and he stared me down. "Do you have a death wish?"

"Tell me who you are and where we are going. NOW," I shouted, and when he glared and turned around, I kicked his back foot out from under him and wrestled him to the ground. We rolled a couple of times and I ended on top that time, with the gun from the back of his pants, I might add. I didn't point it at him. I just wanted him to see that I had moves too.

"What now, sweetheart?" he asked. He bit down on his lower lip. The man was clearly patronizing me at that point. I glared and angled myself lower. We were torso-to-torso, breast-to-breast and nose-to-nose. I could feel his breath, hot on my dried lips. I licked them once before speaking and I swear he stopped breathing for a couple of seconds.

"I'm not going to ask again. Tell me the God-damned truth. Why were you on that plane and are we still in danger?"

He bucked his hips, which felt sort of fun, and then he rolled me over into the dirt and stood up. "I have to go back to camp, I left something and I need it."

"What are you, a spy?"

His eyes narrowed. I might have hit the jackpot.

"Jesus fucking Christ, woman, can't you just shut up for two seconds?"

"No," I shouted. "No I can't, not when you're keeping the truth from me. I need to get home. Her father is probably out of his mind with worry...." Then it dawned on me that a search party was most likely already underway. "What if those Jeeps the other day were out looking for us? What if her father is trying to find us and he can't because you are dragging us around god-knows-where to do god-knows-what?"

"You need water," he said. "You're delusional."

Then he walked off in a different direction. He carried Bella most of the way, and I carried her for the rest of the way. I could hear the rushing water, before I could even see it. Awww, I could almost taste it.

I helped Bella down the rocky terrain to a small pool where a waterfall was trickling down a plateau. The water was fresh, but not drinkable according to Duane. He made a fire quickly and busted open one of the canteens to use as a pan. We boiled the water, and let it cool down while we swam. I needed a swim; it was a chance to get clean and wash my hair.

Bella was so child-like, splashing around in the coolness.

Duane sat on a big rock and just watched. I think he was enjoying watching me swim in my underwear more than anything else. I swam over to him a number of times and urged him to get in, but he refused. Said it wasn't safe.

"What could happen?" I said, and as I said it, I saw it, too. A Jeep with only a driver and one passenger, but this time, it wasn't Government Issue. It was the same red Jeep that we saw in camp when we escaped. That meant that we had to be close to where we started.

I shivered and hunkered down in the grass in my underwear and bra while Duane snuck off to deal with the problem. What neither of us planned on was that bad guy number three was lurking in the bushes just beyond where our fire was. Bella remained on the edge of the lake, huddled under a tree branch that was probably home to a big long snake. Glad I was out of the water. I hate snakes. Ick.

I heard shots fired.

I feared for Duane's life, no matter who he was. He had saved our lives and although he bugged the crap out of me with his covert ops bullshit, I didn't want him to die.

It would have been nice if he would have left a weapon for me, but he didn't, so I had to sneak off behind bad guy number three and brain him with a tree branch. He went down with a thud just as Duane came back, swearing, panting, and holding his left shin. Blood, I saw blood. It was right there, on Duane's pants. I looked up from the blood and kept my eyes directly on his face.

"Fuck," he shouted again and sat down hard in the bushes.

"Bad guy," I motioned over my head and his eyes immediately went to my breasts. After all, I do have a great rack. "What should I do?" I stayed as far away from the blood as I could. "Did you get shot?"

He shook his head and ripped his pants off, turning them into makeshift shorts. He wrapped the extra material around his wound and hobbled over to *unconscious-man* and me. "Kill him."

"Uh, I don't know about that," I said as I stumbled backwards.

"Look out," he groaned, shoved past me, and then did the unthinkable and snapped the guy's neck. Two-feet in front of me, the man died, another South African taken out by the buffoon. I sat down hard in the bushes.

"Did you have to do that?"

"Yes."

He was a man of action and very few words. Which I appreciated at that point, because nothing he could have said would have made any of that any easier on my nerves.

We returned to the cool lake for one more dip while Duane confiscated the Jeep and dumped the dead guys into the bushes. All of them looked the same, tall, blonde white guys wearing Polo shirts and khaki shorts.

"Does this have anything to do with us?" I wanted to know that right off. I didn't suspect that it did, but after all, Bella's grandfather was still in hiding and he had pissed someone off at the highest level.

"What do you mean?" he said and lifted Bella into the backseat. "If you are asking if those guys would have killed you then, yes. They would have killed us all."

"No, that's not what I mean. Do you know who Bella is?"

He looked into the rearview mirror, did a wonderful impression of a poker player and then looked at me. "No."

He took off around the lake. I felt so much better since I was clean and fresh, now if I could just get home, alive.

After what seemed like about an hour, he turned behind a large tree and stopped, cut the ignition and slumped forward over the steering wheel.

"What?" I asked.

"I can't take you with me."

"What do you mean?"

"Get out," he demanded and I, obviously, wasn't about to budge. I was unlucky, but not stupid. Never stupid. "Now. Please." He looked over his shoulder at Bella who started wailing. I slapped him hard in the chest for being such an insensitive jerk. "Now. I mean it Charlie. I can't do this with you two tagging along."

Mercenary, my ass. He had to be an assassin. That's what he was and he must have lost his information on his mark, or his high-powered rifle pen that shoots poisonous darts. I'm a huge Bond fan. Can you tell?

"You are not ditching us in the middle of Africa to go off and do whatever it is you do. Are you insane? She's a child for Christ's sake."

"And you're a very doting nanny," he grinned and pulled his gun out.

Damn, I hated it when he did that.

He leveled the barrel on my chest and said to Bella nicely, "Bella, please get out of the vehicle and tell your nanny to do the same."

"Fuck you," Bella screamed and got out.

Duane and I exchanged a wide-eyed expression...and I got out.

"You're a...." Again, I just couldn't think of a good line, "...dick." I shouted, but I doubt he heard me over the roar of the Jeep engine. "I'm so sorry," I held Bella tightly. "I know you miss your dad and we shouldn't be here right now, but we'll be okay. I know we will." I lied through my teeth, looked down at my feet and saw a gun and a canteen.

I picked them both up, but he was still a *dick*.

Bella and I chose to walk around the under side of the plateau, that way one of us could walk backward, one of us could walk forward and we only had to worry about being jumped from one side because a tall rock wall was to our right.

"Do you really think this has something to do with Grandpa Claude?" Bella asked, and then switched places with me so that I could walk backward for a while. "I know that something has happened and my grandmother and my dad won't tell me. Do you think he's in trouble?"

"Honestly, sweetie, I don't really know. It's either that, or something totally random and we just were in the wrong place at the wrong time." I tried to think of something comforting to say. "Why don't you tell me what is going on. We'll make a game of it and pretend that we are screenwriters and this is just a movie. What would happen next?" I was actually excited about this game and she seemed amused too.

"Okay," she started smiling again. "If this were my movie, Duane would be a secret agent and he would come back and rescue us from the dinosaurs that a madman had been building in the Congo. He would fight the T-Rex, sweep you into his arms and kiss you."

I laughed.

I think I might have had the same fantasy, without the dinosaurs and without clothes. I had no idea how I could be so physically attracted to such a bad, bad man. A man who killed without mercy and dumped us in the Serengeti to fend for ourselves.

Okay, my turn," I said, and switched places with her because I was somehow getting motion sick from walking backward. "Your grandfather is being held captive in an ancient tomb and Duane is an archeologist trying to find Noah's Ark, but he ran across your grandfather instead. Then he had to escape because of booby traps and then lost the map to where the Ark was hidden. Your grandfather offered to help find the Ark if he agreed to keep you safe wherever you go. Then Duane goes back for his treasure, calls your dad and they send a helicopter to pick us up right before we get trampled by a herd of elephants. No kissing occurs at the end of my story because Duane dies in a fiery death while being blasted with poisonous darts and eaten alive by piranhas who feast on his flesh until he's just a skeleton. Then someone takes his bones and rolls over them with a steamroller until they are piles of rubble and then they get incinerated and his ashes are tossed into the ocean for hungry sharks to feed on." I finally took a breath and slapped my hands together in righteous glee.

"You like him," Bella grinned. "*Don't* you?"

I think I blushed, or at least it felt like I blushed.

We picked dates and figs, hung out in the tall grass, and watched the antelope jump up and down. I saw a giraffe for the first time in my life and I saw many bugs the size of my fist.

Bella really seemed to be enjoying herself despite our situation and she finally opened up to me about her parents' split, her life, and the boy she liked at school, but she wasn't sure if he really liked her or if he just wanted to hang out because he might get to see her father. She confided in me that she wished she had a normal dad.

I told her that even normal dads have their problems and that my dad's a doctor and he managed to screw me up, so she should think about talking to a counselor at school, or a friend, or even me. After all, I hoped to be around for another eight months at least so I could finish my degree and have that much more money for a house and the car of my dreams. I had it all drawn out. A black Ford Expedition with running boards, fog lamps and a rack on the front and back for the kids' bikes and camping equipment. Bella liked hearing about my dream and my plan, and I told her that it's good to have a plan because it keeps you focused, and it is okay if the plan doesn't work out exactly as planned; just as long as you are happy.

I think it did some good for Bella to hear what I had done with my life. It's not every day that a confused girl like me picks herself up, dusts herself off and stays on track in pursuit of what she wants most.

I loved listening to Bella's stories too, because it made me feel like a kid again. You know, to have that butterfly feeling in your stomach when a cute boy looks at you; the feeling of innocence and wonder about the great big, unknown world. The big world filled with strange creatures that I still have yet to figure out. Men were still the greatest mystery to me. I just never got close enough to my father or my brothers to get a handle on how they tick. I just knew that men were fun to look at and I hoped that one day I would find a good one to marry.

I stared at the fire and wondered why no one had rescued us yet. Clearly, our plane never made its destination and certainly Roald had to be overwrought with worry, fretting for his daughter. No one would be fretting over me because I didn't even tell anyone I was going to Africa. I was sure my father would somehow blame *me* for getting myself eaten by a lion when he heard news of my death. I was sure in his head it would all be about what I did wrong and he'd concentrate on the negative versus the plus side.

I really couldn't see a plus side to me being Leo's dinner, so I tossed the thought from my mind and concentrated on the mating sounds of the Mandrills. At least I hoped they were mating calls and not some prelude to seizing the dates and figs that we had foraged. Mandrills never looked friendly, no matter how I looked at them. They always just looked pissed off. I guess if my white ass were hanging out there for the world to see, I'd be pretty pissed off too.

At least I ate well during our time alone without Duane the assassin. Bella had filled us up with every kind of fruit we could find and the seared rabbit was divine. Thank God, *dick* left us a gun. We even had peanuts for desert, although I would have preferred sprinkling them on top of an ice cream sundae while sitting on the couch and watching "Star Wars" for the hundredth time. But they were a nice treat and yes, God, I did appreciate them.

I tried to keep focused on the fire and all the amazing colors it made after Bella finally nodded off to sleep. I could feel the hair on the back of my neck standing on end every time I heard a wild animal, which was every second, because I was in Africa, after all. Bella looked calm and content as she slept, despite the fact that a burly looking spider had just crawled onto her leg. I did what any doting nanny would do, scraped it off with a stick, and flung its fury body into the fire. It actually exploded like a tiny bomb going off.

It seemed that I had only just closed my eyes when I felt a tapping on my shoulder. I flung around with gun in hand and Duane once again knocked me to the ground.

"You stupid sonuvabitch," I shouted again because he not only left us alone, he just scared the piss out of me on top of it all. "Damn it, you stupid pri...."

I tried to say prick, I really did but his mouth covered mine in a mind-bending kiss that made my toes curl. His hand was hot on my breast and I wanted him...dead!

"Get off me, you buffoon," I hissed quietly, so as to not wake the child. I spit into the dirt a couple of times to let him know that he had no sexual effect on me what so ever. My pointy nipples told a different story, but it was dark. Maybe he couldn't see them.

"Asshole."

"You have quite a mouth on you for a nanny." He grinned and seemed much more relaxed. He had probably killed a lot more people. "Are you really a nanny?"

"Yes," I said haughtily, and took my seat once again. "And you are...a contract killer?"

"Boy, you aren't going to give it up are you?"

"No." I looked around behind me. "No Jeep?"

"It's over there. I didn't want you to shoot me by mistake." He pointed and helped himself to a candy bar.

My eyes dropped from his pointing hand to the chocolate in his other hand. I moistened my lips and panted.

"You want some of this?" he grinned and put it to his lips. "Come and get it."

I glared. I didn't want it that bad.

Okay, so I did. I wouldn't have minded kissing him again, but I was pissed off beyond belief and wondered why was he being so damned smug and happy all of a sudden. What could have possibly changed?

"Charlie?" he mocked, and moved closer with the piece of chocolate dangling from his lips.

"Duane," I mocked right back. "What kind of a name is Duane Johnston anyway? It sounds nerdy."

"Hey," he bit down on the chocolate, taking half of the chunk into his mouth. I drooled as I watched him enjoying it. Then the piece was only half as big, damn him. "The Rock's name is Dwayne Johnson."

"Yeah, and that's why he renamed himself The Rock," I retorted snottily. "Duane is the dweebiest name I have ever heard and it doesn't even fit you. You should be a ..." He moved closer, so close that I could smell the chocolate. "Dick. That should be your name."

"It's actually Vince." He bit off another chunk and chewed it slowly. "It's almost gone, Charlie."

My God, he is the devil.

"Vince?" I narrowed my eyes. "Vince what?"

"Just Vince," he smiled. "You know, like Cher or Madonna."

Yep, contract killer. I once saw a movie about a professional assassin and he only had one name.

Whatever his name was, moved closer to me and I could feel his knee between my thighs. His butt had to have been on fire because he was that close to the flames. He must have really trusted me.

"You left me and a child alone in the desert with lions and elephants and snakes. You're a sociopath."

"Hey," he scowled, "I'm trying to offer you some chocolate as an apology."

Yeah, chocolate and his tongue. Which would be fine under ordinary circumstances, but I still wanted him dead.

"I wasn't going to leave you out here forever."

"Kiss my ass," I said haughtily and moved backward, so far back that I fell off the stump I was sitting on and right into the dirt. He followed and was precariously perched over my lips again, but the chocolate was gone. *Double damn.*

"You need to learn a little thing, like when to shut up and cherish what you have when you have it."

"Who the hell are you, Confucius?"

He laughed and helped me up. "Seriously, Charlie, where did you learn to use a weapon? You look like such a nice girl."

I batted my eyelashes, sent him an enigmatic smile and yawned. "Can you stay awake?"

"Ha, ha very funny," he groaned.

"Vince," I said.

"Yeah."

"Did you happen to call someone and let them know where we were?"

"No radio, sweetheart. But don't worry; I know where we are now."

Why did that not help me sleep any better?

Chapter Six

The howls at the moon woke me up in the early twilight hours and I wanted to roll over and look up at that stars but Duane...I mean Vince, had an arm perched over my shoulder, so I was afraid to move. I was actually enjoying the comfort and warmth of his body wrapped around me and although I wasn't awake when he got that way, I was certainly not go to put up a fight now. I rolled carefully with my eyes closed under the pretense of still being asleep and lightly slapped my hand across his chest. I burrowed in beside him, staring over his chest as it moved up and down with every breath.

The stars were the most magnificent that I have ever seen them. Each one lit up like a bright beacon in the sky. I watched for a good few minutes before closing my eyes again.

If anything, Vince made a good pillow.

When I woke up later that morning, Vince had his hand up my shirt and he was smiling.

"Buffoon," I groaned and slipped away from his grasp before the girl woke up. "Are we finally going to get the hell out of here today?" I adjusted my bra and hoped my nipples wouldn't stay in that erect state all day. I didn't quite want him thinking that this was ever going to happen again. "So, where are we?" I looked around and saw Africa. Africa was vast.

"Coffee," he groaned and scratched his scruffy chin. "And Advil."

"I have Midol," I offered humorously.

"Ah," he moaned throatily. "I get it now." The smirk on his face really needed to be slapped off and I was just the woman to do it.

"Excuse me?"

"You're on the rag. That's why you didn't want any hanky panky."

Ooooh, I think my face reddened to the deepest shade of crimson. "I didn't want any hanky panky," I used my fingers as quotation marks in the air, "because I don't happen to be attracted to you."

"Ha!"

Bella saved him from a broken nose when she opened her eyes and sat straight up. "Are we going home today?"

"Soon, sweetie." I glared at Vince. "Vince here was just about to tell me where the heck we are."

"Vince?" She stretched and rubbed her eyes. "Who's Vince?"

I pointed at Duane and he bowed.

"Let's go."

Man-of-few-words had done it again. We packed up, headed for the Jeep and within minutes, we stopped along a deep ravine. Vince jumped out and began digging in the dirt. He came back with a dusty duffle bag and kept it concealed in his lap except for the laptop computer that he handed to me.

"What's all this?"

Maps and geological markings were already lighting up the screen. It was like no other laptop that I had ever seen. So, I was probably wrong about the fact that he was a contract killer. I was now thinking CIA, FBI, DEA, NSA, but I ruled out the KGB. I don't think that the KGB exists anymore and Vince was one hundred percent American male, or so I assumed.

I waited a long time for an explanation that I was never going to get, so I stared at the screen until it all made sense. It was some sort of global tracking device and a beacon just ahead, but more than a few miles away was blinking rapidly. It was far more advanced than anything we had used during our special ops in the Army.

"What's that?" I pointed. I wasn't about to give up, and, I was sort of enjoying myself. This was exactly the kind of thing I used to do in the Army: heavy surveillance, some infiltration and extraction, but mostly recon work.

My adrenaline surged, and I forgot how much I had missed that.

The most my adrenaline had surged in my last four years of being a nanny was when the Thompson girls locked me out of the house and then tried to make lunch. Both the daughters of Earl and Rita Thompson were as spoiled as they came, and one afternoon they thought it would be funny to lock me out, so they pushed me outside when I accepted a Fed-Ex package, and then ran around and locked every single door. There were probably ten doors, but there were two of them and only one of me.

I stayed close to the windows so I could see through and I watched them. With bated breath, I watched them and had fantasies about shaving their heads while they slept. The girls were only seven and five, but I could see that they were already well on their way to becoming the next Hilton sisters. To make a long story short, I watched Stacy, the five-year-old, pop a Pop Tart into the toaster, and then try to extract the pastry with a long serrated knife, while it was still toasting. That made my adrenaline surge to the point of tossing a lawn chair through the window and tackling her when the first spark flew.

They fired me for breaking the window and knocking the wind out of that little brat. It didn't matter that I saved her life, it just mattered that two little girls had had me and once again, I had said, "but your kids...."

"That is where *I'm* going." Vince's deep voice brought me back from feeling sorry for myself. He flipped open his duffle and handed me a compass, a couple of dried food packets and a knife. "You can keep the gun."

"Thanks," I said, but his actions utterly confused me. Was he really going to toss us into the wild again with hopes that we could find civilization before the animals ate us alive, or worse, the bad guys came back? "What are you doing?" I asked as he pulled the Jeep into a dark cave and cut the engine.

He looked over at me and this time, he actually looked sorry for what he was about to do.

"No," I shook my head. "NO YOU DON'T," I screamed, and shook him silly with all my might. I clung to the cotton of his tee-shirt and begged him not to do this. Once he got my hands free of his tee-shirt, he frowned at me and I wept like a baby. "Please! I don't know what you are doing, or who you are, but I know that in good conscious you can't just dump us again. We have half a day's water, two pouches of food and nine bullets. We won't survive through the night. How can you live with yourself?"

He yanked me from the passenger seat against my will and hauled me behind a tree. "Charlie, I'm here for one reason and one reason only. That reason does not include rescuing some spoiled teenager and her nanny. Let someone else be the hero because I'm not botching this mission on account of two civvies."

I narrowed my eyes. He most certainly had been military at one point, and could still be. Hell, he could be the Pope for all I knew.

"I'm sorry that it has to be this way. Really I am." He sent me a cautious smile. "You know, this was a lot easier for me when I thought you were just a spoiled rich tourist."

"Is that what you thought of me?"

He shrugged, and why did I care at that particular juncture? "What's your last name?" he asked me.

"Ford," I said. "Why?"

"I'll make this up to you someday, Charlie Ford." Then he kissed me. A long, deep kiss that meant business and had my muscles clenched and ready for battle. He, unfortunately, broke away much sooner than I wanted him to, because my knee hadn't connected with his groin yet.

He lifted the kicking, screaming teenager from the backseat. "Just head west." That was all the son-of-a-bitch had to say to us.

I kicked the dirt. I flipped him the bird. I called him every lousy-stinking-no-good name in the book, and then I threw a rock at the dusty trail that he left behind. If he were that noble of a man, he would have left the Jeep with the woman and child, and *he* would've gone on foot.

If I weren't a noble woman, I would have shot him in the back.

"Men!" I shouted and hugged Bella. "We'll be fine."

"I know," she smirked and pulled something out of her pocket. "Will this help?"

I glanced down at a tiny remote censor and watched the little bleep get bigger and bigger as we walked toward it. Wherever he was going, we were soon to follow.

I smiled brightly at the little kleptomaniac and was genuinely happy that she was so ingenuous. She had swiped it from his bag when he was lecturing me behind the tree. She was one smart pre-teen. We laughed wickedly and held hands before she grinned again and pulled a chocolate bar from her other pocket.

"You're my idol," I said sweetly. "Take that, Jackass." I have never enjoyed chocolate more in my entire life.

We walked. We ran from snakes. We gagged and wheezed when we accidentally swallowed bugs, but by golly, we were getting it done. We even sang some old campfire songs and played the screenwriters game again.

This time Bella dug deep into her soul and exposed her dark side.

"Okay, so Duane...I mean Vince," she giggled wickedly, "is really the bad guy and at the end, he's about to run you over in the Jeep and I throw a rock at his head. He swerves and runs over a baby lion cub and the daddy lion eats him alive while we watch."

This girl was going to need some serious therapy when and if we get home.

"Awesome," I said, but I was really starting to think like a super spy. "Duane really is his name; he's just ashamed because it's so dorky, so he calls himself Vince. He's the head of a specialized task force that is heading up a military coup of Uganda and he's here to assassinate the Prime Minister of Morocco who is here on vacation with his family. He's afraid that I am onto him because I myself am a super spy, so he flees with the fear that I might come for him while he sleeps. The beacon on this little gadget is really a signal from Club Med and when we get there, we will feast on food, drink wine and my father will come to visit, we will talk and laugh and he will listen to all the amazing things that I've done. And then we will hug and he'll tell me he's proud of me and that he loves me." I actually started crying at that point. "And then Vince will show up and I will kick him in the balls, throw him in the pool, slap my hands together and never look back."

I was very surprised that in the past few days, I hadn't seen one airplane fly overhead; not one helicopter came looking for us. It was eerie. I wasn't privy to Africa's laws about rescuing children from the savanna and all I could think was that there was some sort of protocol that they had to follow and the bureaucratic red tape was holding them up. Either that, or we had crossed the line into the Serengeti National Wildlife Refuge and we were going to be cheetah fodder soon.

It was almost nightfall when we reached something that I wished we hadn't reached. I shivered and let out a breath of sheer panic. Fear rippled along my spine.

It was set up the same as the old camp, but there were only three tents and I could see only two red Jeeps. One I could only assume belonged to Vince and that made me very nervous. Perhaps he was with the bad guys all along. Either that, or the bad guys had already captured him and Bella and I were fucked.

Either way we were fucked, but I preferred to think that I hadn't played tonsil hockey with one of the bad guys.

I refused to believe any of part of what was running through my imagination. I do have a very wild one, after all. I didn't want to believe that the bad dudes had captured Vince with his super-lightning-speed moves and panther-like reflexes. Furthermore, I refused to concede. *Give up and let Bella and myself die?*

Sure, we could have backtracked and prayed to be rescued, but by then we would be dead, and the vultures would be pecking at our dehydrated remains.

Not a pretty picture.

I figured we had one chance and one chance only, and that was to steal a Jeep, grab a map of some sort and find civilization.

I instructed Bella to stay under a bush not too far from camp. I gave her the last of the food, told her that I loved her and that if anything happened, or if someone caught her, she should tell them who her father was and that she could get them lots of money.

It was the best I could come up with at the time.

We said a small prayer together, and then it was my time to shine. I had faith that I could do it. I still remembered everything that I learned and, although I never finished the hellacious program, I had been on many real maneuvers and I still had faith that I learned as much as I could under the tutelage of that cocksucker, Master Chief Brick.

I waited until the cover of nightfall and on my first attempt at approaching camp, I stumbled and fell into a pile of elephant dung. Elephant dung doesn't stink quite like dog crap, but it's still more than disgusting and there's a lot more of it.

I heard a small howl from the bushes to my left and hoped that a lone, hungry hyena would not foil my plan. I had no idea about how many bad guys were in camp, so I decided to take inventory before I started blasting away. After all, I had only nine bullets and one fierce-looking knife. I was almost certain that I didn't have the stomach to kill a man up close and personal so I tucked the knife into my waistband and held the gun steady in my hand.

I heard boisterous laughter from the first tent and thankfully, I heard a little hissing sound that made me glance down because that heinous looking snake had just saved my life. Not six inches in front of my left foot was a thick wire either attached to a mine, or attached to an alarm. I didn't want to find out, so I carefully moved around the snake and over the wire. It was now a challenge to crawl through the grass and keep my eyes peeled for assholes and hyenas. Thank God, they both cackled before they attacked, or I would have been a goner.

I seriously feared for Bella's life and my own. I hated that I had put us in this situation and I hated that I hadn't shot Vince when I had the chance. I really wanted him dead.

But not really.

I really didn't want anyone dead, especially not Bella and me.

Especially not Bella.

I sighed and strengthened my resolve.

I could hear three distinctly different voices in tent number one. That meant that I would have to use three bullets. I moved carefully around to tent number two and heard quiet weeping. Very quiet weeping and some mumbled prayers that didn't sound familiar, so I guessed that this tent didn't house Vince.

Now I was moving at the pace of an inchworm. The wind was howling just enough so the sound of the grass flapping together muffled my noises, but I still wasn't taking any chances and remained moving at the speed of a slug. Each step I took felt like it could be my last. At least that was what I kept reminding myself of as I swallowed hard, and tried to get comfortable with the fact that I was going to have to kill in order to survive.

I heard three more male voices in tent number three. Two were of the same South African accent, similar to the men on the plane, and the third one was just grunting and groaning and not much else. This tent, I figured was where they held Vince because, after all, he was a man of few words and I had heard those grunts before. The man liked to grunt. Right then I thought he was grunting because they were torturing him and that meant that I needed two more bullets and I had better not miss.

This was where I needed to start. Once I freed Vince, he could help with the rest of the killing, but right then, I had to hang my head low, take a few deep breaths and when I narrowed my eyes on the back of the tent and saw two tall figures, I waited a split second longer. When I saw a flicker of a lighter and a shadow of a gun pointed toward the ground, I squeezed off a shot and prayed to a higher power. I heard cussing, a thud and then with lightning speed I moved around the tent, waited for bad guy number two to emerge and when he did, I took him out with one precise shot to the head.

It was dark and I didn't see much blood, which was a good thing. Another good thing was that none of the other men from tent number one came running out. I think what happened was that I had just interrupted an execution. I entered the tent and dragged the second dead asshole in with me. I slumped down into the dirt and wiped my forehead dry of sweat.

Vince, hog-tied in the dirt, was face down with a bandana around his eyes.

Won't he be surprised to see me? And damned if I didn't feel energized. I just saved a life and to my surprise, I was delighted that it was Vince's life that I saved.

I guess I liked him more than I thought.

Before letting him know who I was, I grabbed both bad guys' guns, tucked one into my waistband and then ripped the bandana off Vince's bruised and battered face. One eye was completely swollen shut and he looked bad, really bad.

"Jesus Christ," he groaned and tried to sit up. His right ankle had been badly broken and looked as if it was hanging on by a thread. It was horrifying. "Charlie? What the fuck?"

I know it was dark and all, but I swear to all things holy that a single tear rolled down his battered cheek. The entire left side of his face looked like hamburger.

"Shhhh," I demanded and I was enjoying being the one who was calling the shots. Vince was in no way going to be able to run from the tent, and I doubt that I could have carried him. He wasn't a big man by any means, probably four inches taller than me and both our bodies were rippled with muscle, but he was a man and all, so he out-weighed me by at least forty pounds. "Here." I wasn't about to gloat at this point, but I handed him two guns and helped him out of the ropes that bound his hands together. "How many more are there?"

He held up one hand.

There were five more bad guys, but I had a lot more firepower.

"They're going to wonder why Simon and Turk haven't returned to the main tent. We have to get out of here," Vince said through clenched teeth. I knew he was in horrendous pain, and I was proud of myself for not passing out. The elephant shit that I rubbed under my nose was working like a charm.

He grabbed my arm, as I was about to poke my head from the tent. "This way," he said and pointed at the back of the tent.

He had a point.

I pulled the knife from my waistband and quickly cut the thick fabric enough for us to get out. I needed to get Vince into one of those Jeeps or we didn't stand a chance.

I heard footsteps and someone calling for Turk just as I pulled my leg from the tent. All hell was about to break loose, I could feel it in my bones, but I persevered. More shouting resounded around camp. I got Vince safely tucked behind a tree.

"Don't worry about me, just go. The keys are in the Jeep," he demanded.

Yeah, like I was about to do that. I would never leave a team member behind and like it or not, I thought Vince was a good guy.

In the moonlight, I glared into his one good eye and tucked the knife back into my waistband before rolling a couple times in the tall grass and then stopping on the other side of the tent.

Did I happen to mention that I received highest marks in marksmanship? Well I did.

I took out two more South Africans with two more bullets and then remembered that I no longer had to make my ammo count.

Both men fell dramatically and lifelessly to the ground. Someone flipped on a bright light that caught me by surprise, but I jumped back behind the tent and emptied my magazine at the remaining two bad guys who were stupid enough to step into the light.

I then took a moment to calm my nerves, rein in my adrenaline and crawl back over to Vince to grab another gun.

My heart stopped dead in my chest when I saw him slumped over behind the tree. For what seemed like the longest minute of my life, I crawled toward him, praying to God that he wasn't dead. As soon as I was close enough for him to smell me his eyes popped open wide and he raised a gun to my head.

"Shit," I gasped and grabbed the gun from him. "Five, right?" I wanted to make sure.

After all, they had busted up his ankle something fierce and had beaten him senseless. Perhaps he thought he held up ten fingers thanks to the double vision that he most likely had. I took a couple of deep whiffs through my nose to clear my sinuses and took in the aroma of the crap under my nose. "You okay?"

He groaned.

"Charlie?" He grabbed my wrist. "Why are you still here? Go. Get out of here."

I shrugged out of his grasp and that wasn't difficult to do because he had just passed out again.

I crawled around the third tent, stopped and listened for any noises. There were none. It was eerily quiet so I remained out of sight and took cover under the trees around the back of the tents. I continued until I got to the second tent, where I had previously heard the quiet prayers. I peered inside and saw another man, wrapped in nylon cords, clearly battered, tortured and hung up to dry. Another white male was lying at his feet, his hands also wrapped in nylon cords only that man wasn't battered.

I steadied my gun at this man on the floor.

"Oh thank God," he said and rolled over and held up his bound hands. "We have to get out of here. There are more of them." He sounded American, but the only thing wrong with his face was a bloody nose.

If I had a downfall, it would be that I couldn't read people very well. I wouldn't be a good spy. I don't know when people are lying to me and I tend to trust what people tell me. But my gut told me that this guy wasn't being completely honest with me.

Then again, I wasn't about to put a bullet in his brain just because I was unsure.

"Please, hurry."

I needed help.

I didn't speak; I just stood there pointing my gun at his head. He was clearly unarmed and still holding his hands out for me to cut him free.

"You're American, right?" He goaded me on and attempted to stand up. He was too clean. That I noticed right away. The dirt on his pants and shirt looked rubbed on and not soiled in. I know laundry pretty well and that was *new* dirt.

"Sit," I commanded and then carefully groped for a pulse on the tied up African man. He had a pulse, so I instructed whitey to untie his hands and help him down.

He did what I asked without question and then held up his hands again. He hadn't tried anything yet and it still freaked me out that more assholes would be arriving momentarily, so I moved two steps toward him. I heard the high pitch of a bullet whiz by my head and his forehead exploded in a shower of blood.

I did lose consciousness at that point.

When my eyes fluttered open, I tried to focus, then rolled over and hurled into the grass. When I got a hold of my bodily functions, I looked over at Vince, propped up against a bench, holding his gun in one hand and my gun in the other.

I didn't know what to think. I didn't know what to say. I suspected that he was about to say enough for the both of us because he had that look in his eye, the only one that was properly functioning, and he looked pissed.

"That's why chicks should stay home and raise babies."

I had heard that line so many damn times in my life that one more time really didn't bother me all that much.

"Is that all?" I stood up with dignity and grabbed my gun from his grasp. "Don't you want to tell me that we're weaker, we're emotionally unstable and we can't follow orders?"

"You're definitely weaker. You *are* unstable and I told you to get the fuck out of here an hour ago."

"Fuck you, *sir*." I saluted him with defiance and bent down to see how badly he was hurt. He probably misconstrued my nurturing and therefore chalked up one more reason why women should stay home and raise babies.

"What branch?" he whispered into my ear when I checked the gash on the back of his skull.

"Army." I not so gently let his head fall back against the hard wood. "I think you'll live." I stood up and went to the unconscious man on the floor. "I need to get Bella." I looked over my shoulder at Vince. "Do you think it is safe here for the time being? We need food and water and..." I stopped because his gaze dropped below my waist. My khaki colored capris were covered in blood.

"Jesus, Charlie, are you hit?"

"No." I shrugged it off and felt completely humiliated, just one more reason for me to feel inferior to men. I bleed once a month, that's clearly a sign of weakness right there.

"Can I get Bella or not?" I snapped.

He nodded and rolled over a couple of times to finish helping me get the African man completely untangled from his harnesses.

The African's face was even more mangled than Vince's was.

I was still leery about taking the Jeep and making that much noise, but Vince said that he had overheard the gang of asses and they weren't due back until tomorrow at sunset, so I pulled up in front of Bella's bush and she wasn't there. It was pitch black outside and one of the only two clouds in the sky had overshadowed the moon; my guts felt tied in knots. What had I done? Some big animal, or even worse, some big South African had come for her. My heart leapt into my throat.

"Be-ll-a," I shouted loudly and dramatically, sounding a lot like Marlon Brando. After all, the names did rhyme.

Then I heard a rustling in another bush.

Hell, all these bushes looked alike. My arrhythmia stopped and Bella came running toward me.

"Are you okay?" I hugged her tightly and I hadn't been so happy to see anyone in my entire life. Somehow, she had become my mission and come hell or high water, I was going to return her to her father in one piece. "Did anything bite you? Did you get scratched by any weird bushes?" I checked her up and down and hugged her again. "We'll be home soon. I promise. I promise." I pressed a kiss into her hair and thanked God for my father, because if it weren't for my father and his many faults, I would not have rebelled against him and learned how to kill people without hesitation.

I roared back to the campsite and rustled up some fresh water, checked around for any sort of radio. I found some sort of short wave radio, but Vince warned me against using it.

"You don't know who's listening," he said as I helped him take off his shirt. He really looked good without a shirt on, but I kept my mind on the task at hand. Although I never went to medical school, I did learn the basics, so I splinted his ankle the best I could and then jammed a syringe of morphine into the hardness of his thigh.

Bella had to be the one who cleaned up his wounds because I don't *do* blood and there was no amount of elephant crap that would get me to actually play doctor on Vince's mangled face.

I brought enough cots into one tent for everyone to sleep on. I found the main tent and cleared it out, taking everything that I thought we might need, including weapons, maps, Vince's laptop and food. There were mounds of canned food, mostly stew and canned beans, but it was heavenly. I did happen to find two chocolate bars and tucked one aside to torture Vince with, but then again, do men really crave chocolate the way women do? I don't think so, so I ate the second Hershey bar without remorse. I had saved his life tonight, and that was about the last good deed I had in me for the day. I was spent.

Bella filled up on food, climbed in next to Vince while I stayed awake, and listened for strange bumps in the night. I doused the fire thoroughly and laid my head back to look at the stars. At least I knew how to appreciate nature while I was out here in the middle of nowhere. I found Orion and the Big Dipper and tried to remember the rest of my astronomy, but it was hard because I wanted to close my eyes so badly.

I had found quite a bit of first aid supplies and I had drugged Vince to high heaven so I knew it wasn't a possibility to take shifts that night. I was just going to have to suck it up and stay awake.

I began daydreaming about doing this sort of thing in even more exotic lands, like Australia and Central America. I bet the bugs in Central America were even larger than my fists so I started dreaming about room service and driving a black-and-white cruiser up and down the city streets—streets with bathrooms and hot coffee and doughnuts. I would have given anything for a cup of hot coffee and a Krispy Kreme.

I had thought so much about what I wanted to do when I grew up and now that it was less than a year away, it scared the hell out of me. I was actually going to buy a house, put down roots, get a job that I had to actually get dressed for and grow up. My life was about to change dramatically. I had just spent the last three and a half years living in other people's homes, taking care of other people's children and basically getting a free ride. Sure, I worked hard for my paychecks, but the money was astronomical for what I did and the perks were even better. I realized that all those money market accounts and all that money I had saved over the last twelve years was about to be spent. I was going to have a mortgage. I was going to have to pay utilities and buy my own food, pay for my own gas and car insurance. Ahhh. It all sounded so grown up, so unlike me.

    I actually smiled for the first time in days. A lazy smile that made all those small insignificant details seem so far away. Right then, survival was my utmost priority and I had a dire feeling that I would never look at life the same way again. I didn't think I would be taking anything for granted for the rest of my days and perhaps I did want to do more than a run-of-the-mill police officer did. Maybe I wanted more, something wilder, something more dangerous. Something like what Vince did. *Nah.* I laughed in my head. I wasn't that crazy. Besides, I still had no idea what he was up to or who he really was, but I was certainly going to find out.

Chapter Seven

The first chatter of birds jolted me out of my trance at daybreak. It was by far my most favorite time of the day here in Africa. The air was crisp and cool, the animals seemed tamer and more at ease and I liked watching Vince sleep.

"Don't *do* that," he groaned from under his blanket that he had just tossed over his eyes. Clearly, he had transparent eyelids or had extra sensory perception and had sensed that I was watching him sleep again. "Did you stay up all night?"

His face looked much better since Bella had scrubbed the dried blood from his cuts. They hadn't mangled him as badly as I feared. He still looked ruggedly handsome, even with that disapproving scowl in his face.

"I didn't close them once." I yawned, but was ready for answers, not ready for sleep. "How's your pain? I have more morphine." I patted the first aid pouch next to me.

"Why don't you go clean yourself up and Bella can find you some new pants." I guess he had more of a problem with my lack of maxi-pads then he did with his broken ankle.

He nudged Bella in the back.

She stirred and sat upright on her cot. "I had the weirdest dream." She shook her little blonde head and frowned. "Dinosaurs were coming to get us."

I giggled because it had been a long night, and I was happy that she was dreaming about big imaginary beasts rather than real ones, and then I scowled at Vince once I realized how Bella was going to get me new pants. "She's not touching D-E-A-D people."

Vince chuckled and Bella frowned.

"I *can* spell you know," she said.

Vince laughed again and dropped his weary head back onto his cot.

"Sorry," I said. "I'm so used to babysitting toddlers. I forgot."

"My duffle is in the tent that I was kept in. You can have some of my pants," Vince continued once his laughter died down.

"Thank you."

I went into the tent, retrieved the duffel, changed my pants, tore open a couple of pillows and made authentic African maxi pads with the cotton. Then I wondered what tribeswomen wore or maybe they were just lucky enough not to have periods.

I shook my head with a smirk, went through the rest of his duffle, and found more chocolate and a fancy flask with the initials R.M. etched into the bottom. I smelled the flask. It smelled like fine cognac and then I took the duffle to Vince... if that *was* his *real* name.

When I returned after eating his last chocolate bar, he was sitting up helping Bella bandage the African's arms. "Do you know who he is? Why are you here? Who are you following and who is R.M?"

"Jesus." He wiped his brow with the back of his wrist.

It was already scorching hot and I had just made him squirm. "I saved your life yesterday, pal, whether you want to admit it or not."

"I never asked you to," he snapped fiercely.

Well, I wasn't expecting *that* big of a thank you.

"Buffoon," I grumbled through my gnashing teeth. I was so stinking mad I couldn't look at him anymore. I quickly pulled his laptop off the table and flipped it on. A blank home page blinked at me and asked for a password. "Shit," I shouted and pounded my fists down on the metal camp table.

"Did you happen to learn encryption in the *Army?*" He said with conceit, disdain, and something else that I couldn't quite decipher. I think it was just pure bruised pride. A woman had saved his life and now he was going to make me feel inferior for the rest of my life because of it. "I saved your life too, you know. You were about to untie the ringleader. Didn't they teach you anything in the *Army?*"

Okay, so now I was more than convinced. It was the way he kept saying *Army* that tipped me off. He was a Marine or had at least been one at one time. It's no secret that the two don't get along. Sure, we're all on the same team, but the Marines are some of the most hard-core, war-mongering sons-of-bitches I have ever met. However, in a good way. I completely hold them in the highest regard, I just don't like to sit around and bullshit with them because it always ends in a pissing contest or a who-has-the-biggest-dick contest. Needless to say, I don't have one of those so I end up feeling quite small around Marines.

"I'm sorry," I said with my head held high. "I didn't mean to insult you the other day, I was just angry. I don't think Marines are cocksuckers. In fact, I hold them in the highest regard. Present company excluded of course." I meant it to be cocky and tinted with spite and I think I pulled it off, because he pulled me into his lap. Boy, he was fast.

We were then nose to nose again and that must have been when he smelled the chocolate on my breath. "Did you eat my chocolate?" he asked breathlessly. His entire Yoga persona had gone out the window. He was either just as turned on as I was, or he was beyond pissed off that I stole yet another one of his candy bars. I was hoping for turned on.

"Yes." I gulped and smiled. "Are you going to start giving me some answers now?"

He licked his lips. They were dry and coarse and pretty banged up but I really wanted him to kiss me.

Then I turned my head because Bella was gawking at us and I really didn't think he was going to kiss me. I think he was going to rip out my tongue and eat it for breakfast. Yep. He's a Marine all right.

I cleared my throat, got off his lap and grabbed up the supplies. It was time to start loading the Jeeps to get the hell out of there and find a phone. Bella helped me load up the African man who had opened his eyes for a couple of minutes and smiled. Most likely because I had shot his ass full of morphine and he was delusional and thought we were his harem or something. I piled on the boxes of food, all the guns I could find. I smashed the radio to bits and then stacked even more supplies into another Jeep.

Vince looked at me strangely.

"Bella can drive one," I said as I loaded up the rest of the blankets and pillows.

Bella jumped up and down, arms flailing in the air as if she were at an N'Sync concert.

"Can you drive?" Vince narrowed his eyes on the girl.

She nodded emphatically.

I wrapped an arm around her shoulder. "Sure she can. You and she can take one, and I'll take Mystery Man in the other."

"Charlie." his eyes narrowed. I don't think he liked me telling him what to do. Vince liked to be the one in control. He had a penis dangling between his thighs and he wanted me to know it. "Can I talk to you in private?" By the tone of his voice, I was convinced he was actually going to show it to me.

I asked Bella to wait by the other Jeep, but I wanted to keep her in my sights.

"What?" I started on the defensive. He was perched against the hood on the Jeep, keeping his weight off his bad leg. "You can't drive in your condition, can you?" I asked rhetorically.

"No." That must have been hard for him to admit. He swallowed hard. "Do you want the bad news or the *bad* news?"

Nothing could possibly shock me at that point so I asked for the *bad* news first. I stared at him and waited for his response. His head hung low and he shook it from side to side before speaking. At that point, I half expected him to say he was going to ditch us again.

He pulled his laptop to his chest, did some fast fingering and then turned the screen so that I could see it. "This is where we are." He pointed to the screen. To me it just looked like an ordinary map. Big green and brown patches with little black dotted lines and a couple of thin blue lines and a couple of big blue globs that I assumed were bodies of water. "This is where we need to get to." He pointed to another spot on the map. "We could go here, but my guess is that thirty men with semi-automatics would be waiting for us."

"Can't you just signal for an extraction right here?" I asked.

His expression changed. I don't think he liked that I knew his jargon, or his intentions. I think he liked being Rambo.

"Didn't you pay attention during class little girl?"

My blood boiled in my veins. One—I hated being called little girl. My brother Dave used to call me that when I wanted to play football with the boys in the backyard or follow them to the pond to catch frogs. Two—I hated that he was right. I hadn't paid attention and right after I opened my mouth and suggested it, I felt like an ignoramus.

"I know." I rolled my eyes. "There's protocol, procedures and little imaginary lines in the sand." I looked at him and I think he was impressed. Good for me. "It's your show. You tell me what you think we should do."

He scratched his chin. He had a nice chin. It was very manly. I can't believe that even for one second I ever thought he was a nerd. "We could go west, but it's possibly a two-day drive and we probably don't have enough gas."

Okay. I looked at the sky and took a deep breath. Perhaps I did pay attention in Yoga class.

Bad guys with guns or we take our chances in the wild. We had vehicles, at least for a while; we had food, water and pillows. "I vote for heading west."

"Are you sure?"

"Um, let me think about that?" I narrowed my eyes. "Thirty men with guns?"

There was a long moment of silence between us until he looked up from the screen and looked right into my brown eyes.

"Thanks."

I don't know why he said it but he did.

"For what?"

I liked the genuine smile on his face just about as much as I liked his hand on the back of my neck.

"For saving my life." He rubbed his coarse thumb up and down the side of my throat.

Wow.

He dropped his hand from my neck when Bella cleared her throat loudly. I think she was becoming uncomfortable watching over the African gent. Either that or she didn't want to witness me making out with Secret Agent Man. Hell, she'd already witnessed me kissing her father, she probably already thought I was a ho as it was.

Bummer. I thought for sure he was going to kiss me again.

"Who is this guy?" I asked Vince, but he didn't answer.

He climbed into the passenger seat of Jeep number two.

Bella bolted into the driver's side. Elation lit up her face. She started the engine and beamed over at me. I loved to see her smile.

"Easy now," I heard Vince say, and then I started my own engine and we were off.

The African man woke up a number of times, vomited out the side of the Jeep, and then passed out again. I stopped a couple of times, to give him water and readjust his head on the blanket. I hoped that it was the morphine making him sleep and not a prelude to death. I didn't want anyone else to die on our little expedition. I knew that Bella and I would be okay and I had a strong feeling that Vince would survive, but I was beginning to wonder about the Mystery Man. I then began wondering if Mystery Man was the key to this entire mess. After all, he was the only dark-skinned one that the South Africans hadn't killed off. Clearly, he had been tortured within an inch of his life and I felt proud that I had showed up when I did.

I looked behind me at this point and Bella seemed to be holding her own.

Vince on the other hand, looked downright petrified. Every so often, I would hear her yelp with excitement and she would speed up ahead of me, wave and then he would wave his hands frantically and she would slow down.

When the sun was beating down directly from above, and I had finished singing every lyric to every television show I had ever seen, I pulled over under the canopy of a large tree and cut the engine just as I finished with...*here on Gilligan's Isle.*

I could hear rushing water in the distance and I was hot.

"We can stop here for lunch," I said, as I jumped down from my Jeep, and shimmied my ass because it had fallen asleep.

"Stop for lunch?" Vince growled. "What do you think this is? Summer camp?"

"The child needs to eat."

I could hear Bella's stomach growl even over his exaggerated grunts.

He watched from the Jeep with gun in hand while I fed Bella some chili and fruit.

I then took off down the hill toward the rushing water. I'd always had a predisposition to water, even as a kid. My mother used to scream and yell at me because I wouldn't get out of the bathtub when she wanted me too. Then when I was older, she would scream and yell at me because I never got out of the pool. What can I say? I'm part fish.

The water felt so wonderful against my hot skin. I peeled off all my clothes, washed each piece against a coarse stone and laid them on a flat rock to dry while I gallivanted around in the cold water. Bella joined me and, yeah, for a minute, it felt a bit like summer camp. I, for once, was having fun and taking the time to stop and smell the roses. I needed to clear my head and take inventory of what was most important to me.

I was shocked to admit that my family was the most important thing to me. I really wanted to make amends with my brothers and get to know their wives and children. Little Randy and Carla were already three and five and I had only seen them once. Dave's little boy, Marcus, had just turned one and I didn't even bother to send the little guy a birthday card with money in it. I wasn't doing a very good job as Aunt Charlie. I needed to stop being so damn self-involved and stop blaming my father for everything. Laying my head back in the water for a moment, I truly appreciated that I was alive to feel the things that I was feeling.

For once, I felt peaceful about the fact that I was a woman. I reached my wrinkled hands up and placed them on my bare breasts and for the first time in my life, I was glad I had breasts. Breasts are beautiful. They felt full and firm and by God, I was proud to be a woman.

"What are you doing?"

I heard a slight sensual growl in his tone. I looked over without removing my hands from my breasts and rolled over so I was once again submerged under the water.

"What does it look like I'm doing?" I said haughtily. My face flushed slightly.

He grinned.

He looked fantastic leaned up against that tree dangling his gun from his fingertips. It was the most relaxed I had seen him since the first day in the tent when he quickly ruined my image of him as a gentle, sensitive nerd.

"We should get going," he said, but didn't make a move to crawl back up the hill. "Are you coming?" He grinned shamelessly.

"Uh," I squealed. "I'm naked."

"I can see that." His grin widened and Bella's screaming interrupted us.

"Snnaakkee," I heard her scream loudly, and I have never seen anyone run so fast in my life. She was by Vince's side in a matter of seconds.

He let Bella help him up the hill and I stayed behind to get dressed. It felt wonderful to be clean again, but it didn't last long thanks to the humidity and the dust.

Mystery Man was still perched in the same position when I returned. I had contrived a makeshift canopy for the Jeep so he wasn't exposed to the hot rays of the sun. I managed to wake him long enough to get a couple bites of food down his throat and several gulps of water. He was definitely perking up.

Before we took off, Bella pulled up beside me. Vince looked over at the man.

"Is he hanging in there?"

"Yeah," I said. "I think he'll be fine."

"Good." Vince looked relieved, and that strengthened my suspicions that Mystery Man was the key and that this little African fiasco had nothing to do with Bella's grandfather.

Dusk came and went while I helped Mystery Man onto a blanket by the fire.

"Does he have a name or should I keep calling him Mystery Man?" I was hoping that Vince would divulge something to me at this point. "Can you tell me anything? I'm dying here. I'll be satisfied with one tiny bit of data. Paaalleease?" Feminine whining was something I rarely used, but it seemed fitting.

Vince just grinned and helped himself to more chili. I could tell that he wasn't about to tell me one little shred about what he was doing. I think he liked to watch me squirm and he seemed like a true professional, whatever that might be in this case.

Bella took a seat beside me and curled up against my shoulder. I loved that. "You okay?"

"I miss my dad." She started crying. "And I miss my mom. I even miss Gregory and those stupid dogs." She wailed harder and I tightened my grip on her frail shoulder.

I could tell from her build and tall frame already that she took after her father's side of the family. I wasn't even sure what nationality Roald Munson was. I don't think he was Hungarian or French like his mother. Perhaps he was Scandinavian. After all, he did look like a Viking. Bella's long blonde hair blew slightly in the wind before I grabbed hold of it and twisted it into a braid.

"Thanks," she said as I tied a piece of fabric around it to hold it in place. I almost wept at the genuine smile she gave me.

I do want a daughter after all. Girls are great.

Vince watched the stew on the fire and I snuck off to get something from his duffel that I just really had to have.

"That's mine." He grabbed the flask from my hand and took a big swig. Then a sexy smile lit up his face and he handed it back to me.

"Who did you swipe this from?" I asked after I felt the warm tingle of alcohol tickle my blood.

"It's mine," he said.

My eyes opened wide. *Son of a bitch.* "Ron?"

He tilted his head in confusion.

"Rick?"

He laughed aloud and took another swig.

"Robert?" I asked.

"Ryan," he finally said through clenched teeth. "Ryan McNeil, it's nice to meet you."

"You're a pig." I laughed because it felt good to laugh and he looked so cute.

"Sorry. I wasn't sure I could trust you," he said and I actually believed him. I'd probably regret it in the morning, but I believed him just the same.

I looked over at Bella. She was sleeping soundly. I covered her with a blanket and kissed her cheek before tossing another couple of twigs onto the fire.

When I returned to my seat, Ryan was lying on his blanket, the last blanket at that. I guess I was sleeping in the grass.

"So, who is she?" he asked.

I had to take a deep breath because the alcohol was going to my head a lot faster than normal. Then paranoia took over my brain and I started thinking that it wasn't cognac, it was truth serum and I was about to be interrogated by the IRS.

"Roald Munson's daughter," I said as I sat back down and grabbed the flask. I liked how I was feeling and so what if I was about to divulge all my secrets. I didn't have that many anyway.

He grinned and leaned up on his elbow. "That's Nicole Harrison's daughter?" He looked over at Annabelle and whistled.

I didn't really look at it like that since the whore took off with another man and abandoned her only child. "I guess so." *Technically, but not in my mind.* In my mind, mothers don't just up and leave their children, especially their daughters.

"So, I take it that you thought this was just some Hollywood kidnapping?"

"Honestly, I didn't know what to think until you started breaking peoples' fucking necks. At first I thought that it had something to do with her grandfather, but then all this weird shit started happening with you and now I'm totally fucking convinced that Mystery Man over there is really the key to this whole fucked up situation."

"You cuss a lot more when you're drunk." He grinned and probably thought he was going to get lucky. I sent him a devilish, yet sensual glare.

"I'm not drunk," I said defiantly, but I lied.

"So, who's her grandfather?" Ryan was still sharp as a tack and I was getting more and more numb.

"Claude Munson. He is some diplomat who apparently halted some major coup in Armenia and is now on the run from some pretty intense people. I've heard a couple of different rumors, but I don't know who to believe. Not that it matters, I don't think this is connected."

"Never heard of him."

That was probably a good sign. If the spy-dude hadn't known about Bella, then chances were she was safe from the wild-*Turkians*, or whoever was after her grandfather. I started laughing at that point because I was feeling pretty loose and for the life of me, I couldn't think of what inhabitants of Turkey called themselves. They most likely just called themselves Turkeys for all I knew.

Turks, I slapped my knee when the answer finally came to me.

Ryan gave me a quick glance. I looked at his face and decided I liked Vince better. He didn't look like a Ryan.

I leaned back against the rock behind me and looked directly through the fire and into his eyes. He had great eyes. Very large and dark and his lashes were longer and darker than mine were when I was wearing mascara. It just wasn't fair. "So, who is he?" I leaned forward on my elbows. "I promise I won't ask you another thing." I thought I could keep that promise, but I wasn't completely sure so I crossed my fingers and hoped he couldn't see them over the bright amber flames.

"Let me ask you something first." He sat up and adjusted his position before taking a long pull from the flask. "How did you manage to kill six men all by yourself?"

I closed my eyes. I didn't like the term *kill*. It sounded barbaric and so unlike anything that I would ever do. I reopened them and wanted to be closer to him. I wasn't thinking about how sexy he was sitting there all bashed and bruised. I was thinking about comfort and companionship. I was lonely and after the previous night, I just needed a hug.

I got up slowly and moved over to the blanket, keeping my eyes directly on his. My expression must have softened and my vulnerability must have been clear in my gaze because he held out his hand and I took it. I curled into the V that his legs made and leaned back against his chest. I still hadn't breathed since I fled to his arms and when his arm tightened against my waist, I finally exhaled and relaxed my shoulders.

I felt safe in his arms. Then I took another swig of cognac and stared into the fire for a minute or two. "It wasn't my first time," I finally confessed and my throat tightened when he tensed. I felt a change in his body, but his arm stayed wrapped tightly around me, and he gently, yet urgently pressed a kiss against my temple.

"Where?"

"Bosnia."

No words were exchanged after that for a heartbeat or two. We just sat in silence and looked into the fire. The howls at the full moon had me shivering and leaning even closer to his chest, if that was even possible.

I didn't really feel like getting into a pissing contest with this Marine, so I tried to change the subject. "Do you want to take the first shift?"

"What made you join the Army?" He apparently didn't want to change the subject.

I blew out a breath in resignation.

What the hell, I was drunk, I was in the arms of a secret agent man that I would never see again and I had just survived the most hellacious week of my life.

"My father said 'college or the Army.' I was a rebel and didn't like the way he demanded that I go to college and make something of myself, so I joined in defiance."

"That answers why you joined," he whispered. His breath was hot against the back of my neck, sending small shockwaves somewhere south of my navel. "Why did you stay?"

"I loved it after I got through the first year. I learned a lot about who I was and what I wanted to do with my life. Besides, I was pretty damn good at what I did," I said with pride. "How about you?"

"I always knew I wanted to be a Marine."

I should have guessed that. "How long were you in for?"

I could feel his hot breath on my neck again. "How do you know I'm not still with the Marines?"

"I don't," I said and shrugged my shoulders. "I was just grasping at straws, hoping you would tell me what the heck you are doing out here."

"I could tell you." I could sense that he was smiling because of his playful tone. "But then I'd have to kill you."

"Ha, ha." I slapped his arm and leaned my head against his collarbone. I hadn't had a moment of intimacy like this with a man in years. It seemed odd that I was curled up in practically a stranger's arms, but I liked it...a lot.

"What are your plans when we finally get out of here?" he asked as his fingers tickled up and down my bare arm. It felt nice.

"I have two more semesters at UCONN until I finish my master's degree, so I hope I won't get fired when I get back because I'm...*so close.*" I closed my eyes and emphasized that last part. I had worked so damn hard to get where I was and I really didn't want to leave Bella. She needed me.

I squeezed my eyes shut to discourage the tears but they came anyway. I don't even fully understand why. I hadn't cried when I killed six men. I hadn't cried when brain matter erupted from a man's head in front of my eyes so why now, what the hell?

I figured a man like Ryan would be uncomfortable with a woman breaking down in front of him, so I reined in my emotions and took a couple of deep breaths.

"You okay?"

"Fine," I snapped because I wasn't.

"I'll take the first watch." He moved away from me and hobbled over to the rock with gun in hand. "You get some sleep, I might need you tomorrow and I need you sharp."

I didn't know what he meant by that, and I hoped that he hadn't kept something important from me.

Then again, he was a master of deception.

I woke up with a crick in my side and rolled over before I realized that the fire was almost completely out. I sat up and looked over at Secret Agent Man. He was sawing logs from an upright position. Head slumped forward on his chest. It looked incredibly uncomfortable. I got up, stretched my back and tossed more wood on the fire to keep the animals from eating us while we slept.

Ryan woke abruptly just as I was lying back down. "Sorry," he said with a yawn.

I didn't blame him. He had to be in horrendous pain and after all, we did finish off that flask of cognac. "Don't worry about it. The fire should be fine until morning. Go back to sleep."

He crawled around the fire and nudged me with his knee. I guess I wasn't the only one looking for companionship and comfort. He pulled me close in a comfortable spooning position and we fell asleep within minutes.

Ryan must have awakened early, because when I heard the first moan of a peacock, I immediately noticed that I was missing something.

"We need to get going." He had already managed to cook up a can of beans and had Bella fed.

I needed water, coffee and a couple of Vitamin Bs. Hangovers suck in civilization, but they are murder in the savanna. The sun was already relentlessly beating down from the sky, and I swear that it had grown since yesterday. In fact, I think it was still growing and eventually, it was going to swallow us up and deep-fry us like a batch of French fries.

I swiped my brow with the back of my hand. Ryan handed me a canteen and I sipped slowly, taking every drop into my throat with control. We still had at least one more day out here and it wouldn't be too much longer before the Jeeps ran out of gas.

Bella helped me with the African gentleman and we got him into the backseat without incident. It was so much easier when he was awake.

"Hello," I said as a kind greeting. "I'm Charlie." I hoped he spoke English, because I was driving him again that day and I'd hoped to have a few questions answered. I just couldn't let it go that I wasn't privy to this super secret operation. I don't give up. I am a woman after all and damn proud of it.

"Armand," he spoke slowly and nodded in acknowledgment. His voice was forced and raspy. "Where are we?"

I loved his accent. *Very cool.* I shrugged. "I have no idea." I could see over my shoulder that Secret Agent Man was growing more and more nervous.

"You know," I heard him say and then he jumped on one foot over to my side, "I think I might be okay to drive today. Why don't you give Bella a break and I'll take...," he looked over at Armand as if he didn't know his name. *Yeah right.*

"Armand," the African man spoke again, and Ryan nodded.

"I'll take Armand."

Boy, he was so slick, but I had to agree because the terrain was looking portentous and we were nearing a ridge that seemed impassable. If we lost a vehicle at that point, I didn't see how we would be able to make it to the little imaginary line in the sand.

"Fine." I nodded as a kind gesture to Armand and then glared at Ryan. "Yell, if you have trouble and...and... don't crash."

I am so *not* smooth. I just can't come up with good zingers. I shook my head back and forth in resignation as I approached the other Jeep. Bella had already moved over. She probably saw the scowl on my face and knew that I wouldn't be up to arguing.

"You okay?"

"I will be when I get you out of here." I smiled and started the engine.

We needed the double gas tanks on the back of the Jeeps at that point. We had just made it over the precarious ridge and I do have to say that those corny Jeep commercials on TV don't lie. I was amazed at where I could drive in that thing. I may have to rethink my Ford Expedition idea and go for one of these babies. I was really enjoying how it handled.

I waved to Ryan when the main tank read empty and then I pulled over under a tree to hook up the backup tank. It was a quick maneuver and then I moved over and did it for the crippled men. Ryan was driving incredibly well for someone with a broken appendage, he cringed only a couple of times.

Okay, I have to admit he was much stronger than I was in every way. I, for one would be crying for my father, the doctor, if my ankle was that swollen and blue and twisted. The sight of it alone had me wincing in pain, but Ryan? Wow, he was amazing. It was probably that whole Yoga–Zen mentality and he just willed himself not to feel pain.

When the sun was finally behind us, we stopped for lunch. Ryan demanded that we keep going and was adamant about it this time, so adamant that his gun kept rising in the air again and he was saying *fuck* every other word.

"Jesus fucking Christ, Charlie. We have to keep fucking going. It's not much fucking further."

"Eat," I told Bella and handed her a can of beans. Cold beans, because buffoon refused to let me build a fire.

"What's the gosh dang deal?" Since I was close to civilization again, I knew it was time to clean up my potty mouth and return to Poppin's mode. "You said it wasn't that much further, and the bad guys are way over there." I pointed north.

He flushed slightly and he wouldn't meet my gaze.

That's when I barreled toward his Jeep, wrapped my fingers in the cotton of his filthy tee-shirt and yanked hard. His nose bumped mine and I swallowed the lump in my throat.

"Dude." I can't believe that I uttered that word, but I did. So sue me. "You said that there were most likely thirty men with guns to the north, so we went the long way. We came west. We're almost there. Are you not giving me all the information?"

He was clearly becoming irritated with my ranting and the fact that I was strangling him with his own shirt. "I never said there weren't *un-friendlies* to the west. You just assumed."

I hauled back and punched him clean in the jaw.

"Chaka Khan!" I shouted loudly and retracted my throbbing fist. "OUCH," I screamed at the sky, and shook the pain out with a couple flicks of my wrist.

He was clearly rattled. I could tell that by the look in his eye, it wasn't quite focusing on my face. "What the hell did you do that for?" he sputtered once he realigned his jaw.

"Ooohhh." As if he didn't know. "I wanted to hit someone and it certainly wasn't going to be Bella or Armand, so I chose you. *You*, the man who has been lying to me since the minute we met. *You* are the man who convinced me to trust you. *You*, the man who makes me so darn mad I want to spit. *You. Deserved. It.*"

I was completely irrational at that point and began pacing in front of the Jeep and talking to myself. Out loud for the world to hear.

"We're going die." I shook my head and kicked the dirt. "Oh my God, this is it. We're all gonna to die and it's all *my* fault," I continued on, still staring at the dirt as I chewed on my fingernails. "I should have shot him when I had the chance. Hell, I've had lots of chances. I could have just pulled the trigger while he slept, and my God...I let him kiss me. What the hell was that about? What was I waiting for? Shit," I yelled and turned on my heel and kept on pacing all the while raking my fingers through my oily hair. "Brick always said that I hesitated too much. He said it was my downfall, that if I just used my instincts more and didn't try to rationalize so much, I could have been a hell of a contender. He said I had gumption and grit and yeah, sure he mentioned that I had a nice rack once or twice...I mean I do." I looked over at Ryan and Armand who were staring at me with open mouths. "I do. I do have a nice rack, don't I?" I saw Secret Agent Man nod, and Armand just looked confused. Clearly, he had never witnessed a female have a nervous breakdown before, and I'm quite positive that he didn't know what a *rack* was.

I continued once I got the vigorous nod from Ryan. "What's wrong with that anyway? Why was I so hell-bent on pleasing Brick? He was just my superior. He wasn't my dad." I tossed my head back and slapped my palm to my forehead. "I was good. I could have remained a part of the team, but no..."

The slap Bella gave me was something right out of an old black-and-white movie. She put her hands on both of my shoulders and gave me a quick shaking that snapped me out of my hissy fit.

"Get a hold of yourself. We are not going to die. I haven't kissed a boy yet—I haven't gotten my ears pierced—I haven't met Justin Timberlake. I want to go home. You have to get me home, Charlie. You promised."

Thank God for Bella. Bella the drama queen had just saved all of our asses, because I was heading for a catatonic state; and who would step up and be the hero then?

Hell, Ryan couldn't even step from the vehicle.

Damn! I was so mad at him.

"Ladies," Ryan shouted and got serious. "My guess is that since we haven't spotted anybody yet, we might not, but there's always that chance, so I think we should keep going."

He had a point, again. I'm glad I hadn't shot him after all.

"Fine." I got back into my Jeep and followed him. It wasn't too much longer before we ran into a small problem.

"*Oh, my God,*" Bella screamed, and clutched the dashboard with white knuckles. What looked like hundreds upon hundreds of wildebeest were blocking our path. None of them even looked fazed that we were approaching their feeding ground, but in time, I was sure one of them would make a stink, and then they would trample us all. I pulled up next to Ryan, but didn't dare look him in the eye. I was still beyond angry and on the verge of tears again. I mostly blamed this all on him.

My fear was that somehow, he had crawled under my skin and somehow, it still mattered to me what he thought of me. I wanted to remain in control. I wanted to be strong and dependable. I wanted to be the steadfast hero who didn't cry at the drop of a hat. "Well," I groaned. "What now?"

"We wait," he said quietly, then cut the engine. Surely, he couldn't be an expert on the feeding habits of the wildebeest on top of everything else. There must be something that I could do better than him. I stared at the side of his head and tried to think of something.

"Where did you fuck up?" I asked, trying desperately to level the playing field by dredging up his mistakes.

He narrowed his eyes. "How did you get past the trip wire?"

"I paid attention in class," I retorted, and was so damn proud of myself that my lips bowed into a smug smile. If that wasn't a zinger, I don't know what was. I could feel his gaze and out of the corner of my eye, I saw him smile.

"You're an amazing woman, Charlie Ford," he chuckled lightly.

I couldn't believe he just paid me a compliment. I tried not to blush. I tried not to smile. I failed miserably.

"Thanks. You're not too bad yourself."

I leaned back and smelled the roses while Ryan extended the antennae on his portable laptop computer thingy. It really didn't smell like roses out on the plains of Africa. It smelled more like elephant dung and sweaty feet. I peered over my toes to get a look-see at what Secret Agent Man was doing.

He punched a couple of buttons and entered what looked like coordinates and a message that he was bringing civilians back with him. Something to the effect of "be advised, will need medical attention and cargo is intact."

He looked over at me, closed the computer, and handed it to me. "It's starbucks."

"What's starbucks?"

"It's the password. In case I don't make it."

Hearing him say that was like piercing my heart with a dagger. My heart normally didn't ache the way it had this week and placing my hand on my breast, I inhaled sharply and didn't even want to think about that possibility.

"You'll make it."

"I'm just covering my bases." He had the poker face down to a science. "We have about six hours before the team moves in and I don't want to take any chances, so please get Armand into your Jeep and I'll drive solo just in case."

Then I got scared. One minute he was telling me that we were probably safe and then he was talking about making a contingency plan in case he *died!*

"We're going to make it. You got us this far, didn't you?"

"Actually, you got us this far, Charlie." His eyes lit up with a passion that I hadn't seen before. "I screwed up, Charlie. If it hadn't been for you, I'd be dead and my mission would've failed. I didn't look down. It was stupid."

"So, what are you saying? You screwed up, so you don't deserve to make it back?"

"No." He swallowed hard. "Just get Armand into that chopper. The South Africans won't kill him; they need him alive...at least for now." He didn't blink when he told me this. "Promise me."

I felt like he was handing me the earth and saying, "Don't drop it." Sweat rapidly dripped from my brow. I brushed it off with my hand and then leaned out the side of the Jeep to touch his shoulder. I had hated the sight of him half an hour before and suddenly I wanted to hug him and tell him that it would be okay. *I'm a wonderfully forgiving person.*

Chapter Eight

I could see a cloud of dust on the other side of the infinite number of wildebeest and it was either an elephant herd, and the gangs of animals were about to rumble, or it was Jeeps kicking up all that dust. I chose to believe the latter and so did Ryan.

We quickly peeled out and got to a shady area beside a vertical rock wall that seemed to touch the bright blue sky.

Shit, shit, shit! I ran my clammy hands across my jeans and saw Ryan run his hands through his hair. He looked resigned, as if he was about to jump into their path on a suicide mission of sorts.

"Help me get Armand into your Jeep."

I jumped out and did what I was told for once. Bella helped me and soon it was the three of us and *one Ryan*. He pulled three handguns out from under his seat, and set one on the dash. Clearly, he hadn't paid attention in class, because he wasn't thinking like a sniper.

I pulled a high-powered rifle from the back and slammed a couple of rounds into the chamber before Ryan knew what I was doing.

"No," he shouted. "Your job is to get Armand to the extraction point."

"Bullshit," I snapped right back. "I'm not going to let you sacrifice yourself because you tripped on one God-damned wire. It could have happened to anyone and you don't have to do this alone."

Anger grew in his eyes, along with something else. Perhaps it was fear. Perhaps it was a warm fuzzy feeling of love for me. I don't know. I'm not a man. Besides, who knows what goes through a secret agent man's head when he's about to commit suicide?

"Charlie, for God's sake, this is what I do. I take chances like this, because I have to. I choose to and you have to listen to me for once and do what I'm fucking telling you, God damn it."

"I don't take orders from you," I said briskly and a bit breathlessly. I was worried about him. I actually cared if he lived or died and I believed that if he went out there alone, he *was* going to die. "Don't you believe in teamwork?"

"You're a nanny for fuck's sake. Give it up, Charlie. You're not in the Army anymore. Why are you still trying to prove yourself to me?" he yelled, but then his voice cracked. "You had me at Buffoon."

I laughed and choked back tears.

"Don't start crying on me now, please, Charlie. For once, just do as I ask and get Armand to that chopper. Hundreds of thousands of people are counting on him getting home alive and I'm just one man. One." He held up a single digit.

This was precisely why women need to stay home and raise babies. I was not about to let someone I cared about die, and it mattered not how many times he begged me, I knew he couldn't do this alone, not in his condition and not five against one.

We could clearly see the Jeeps by then. They had stopped on the other side of the herd, waiting just as we had been doing.

"Fine." I held my head high and lied straight through my grimy teeth. The gunk build up was horrendous and I couldn't wait to visit the dentist for a good thorough scouring.

"Okay." He nodded and gave me his version of the plan. I had thoughts of my own, but I wasn't about to share them with the likes of him. He was just too stubborn; that just comes with the territory of having one of *those things* between his thighs.

Bella remained out of earshot in the Jeep with Armand. I looked back at them from the hood of Ryan's Jeep and smiled to ease her anxiety.

"Any questions?" he asked.

"Just one," I said.

Our gazes locked for a brief moment, so, okay, I had more than one question. I had about fifty but that was not the time.

"Why are you such a stubborn ass?"

"Once a Marine, always a Marine." He winked and took off, leaving me in a cloud of dust.

"No. You're a man," I shouted and kicked the dirt in frustration. I looked over at Bella and gave her another smile before grabbing the rifle, a bag of ammo and a fig or two.

I took off on foot for the highest peak I could reach without falling and breaking my neck. That was my specialty, what the Army trained me to do. I was once in the top ten percent of all military snipers. If I had a rifle, a scope and a bag of sunflower seeds, I could sit and shoot people all day long. I had steady hands, an eye for detail and a highly accurate shot that rarely missed. *Plus, I was one, sneaky bitch!*

I could see the enemy's Jeeps clearly and none of the men were in any hurry to disturb the herd. One even tipped back in his seat, looking up at the sky.

The more I thought about it, the more I hated Ryan's plan. Ryan's plan sucked.

I tried channeling my inner spirits of good luck and although I had never been called lucky in my life, I knew that had to change at some point, so I got in position atop the cliff and took out the driver of the first Jeep in one precise shot. It seemed all too easy for me, but I was still afraid for Ryan's life. He was pretty much a sitting duck if we did it his way and I wasn't about to let that happen. I guess I was never good at following orders. Sure, I did it, but I hated it.

I reloaded my weapon while chaos ensued on the other side of the herd. Men were standing up in their seats, struggling to arm themselves, and jumping behind their vehicles.

I took another shot and accidentally killed a wildebeest. *My bad.*

"Sorry," I muttered to God about taking the life of such a magnificent creature, but really, they're kind of ugly. I reloaded and took out two tires with two more bullets. I still had a handful of ammo and all the time in the world. One of their own dropping into the dirt clearly hadn't upset the beasts and they just continued on, gnawing on the grass and pooping every five seconds. "Damn, that's a lot of shit," I growled and reloaded. I hit one of the Jeeps, sending the entire thing into the air, because I had hit the gas tank. "Nice shot," I said aloud and looked over to see Ryan still making his way across the vast field to get into position for when the herd passed. The herd simply looked up from it's grazing at that time and then continued on. It was an amazing sight to see.

"Ah, hell," I mumbled under my breath.

Mother Nature had just tossed a wrench into the works. Hunched under the tall grass were two lions. I could either take them both out, and I really didn't want to mess with Mother Nature's survival of the fittest rule, or I could pray that when the beasts started running, they would run over the bad guys and not Secret Agent Man.

I chose to wait a minute and pray to God for the answer.

I guess Brick was right about me rationalizing too much because the mama lions were hungry and decided to pounce while I was in mid-prayer. I hesitated and now I was crossing my fingers and hoping for the best. Dust billowed into the sky as I had never seen before and I saw Ryan taking off toward a couple of trees. The herd seemed to be going in the opposite direction and had the bad guys on the run. There were only three left standing now. Two had just cowered under the Jeep, but the third one... "Yow, that had to hurt."

Now there were two bad guys. Two I could deal with.

The herd finally mellowed out on the other side of the small stream after the lions took down a feeble, limping member of their family and although I felt sorry for the frail animal, I knew it was nature's way. I also knew that bad guys were getting into their Jeep and heading toward Ryan, despite their two flat tires.

I took another shot before they reached the trees and when the Jeep hit a termite mound and rolled over, I knew for sure that I had hit the driver, but for good measure, I aimed for the back of the Jeep and put a bullet into the gas tank. The red vehicle shot through the air like something out of a movie and I climbed back down the cliff, tucked the rifle under the seat, thanked God for my father...*again,* and headed toward Secret Agent Man.

He wasn't as happy to see me as I was to see him, but that changed when I sent him an incredibly sexy, cocky smile.

"Woman." He shook his head from side to side with a smirk. "What do I have to do to get you to follow my orders?"

I didn't have the heart to tell him that nothing short of marriage would get me to love, honor and *obey* another man for the rest of my life.

Bella climbed out and jumped into the Jeep with him. "Can we go home now?"

I laughed. At least she didn't say, "Are we there yet?"

Armand and I had a nice chat on the two-hour drive toward that invisible little line in the sand. I learned all sorts of interesting things about the kingdom that he ruled. He was actually Prince Armand and ruled Gaborone, a small territory that I had never heard of, somewhere north of South Africa. Apparently, he had been traveling incognito since the fear of his assassination had frightened members of his parliament. I clearly understood why the hijackers executed the other African men. They were part of his traveling secret service. Obviously, the people of his country could learn a thing or two from our secret service about protecting their leader. I still didn't understand why Ryan was on that plane, unless he was there as back up because whatever three-letter agency he worked for didn't trust Armand's bodyguards. Armand couldn't help me out with my inquiry and I figured that I would never fully understand what Secret Agent Man was doing. It didn't matter, then. I could almost taste freedom, I could almost smell pancakes with real maple syrup and I could most definitely smell gas.

I sniffed the air.

Uh oh! My Jeep sputtered, stalled, and then died completely. Ryan's on the other hand seemed to be doing fine. He pulled up beside me and grinned.

"Problem, little lady?"

"Bite me!" I couldn't help it. I was just having a semi-orgasmic fantasy about real food and then I would just have to wait that much longer. Shit.

"Hop in," Ryan said.

I helped Bella move all the supplies from the dead Jeep into the one that was still running. I helped my new friend, Armand, into the passenger seat and then crawled in beside Bella in the back. The humidity had me sweating in strange places. The clouds that had moved in above looked dark and ominous.

Two hundred feet later, and just after I had sopped up the rest of my sweat, Ryan's Jeep sputtered, stalled and then died. I had known that was coming, but I had high hopes for pancakes and bacon. "Now what?" I inquired.

"Now, we walk," Secret Agent Man stated the obvious, and had both Bella and I rolling our eyes at him.

"How are *you* going to walk?"

"You're going to carry me, sweetheart."

"Ha," I said, but I think he was serious. "Really?"

"You can do it, can't you?" He was smiling now and testing my patience. What else was new? He'd been testing my patience since he demanded that I give him my purse on the airplane.

I balked, I snorted and then I giggled. "You're a pain in the ass."

"Don't I know it? Now come here, honey."

I hate to admit this, but I rather liked it when he called me honey. Sweetheart—not so much, but honey just sounded like music to my ears. I packed Bella up with as much as she could drag behind her and then I looked over at Armand. "Who's going to carry him?"

Ryan looked at Armand, who looked frail, weak, and ready to pass out again.

"You can drag him behind you on a blanket."

"Who do I look like, the Incredible Hulk?"

"I can help Ryan," Bella stepped up to the plate and eased under Ryan's armpit. I hadn't been more proud of her than I was right at that particular moment. She had been a heck of a trooper. She hadn't whined about getting her hair dirty. She hadn't moaned about missing MTV, or the fact that bad men were trying to kill us. I thought she was an amazing girl with more resilience than most adults I know.

"Thanks," I said and then I wrapped two corners of the blanket around my wrists and told Armand to get on and hold on tight. The road was going to be bumpy.

"I will walk." The tone of his voice was regal and proud. His chin tilted toward the sky. "I can make it."

And he did.

An hour and a half later, we took a different path to the left and ended up crossing a small stream. The night sky made it difficult to see and rain had just started pouring down on top of us with drops the size of gumballs. It was getting more and more difficult to hold Ryan up, more so now he was drenched. I could see that he was clearly exhausted, but so was I.

He collapsed from my grasp and landed in a heap just on the other side of the creek.

"We can't stop now. I want pancakes, and bacon and fresh squeezed orange juice." I dropped to my knees beside him and wiped the soaked hair from his eyes. He really did have beautiful eyes and right then, they looked relieved and almost happy.

"We made it," he groaned and laid back into a puddle. The drops of rain relentlessly pelted down from the sky and I could see them hit his elated face one at a time. It seemed that everything slowed to slow motion and suddenly I was really...sad.

I heard the familiar whooping sound of a chopper just a couple of minutes after I realized that I was sad. And then suddenly I wasn't. I was so friggin' happy that I pulled Bella into my arms and jumped up and down as if I was at an N'Sync concert. "Oh my God," I cried into her hair. "We're going home."

She laughed and told me that she loved me and we hugged and hugged and looked up to see a big black burly looking helicopter land in the clearing up ahead. Four soldiers with big guns jumped out and secured the area, and then two medics jumped out and helped Bella into the chopper, followed by Armand, Ryan and finally myself.

"Nice to see you again, sir," one of the soldiers yelled over the noise, and saluted Ryan. Ryan saluted the young man, smiled and leaned back in his seat. His eyes closed before we even lifted off and I was disturbingly sad again.

I sat back and held Bella in my arms as we lifted off the African soil. I closed my eyes at that point and trusted that God would not let us die in a helicopter accident after all we had been through.

What seemed like an eternity later, we set down on an aircraft carrier in the dead of night in a torrential downpour that didn't seem like it would ever end.

I kept Bella close as they helped us from the chopper. I saw some people brusquely shuffle Armand behind closed doors. I saw Ryan receiving the medical attention that he desperately needed, but I didn't see any pancakes or bacon and damn, if that didn't piss me off.

A uniformed officer introduced himself as a liaison and took Bella and me to a private area where we waited for directions as to what to do next. It wasn't my first time on an aircraft carrier, so I wasn't quite as awestruck as Bella was.

"I really need to call her father," I said to the MP who was guarding our stuffy room. It was a tiny cabin with two bunks and I don't know what or who they were guarding us from, but I wasn't getting any answers and I needed to use the phone. "Hey," I yelled again, but no one responded. Then, I just felt ignored and imprisoned to boot.

Bella was already asleep, curled up on a cot after devouring the sandwich they had brought her. I finished mine in four seconds flat and then pounded on the door again.

"Where's Ryan? I want to speak to Ryan."

A few minutes later, after I had given up on speaking to anyone with a pulse, a different uniformed officer entered our tiny room and stood at ease in front of me.

"Can I get a phone call?" I asked snootily, and played the deranged tourist card. "Can I call her father and call off the search party please?"

"You will be taken to Athens in the morning, just hold tight."

"Can I at least talk to Ryan?" I wanted Ryan. I wanted him to tell me that he was going to miss me. I wanted to see his face one more time.

The officer cocked a brow in confusion.

"Ryan McNeil, the man who came in with us. You know...don't you?"

Maybe he didn't know. Perhaps Ryan McNeil was just a figment of my imagination, so to speak. It was entirely possible that he was a spook, or just a friend I made up because I was so lonely. Perhaps, I have schizophrenia and I contrived him out of thin air like in that "Beautiful Mind" movie.

So, I was delirious and I then saw that there was more to life than movies. "Do. You. Know. Who. I. Am. Talking. About?" I asked my question clearly, so there was no mistaking what I was saying.

"Miss, I understand you have just spent a couple of hectic days away from home, but I don't appreciate your condescending tone."

A couple of hectic days away from home, huh, is that what just happened to me? I don't *fucking* think so. I reined in my anger before it got the best of me and got me thrown into a four-by-six room with a cellmate named Bertha.

Tears steadily streamed down my cheek and I nodded and gave up my battle. I was too damned exhausted.

I curled up on my cot and let it all out. I cried and cried until my tear ducts were dry and I could no longer breathe through my nose. I slept soundly for being in a windowless room with no fresh air. I was afraid to open my eyes in the morning because I was afraid that I was dreaming.

A knock on the door woke me before Bella opened her eyes.

"Miss, I have orders to take you and the girl to Athens now."

I wiped my eyes and could tell that they were mighty puffy that morning. "Can I call her father?"

"Not from here, Miss. You'll have to wait until you reach the mainland."

"Protocol *smotocol*, I just want to tell the poor man that his daughter is safe."

I don't think he appreciated my tone either. He groaned and left me alone, for the time being anyway. He came back with two more officers. I guess I was too much of a woman for him to handle alone.

I nudged Bella with my arm and woke her up gently so the three strange men standing in the doorway wouldn't frighten her.

"Can I at least see Ryan before we leave?"

"Ryan, ma'am?"

Why were they all so hell-bent on making me feel as if I was going insane?

"Okay, then can I say goodbye to Prince Armand?"

Both sets of eyes darted from me to each other and back to me again.

The navy has a horrible way of showing hospitality to heroes at large. Then again, they had no idea that I was a hero. Wow, that's the first time that I had ever thought of myself that way, but I was. Cool.

I forced a smile. "I'm not leaving unless you let me see Ryan and Armand." I did my best at standing my ground and crossed my arms triumphantly in front of my chest. My clothes were filthy. That's weird; they didn't seem all that dirty in Africa.

Both men grunted and left the room. I was then escorted to the main deck by a young man who couldn't keep his eyes off Bella's behind.

"She's twelve," I said spitefully, and placed a proprietary arm around the young girl's shoulder. "Pervert," I said under my breath, then turned the corner and met a very stern looking man who did a wonderful imitation of my father. "Look, I just want to say goodbye to Ryan and Armand before we go. He did save our lives after all."

The man said nothing and continued staring at me. He nodded to another man who escorted Bella from the room. I took a seat because the man asked me to and for once, I was doing what I had been told to do. No need for me to make a stink aboard an aircraft carrier that housed more soldiers then I could count.

"Charlie, is it?" He pushed a plate of muffins at me and poured me some coffee.

That coffee was the best coffee I had ever tasted. The muffin needed some work, but the coffee was heavenly. I sipped it slowly and appreciated every drop. "Armand sends his thanks and good wishes. He's already...well let's just say, he's safe now."

I got it. I was no longer privy to any information because I was a civilian and a woman.

I still need to work on that giant chip on my shoulder, don't I? "And Ryan?" I asked.

His eyes narrowed. "I'm not quite sure who you mean."

I slammed both my hands down on the table at that point and stood up in an aggressive manner. "The man that we were brought in with, you know... Secret Agent Man."

His head tipped back when he laughed. "Oh, him."

"Yeah, him, can I please talk to *him*?" I begged at that point.

"He's also...well--*safe*."

I let out an exasperated breath and choked back my tears. Ryan was gone, just like that, no, *Thanks again,*

Charlie, for saving my ass, no, *See you around,* no big hug goodbye. Hell, not even a, *Have a nice life.* "I guess we can go then."

"We have a liaison waiting for you in Athens. She'll take you to the embassy, where you can get cleaned up and make your phone calls."

"Thanks." I extended my hand, because it was the nice thing to do. "Thanks for coming to get us."

"It was our pleasure." He smiled and then winked. "Thanks for saving...*his* life."

So, Ryan wasn't his real name. I got it. I still felt sad, but I was glad to be going back in civilization.

I hoped they had good pancakes in Greece.

Bella and I had once or twice played a little game about turning our misfortunes into Hollywood box office hits and if my life were, in fact, a movie on the big screen, then the following might have happened.

One—the soldiers aboard the aircraft carrier would have lifted me onto their shoulders and paraded me around because I had helped save the day. It would have looked something like the end of "Top Gun" when Maverick and Iceman reunited with Hollywood and Wolfman and did that male bonding backslapping and all that.

Two—Steven Segal would have made me a big plate of pancakes and pepper bacon and most likely would have squeezed me some fresh orange juice using his biceps and forearms as the juicing-vice.

Three—Ryan would have run out onto the platform just as I was about to board the chopper, screaming my name. I would have turned in a dramatic way, not hearing my name over the whooping of the chopper blades, but rather sensing that he was coming for me. Once I reached his arms, the kiss would have been long and hard, demanding, yet tender. My knees would have buckled, I would've cried against his cheek and told him how much I wanted him...yada, yada, yada.

I can tell you this. None of those things happened. I extended my arm to the soldier who was helping me into the chopper and I turned just one last time to see if perhaps my luck had changed. I sighed deeply and turned back around, stepped up into the chopper and held Bella's hand all the way to Greece. The Mediterranean Sea looked amazing from high in the air. It felt as if we were only in the air ten minutes before we landed. I guess I was more excited than I thought.

The liaison's name was Brianna Stephanopoulis. *How nice.* She was gorgeous and very well put together. I, on the other hand, had just spent a week in Africa without tampons, mascara or a mirror. I was quite frightened about how bad I must have looked, and made sure that I avoided all mirrors in the town car, all windows that might have reflected my horrific image and I tried not to look directly into anyone's mirrored sunglasses. The drive to the embassy only took twenty minutes. We were asked many questions. My bag was taken from me and again, I felt I got the short end of the stick. So, what else is new?

I literally shrieked aloud when I finally looked in the mirror once we reached the embassy. Bella collapsed onto the bed and grabbed the phone.

"She said we needed to talk to the ambassador before we got to make any calls." I warned, and stripped down to my bare naked, dirty, grimy birthday suit. Man, the dirt that came off my body and out of my cracks was disturbing. Bella shouted every once in awhile that I was taking too long, but I didn't care. I still had dirt behind my ears, between my toes and ground so far down under my nail beds that it would take a backhoe to dig it all out. "Ahhh," I stood under the water so long I looked wrinkled beyond recognition.

A nice elderly woman, who reminded me of my grandma Sara, took our dirty clothes in exchange for robes, and if I had any other clothes to wear I would have told her to burn them, but I didn't. Besides, the jeans belonged to Secret Agent Man and they were the only shred of physical proof that what happened actually happened.

Wrapped in a towel, I sank down on the bed next to Bella who had just flipped on the TV. Teenagers do have priorities after all. She flipped the channels quickly, but something caught my eye. "Go back," I shouted and stood up in front of the TV. I had already chewed my nails down to the nub, but I managed to bite off a chunk to chew on. Bella found the station I wanted and turned it up when she saw her father's picture in the corner behind the newscaster. We both leaned toward the TV with wide eyes and listened to the blonde news commentator as she went on.

"All of Hollywood is still shook up by news of the death of action-film-star Roald Munson and his estranged wife, Nicole Harrison's daughter. A spokesperson for Munson says he is not taking any questions at this time, and would like to thank everyone for their thoughts and prayers. No word yet on how the charter plane went down in central Rwanda and there has been no comment from Nicole Harrison at this time."

We both looked at each other with wide eyes and dropped jaws. Bella burst into tears, but I remained okay. I just prayed that my parents hadn't been notified. Surely, no one would have thought to call them. I was positive that Roald was too busy mourning his daughter to make that phone call.

Shit, shit, shit. I let the tears roll down my cheeks, because I had sent that letter. What if my parents learned of my death and then read that letter? Ohhhh, I couldn't imagine how they must have felt, receiving a letter like that from the grave, no less.

"Calm down." I finally had to pull back from Bella because she sounded hysterical. "You aren't dead. You're alive and your mom and dad are going to be so happy to hear from you."

She looked up at me with tear-stained cheeks. "I want my dad."

"Me, too," I said. "Me, too."

We finished our debriefing with a couple of ambassadors, a French guy with bad teeth and a couple of men in uniform. I wasn't sure what to tell them and what not to tell them so I kept certain things to myself; like the fact that I killed some people.

One of the men was American, Air Force by the looks of his uniform. I pulled him aside when we broke for coffee. "What do you know about Prince Armand?"

He looked at me as if I were speaking in code. "Miss Ford, we should be concentrating on reuniting you with your families, not with tall tales about Armand."

I got the distinct feeling that either he didn't believe a word I said, or it was so hush, hush that he might have to hire someone to rub me out because I knew too much.

I prefer my first theory.

When they finally gave us permission to make our phone calls, I dialed my father's number from the private office that they let me use and I got my dad on the fourth ring.

"Dad," I cried into the phone and began weeping uncontrollably. "It's so good to hear your voice."

"Did you get fired again?" he asked.

Evidently, he hadn't heard of my mysterious death and even more clearly, he hadn't received my letter. I don't know how long it takes airmail to reach Oregon from Africa, but it made sense that it takes longer than a week.

"No," I laughed and wiped my tears. "How is everyone?"

So, he probably thought I was having a breakdown of sorts, because I was asking all sorts of questions about Dave and Josh and their kids and I never do that. I went on and on and then told him that he had mail coming and if he would please take the time to read it without interruptions I would really appreciate it and then I asked to talk to my mom, but she was out. She's always out, good for her. The woman knows how to live.

I hung up completely satisfied and elated that news of my fiasco hadn't reached Bend, Oregon, yet.

Bella ran into the room a minute later, crying and screeching at the top of her lungs.

"He hung up on me."

"Who did?" I asked, clearly angered and confused.

"Thomas!"

"Thomas? Who's Thomas?"

"He's my dad's personal assistant. My dad never answers his own phone, he has people to do that and he...hung up...on meeee." Her sobs were long-winded and drawn out.

"What did you say to him?"

"I said, 'Hi Thomas, can I speak to my dad?'" she moaned breathlessly. "And then he screamed at me that it wasn't funny and I shouldn't call again."

I couldn't help the laugh. I knew it was insensitive, but I should have insisted that I make that phone call. After all, the man thought she was dead. He most likely figured it was a horrible, distasteful hoax.

"I'll call him. What's his number?"

I dialed and when Thomas answered, I flubbed my words a bit, and then blurted out that Bella was alive. That we were in Greece and please don't hang up.

He hung up.

We tried the number for her mother's assistant next. "Hello, I'm calling from Athens, Greece, to let you know that Annabelle and her nanny are both alive and well, and she really wishes to speak to Nicole."

Click.

"We aren't doing too hot here, are we?" I shrugged my shoulders and then we both burst into laughter because it was so absurd. Then we calmed down, sucked down a couple of Italian sodas and put our heads together.

"We should just call the police in Greenwich, have them go to my dad's house and make him listen."

"Good plan, but is your dad in Greenwich?"

"Why wouldn't he be?"

I scratched my chin and I think I unearthed more dirt. I needed another shower. "I bet he's with your mom."

"Really?" She looked elated.

I'm a big boob. I just got her hopes up that her parents were reconciling when I just meant that they were probably together to plan her funeral, Big Boob. "Okay, so we need to find out where they are?"

Where the hell was Secret Agent Man when I needed him most?

"Gregory," I said as I snapped my fingers.

I called the house and got the machine. Probably not a good idea to leave such news on an answering machine, I coughed a couple of times and hung up.

"Your mom's house?"

She rattled off the number and I dialed and got a voice mail for Braden Booker and his slut of the week, which was Nicole Harrison. Sheesh, I had daggers for that woman and I had never even met her. I'm a tad on the judgmental side, especially now that I absolutely adore Annabelle.

Again, I didn't feel the urge to leave such a message on Braden's machine.

I thought this would be so easy. I thought we would get home, take a shower, have some pancakes and go to the mall. I was so damn wrong.

The men on the aircraft carrier had searched my handbag thoroughly. The room full of diplomatic people had taken our passports. They also confiscated my credit cards, driver's license and Blockbuster coupons in that room and I felt so violated that all my body cavities ached as if I had been searched by the DEA in Miami. Not a pretty picture and then, we couldn't even convince one single person in Hollywood that we were alive.

"We should just call the National Enquirer. I'm sure they would love to get this scoop," I suggested as a joke, and Bella perked up. "I was kidding."

"Well, if we called the press here in Greece and they came and took a statement from us, then my parents would actually see that I was alive and they'd come get us. It could work."

Sure, it could work, but it seemed so dramatic. Then again, Bella loved drama. I was sure in ten years she'd be the next big ticket in Hollywood. She had the looks, she had the genes and she was, after all, the daughter of not one, but *two* Hollywood stars.

"Let's just keep trying with the phone for awhile and then as a last resort, we'll call the paparazzi, okay?"

"Okay," she replied.

I tried Gregory again at the house, no answer. I called my brother in Austria, but he was at football practice. His wife, Julie, said that she had heard that Annabelle had died, along with a number of other unnamed passengers, but no mention of me, the nanny. Sheesh, even in death I was ignored.

I called Dave in Seattle. He was at the hospital and his wife, Carrie, didn't watch television so I didn't even ask her if she had heard anything. Then I called Gregory again. I called Braden's house. I called Thomas again, but no one answered.

"We should call your grandmother."

"Yes." Bella grabbed the phone and dialed grandma's house in Belgium. "Gammy, are you there? Gammy pick up please, it's Bella. I'm okay. I'm here in Athens with Charlie and we're fine. Gammy?" Bella started crying again and hung up. Bella wrote down every single number that she knew from memory. Her father's agent, her father's publicist, her father's hair guy, and finally her mother's publicist answered with a solemn voice. Only it wasn't a real person, it was a recording saying that Miss Harrison would be out of touch until the funeral and that any correspondence could go to a PO Box in Hollywood, please, thank you for your kind prayers and goodbye. Dang.

Bella tried Gammy two more times and left two more messages that were tearful.

"She's probably with your dad, wherever he is."

I waited another hour before trying Thomas again, and there still was no answer. At that point, I climbed into my clean clothes that they had brought me and demanded to speak to someone who could help us with our dilemma. They put me in touch with an American named Sam Watters.

"Annabelle Munson." He smiled and extended his hand. "You're the hottest topic of conversation this week."

"It's actually Squire," I said. "Look, we've tried everyone that she knows and they either hang up on us or no one is answering. Can you help us out?"

"I think your best shot is to call the police and let them handle this."

"We don't know where either of her parents are. They could be anywhere in the U.S., or their place in St. Thomas, or Paris. We've just been through hell. We just want to go home." Fatigue was starting to set in and I really wanted to see Vince again. I thought I liked Vince best. Duane is the one who kissed me, but then again, Ryan was the one who snuggled next to me by the campfire. Well, and it was actually Duane who saved our lives in the first place. Oh, I just want *him* back.

I slumped over in Sam Watters' office and caught my cheek in my palm. "I just want to go home."

"Me, too." Bella could clearly sense my pain.

"Alright, I'll make some calls to some people I know in New York and we will see what we can do. Why don't you two go out and get some fresh air. Athens is amazing and it looks like you could both use some new clothes."

To my surprise, he handed me my purse back. I rarely used my MasterCard and right then seemed like as good a time as any to max it out.

Bella perked up at the sound of that and off we went. We stopped off in our guest room and I made one last ditch attempt to call Gregory again. Nope. He still wasn't home.

Athens *was* amazing. It is more beautiful than I ever imagined. The streets look ancient and everywhere I looked, there was yet another beautiful man who looked like Vince. Black hair, deep dark eyes and chiseled chins everywhere I looked. Yep, I had Secret Agent Man on my mind and I couldn't shake him. I did my best at distracting myself at a corner boutique where I bought new mascara, some pretty, mauve nail polish and a silk scarf to wrap in my chin-length dark hair.

I've never been one of those super-girly women who enjoyed manicures, pedicures and facials, but it sure seemed like a good idea when Bella suggested it. I think we spent an entire three hours in that spa and if our bond wasn't strong before we went, it was even stronger when we emerged. I could see us possibly staying in touch for the rest of our lives. Hell, when she turns twenty-one, I want to be there. When she falls in love for the first time, I want to be there and when her heart gets stomped on by some creep named Rico, I want to be there to help pick up the pieces. I know I'm eighteen years her elder and her nanny of all things, but I have never in my life felt more connected to another female than I did to Bella.

"Do you just want to get on a plane and go home?" I suggested as I stepped into a pretty, plum-colored sundress that cradled my breasts perfectly. I felt like a woman. It was not the typical thing that I would wear, but hell, when in Rome....Okay, okay, so we were in Athens.

"I dunno." Bella shrugged and smiled at me. "I like it. You look so pretty."

"Thanks," I gushed at the sweet girl who made my life hell the last time I took her shopping. We'd come a long way together; at least something positive came out of that whole mess. In fact, many positive things emerged from one traumatic week spent on the Dark Continent. Right then I was thinking that I was almost glad that it happened. Not glad how it ended, though. I really need to find happier endings.

We stopped for a quick shot of ouzo. I'd never had ouzo before but I was in Greece and they offered it on about every corner. I finally had something similar to good old American pancakes, but it wasn't quite the same. Bella filled up on Italian sodas, a giant gyro and a bed of greens with olive oil and feta cheese.

"I'm so full." I leaned over and gave Bella a pinch on the cheek. "We should get back."

She actually laid her head back onto the back of the chair and closed her eyes. She amazed me sometimes. I think she was smelling the roses. "You okay?"

"Fine."

And I think she really will be.

Things weren't as they should have been when we returned to the embassy. People with cameras filled the steps leading up to the main gate. Paparazzi. Holy shit, I had never seen such a mob since....well, since the wildebeests in Africa. I didn't turn quickly enough to get us out of eye-sight of the crowd and soon, guards with riot gear arrived and we were safely shuffled inside.

I dropped my shopping bag to the floor and inhaled sharply. "That was your bright idea?" I slammed my palms against Sam Watters' jacket lapels. "That wasn't very smart."

"I didn't," Sam confessed. "I swear, I made some calls to some people in New York and D.C. and then people just started calling out of nowhere. They had heard a rumor that the Munson girl was in Athens and that she was trying to reach her parents. The AP is jammed with calls and reports and even CNN has made inquiries. This is the biggest thing since..."

"Watergate," I shouted with hands on hips. This was what was wrong with Americans. They are gossip hounds. "Come on." I grabbed Bella by the wrist. We went to our guest room and called Gregory. This time he was home.

"Hello," he said solemnly.

"Gregory, it's me. Charlie...Don't hang up," I yelled when I heard a high-pitched squeak. I didn't hear a thud or the phone hit the floor so I was convinced that he hadn't fainted.

"That's not funny," he shouted. "Who is this? Why are you doing this?"

"Jesus, Gregoire." I knew that was his real name, but he changed it because it sounded *too* gay. "Listen to me, it's me. Charlie Ford. And I can prove it."

I heard heavy breathing. Most likely, he was thinking very hard.

"Where do we keep the dog food?" he said as a test.

"In the kitchen pantry in a big tub, labeled 'dog food.'" I said, pretty pleased with myself and happy that he was about to believe me.

"Anyone could know that. Where..." he began again, but as I saw Bella turn on the TV and we saw our cowering faces, I knew I didn't have much time.

"I know that you keep lavender-scented bath beads under the purple towels in the guest bathroom." There was silence, more breathing and then a high-pitched squeal that nearly shattered my eardrum.

"Oh gawd, Charlie. Is Annabelle alive?"

Duh.

"Yes. We're both fine. We're in Athens and the paparazzi just invaded the embassy. I've been trying to get through to Roald and Nicole all day. Where the hell are they?"

"They're at their summer place in Taos. I think they might be reconciling."

Planning funeral arrangements sounded more feasible, but it could happen.

"Can you get through to them before they hear it on TV?"

"Sure, I'll do my best. Give me the number there and I'll have him call you. Oh, God." He was now crying. I could hear the loud sobs over the phone. "Is she there? Can I talk to her?"

I handed the phone to a newly reprieved Bella, who was just as tearful. I gave them a couple of minutes to chat and stared out the window at the mob of reporters, all of whom wanted the scoop of the century. I, for one, was not going to give it to them. Bella was my responsibility and I didn't want her to be disturbed.

Bella laughed a lot on the phone. I heard her apologize to him for being such a brat and then they cried some more and I grabbed the phone.

"Why? I mean how?" I was so tongue-tied. "Why did he think we were dead?"

"The charter company in Kenya said that the plane went down over the mountains and no one survived. They showed her father photos of the crashed plane, incinerated beyond recognition. He had no choice but to believe them. What happened? Where have you been?"

"It's such a long story; I'll tell you when we get back. See you soon I hope."

I disconnected and waited thirteen minutes before Sam Watters knocked on the door.

"Mr. Munson is on the phone."

I'd seen Bella cry a lot the past week. I had seen her at her lowest, her saddest and at that moment I was seeing her at the highest of her highs. She couldn't even speak when she heard her father's voice. I, too, wept like a child and pressed my cheek against hers so that I could hear their conversation. I held her shoulder tightly as he wept loudly and told her how much he loved her. It was something so incredibly moving that it warmed my heart.

After a half an hour, she finally handed me the phone so he could arrange for their reunion.

"Charlie?"

"Yes." I felt good about myself at that point, so I was confident that he wasn't going to blurt out those all too familiar words, "*You're fired.*"

"Thank you for bringing her home safely. I can't wait to hear all about it. Thank you. I owe you my life."

"It was my pleasure."

Chapter Nine

We didn't have much to pack up. Just the couple of new outfits that we had just bought, my new makeup, some snacks for the trip home. I knew that we had quite a bit of time to kill before Roald and Nicole arrived, but I also knew that I couldn't take Annabelle outside the walls. We did however take a walk downstairs to sit and watch the sunset off the back patio. There were three guards standing watch over the veranda. I felt calm and centered. Almost Zen-like. I couldn't help the giggle and then Duane popped into my head. Duane with his thick, Coke-bottle glasses and matted down hair that he parted directly down the center of his head. That stupid shirt he was wearing and the husky tone of his voice when he demanded that I hand over my purse.

I clutched my bag towards my chest as I watched the first twinkle of the first star. No matter how dirty and grimy it was, I didn't feel the need to rush out and buy a new one. The bag that I was holding had a story to tell. It had brought us food when we were hungry, gave me Midol when I was bloated and held the key to our escape. I sure was glad at that point that I had bought the metal nail file instead of the paper emery boards like I usually purchase. My thought when I bought it special for the trip was that I might need to dig some dirt out from under my fingernails and it looked as if it could get the job done.

I was so thankful for everything I had. Without releasing my bag from my grasp, I looked over at Bella and held out my hand. "What are you thinking about?"

"If this was a movie, I'd be sitting under the stars with Justin Timberlake."

I smiled and clutched my bag.

"If this were a movie...." I didn't and couldn't finish my story because it involved Secret Agent Man, a bed, and an XXX rating. I grinned sheepishly.

"You miss him, don't you?"

Was I that obvious, or was she just one smart pre-teen? I just nodded and closed my eyes. If only my life were a movie. If only. If only.

Minutes later, I heard a loud crash. I looked back and saw a young boy holding a tray with what I assumed was our dinner.

"Sorry," he said sheepishly. "I'll be right back."

I know we were babes and all, but come on. We're starving.

When he didn't return promptly, I got up to see what was taking so long and when I did, the French guy with bad teeth approached me and said I was to come with him. He smelled like musk and cat urine. For all I knew, it was his cologne. I'd once or twice heard that Europeans have different hygiene habits than us Americans. Usually, I wouldn't mind, but his odor was making me gag.

"Miss Ford." He extended his hand and when I took it, he brought it too his lips and kissed the back of it. Yuck. "I'm Christian DuLucere. Would you please come with me?"

I pulled Bella along with me and when we got to the foyer, another man approached us.

"I'm to take you to the airport to await your flight to meet Mr. Munson."

Okay. I figured that Roald would actually come pick us up himself, but he never said he would. He just said he would arrange for our reunion.

"Isn't he meeting us here?"

"He can't take that chance with the media attention and all. Please come with me."

I shrugged and held Bella's hand while we said goodbye to Sam and the rest of the staff. I waved behind me and stepped into the stretch limo that was waiting behind the gate on the south side of the building. The paparazzi were still camped out front, out the west side and across the street. Sitting there like vultures. The sight made my stomach turn and I completely understood Roald's hesitation.

I didn't start feeling uncomfortable about our companions until we pulled out into the street and I could no longer see the American flag waving from the tall pole atop the building. Then I was at the mercy of three men in cheap suits. One of whom was glaring at me from behind his bifocals.

I enjoyed the limo ride up until we reached the airport. Then for some reason, something didn't sit right in my gut. Perchance, it was the lamb-meat gyro that I had for lunch, perhaps it was all the ouzo I had been drinking, or perhaps it was my keen instincts that something was amiss.

I chose the latter as we approached a private plane. I held on tight to Bella's hand and demanded to speak to Bella's father before we got on the plane.

"Would it be alright if I spoke to her father? You know, just to reaffirm to him that the girl is okay."

Both men exchanged questioning glances. I think I must have confused them. Perhaps they weren't used to their passengers making such strange requests.

"Mr. Munson can't be reached. You'll see him soon enough."

Why did I get the feeling that he was lying to me? I can tell you why. Because when I still refused to take my hand off the *Oh, shit* handle in the limo, a long silver gun, equipped nicely with a sleek silencer poked me in the nose.

"You have got to be kidding me!" I shouted at the Lord, and closed my eyes before stepping out and keeping Bella right by my side. "What the hell is wrong with you?" I mumbled to God one more time and hoped he would answer with a strong bolt of lightning that I hoped would zap the guy with the gun.

Both men looked at me with inquiring gazes. They must not have been privy to the hell that we had just been through. What was happening was completely implausible, even for the movies.

I stared at the man with the gun; willing God to make amends with his godly bolt of lightning. No such luck.

"We're waiting." He nudged me in the back and to my surprise; Bella was much cooler than I was.

CIA ran through my mind. As did KGB, for old times sake. Perhaps it did still exist; they just didn't want us to know about it. Then I even thought British Secret Service and half-expected James Bond to emerge from the small jet. Again, no such luck.

I really did have faith that God would not let someone kidnap Bella and me twice in the same week, so I chalked it up to Secret Agent Man and figured this was just his idea of foreplay.

The plane was so much nicer than the last one we had been on. It had soft leather seats, tables, a fridge, a couch and a bathroom with, I was guessing, running water. The men didn't seem quite as rude as my former captors did, so I sat down beside Bella on the couch. They were kind enough to offer us some snacks, which we both declined. They took my bag from me and rummaged through it before they tossed it into an overhead compartment. I do have to say that they did this horrifying experience so much more tastefully than our last captors.

"May I ask where you are taking us?" Because I assumed it wasn't back to the States, to her father and mother, to my parents even. Neither of the men flinched. My stomach rolled up into my throat when we were finally airborne. Bella was still so eerily quiet, I checked to see if she was still breathing. "We're going to be okay. I'm sure of it."

Was I sure of it? Not entirely: sixty-percent positive that we were going to survive and perhaps ninety-nine-percent positive that I would never ever board another plane for the rest of my life. Not with the way my luck had been going lately.

"We'll be there shortly." The one with the bifocals had a voice after all. "You vant drink?"

I recognized his dialect. He was most certainly speaking dumb-shit. The only other person I had ever heard speak dumb-shit was a very popular heavy-weight boxer who will remain unnamed.

I shook my head back and forth. I knew better than to accept martinis from strange men who spoke dumb-shit. I'd seen every James Bond movie ever made. Twice.

The flight to wherever wasn't that long. My new watch said 9:00 P.M. when we boarded and then it said 10:00 P.M when we touched down. I've got one of those classy, yet sporty, watches that tells the time in three different time zones; very handy when you're being kidnapped and dragged all over hell and back.

I didn't feel the need to make trouble at that juncture because for all I knew we were in Russia, Turkey or the Czech Republic. What I did know was that I had maxed out my MasterCard on clothes, facials and mascara and I doubted that anyone would take a personal check from Greenwich, Connecticut, so we were at the mercy of our captors...for the time being at least. Besides, our passports were in my bag, stored safely in the overhead compartment and I didn't want to take the chance that we'd be stranded in a back-ass foreign country with no identification. That scared me more than Bifocal Man with a gun.

I figured that if they wanted us dead, we would be road kill already.

The rain set a dreary tone to the night. I was beyond confused as to what was going on. Two more nicely dressed men in suits and long overcoats met the three original men. With Bella by my side, I emerged from the plane, walked down the stairs and was drenched from head to toe before reaching the bottom. Each step I took, I stepped carefully as I looked around and got a feel for our surroundings. None of the road signs were in English; most of them were just jumbled letters in my mind and blurry due to the horizontal rainfall. The wind whipped around us and had us shivering in our sundresses. I think I preferred the heat in Africa to that torrential downpour: as did Bella, from the look on her face and the chattering of her teeth.

I watched three of the men disappear; when they came back, a large, dark sports utility vehicle followed them. Each one of the men was on edge and keeping their eyes peeled with hands in pockets. I assumed they were holding guns in those same pockets.

If this was Secret Agent Man's idea of a prelude to hot sex, I think I'll end up popping him on the chin again.

Actually the more I thought about it, the more I talked myself out of my fun theory of seeing him again. This seemed all too real and all too scary. The worst part was that I didn't have a gun this time.

I feel better when I'm holding a gun.

I needed a gun.

I glanced over at Bella and sent her a weak smile. It was the best I could do under the circumstances. She grabbed my arm when the man with bifocal glasses ushered us into the big tough-looking truck.

I had ideas about a nice SUV like that someday, but then I was thinking I would rather have a tiny pink Miata convertible. Miatas look safe and fun. This monstrosity reeked of international espionage.

    I stared at the back of the men's heads and wondered if I had enough strength to snap their necks as I had seen Ryan do. I doubted it, so I kept my hands to myself and watched out the tinted windows into the dark, rainy night.

What I remember about making it into a hotel room isn't much because at that time, pillowcases shrouded our heads and they led us with our hands tied. That was by far the scariest thing that had ever happened to me. I didn't like it. The shroud messed up my hair and made it hard for me to breathe. I'm the kind of person who needs cool, fresh air to keep me calm and panic free.

    When they finally pulled the cloth off my head, I nearly hyperventilated and began screaming at the man who was standing just feet in front of me.

    "Assholes," I shouted, and moved viciously toward the man until he knocked me on my ass. I landed with a thud on the hardwood floor, watched the door swing shut and Bella the Brave helped me to my feet.

    "Why are you so calm about this? I'm sorry, I could handle that shit in Africa, but this is just spooky. Are you okay? Are you breathing?"

    Bella nodded and slumped down onto the bed. "We're in Armenia."

    Thank God for Gammy. Bella spoke four languages thanks to Gammy. Suddenly, I felt so much better. The color came back to my face and my heart rate dropped back down to normal.

    "Where exactly in Armenia?"

    "I'm not sure about that. I tried to read the signs the best I could and I know we are far from Yerevan. I've been here before. I think this is where Gammy and Pappi took me to the ballet. I recognized the markings on the side of the hangar. Do you think Pappi's in trouble?"

I nodded because I never lie to Bella. Besides, she knew. She knew that this was no coincidence. Being nabbed in Athens had direct connections to Claude Munson's political Houdini act.

I thought this would be a good time to say a prayer and ask for Secret Agent Man to appear in front of my face. This was definite spy stuff, not my cup of tea. I took inventory of my life, again, and decided at that moment that someone else was going to have to save the day, 'cause it wasn't going to be me.

I sank down on the bed. At least there was a bed. There was a bathroom with running water, a couple of bottles of Evian on top of the television, and a phone.

I picked it up just for the hell of it and a raspy voice spoke. "Vat you need?" I loved his accent, but I was kind of hoping for a direct line to the FBI.

"The girl and I would like some food...please."

Things could be worse. In fact, they could be much worse. I laid back on the bed; Bella grabbed the guest services book and flipped through it. She read it all to me.

"Cool," I said with a grin. "I really need to workout. You think they will actually let us use the workout room?" I rolled my eyes and then rolled over. "You okay?"

"Yeah." She smiled and lay down beside me. "We have food and water and a shower. Let's just pretend we're on holiday."

"I guess that could work." I smiled, but I really wanted to go home. I wanted to be free. I enjoyed freedom and that was why I lived in America, damn it, damn it, damn it. I did have the worst luck in the world.

Dinner arrived and consisted of a couple of steaks, mashed potatoes and a plate of fresh vegetables and dill dip. I felt stuffed to the brim, but I still wanted to go home.

That night we watched "Friends." I couldn't understand a word that they said, but Bella laughed a lot. It was actually very funny to see Joey's voice dubbed by a man with a high squeaky voice speaking French. I knew it was French because I know the words 'oui' and 'non'. That's about it. Again, I would have liked to be in a country where I actually understood the language.

"Where was your dad born?" I asked, because I was curious and I never liked "Frasier," so I turned off the television.

"Brussels, Belgium."

"Really?" That surprised me.

"Pappi is from Armenia, Gammy is from Belgium and when he was with Interpol, he was stationed in Belgium. He met Gammy and she had Daddy a year later." Bella smiled wickedly. "They weren't even married. They never did get married. Gammy was supposed to marry some other rich dude, but she fell in love with Claude. Very romantic." Her eyes blinked as if she were thinking about Justin Timberlake again.

"Who told you all that? Your dad?"

"No," she scoffed. "Gammy told me last summer. Gammy tells me everything. She's actually my best friend," she said and then turned to me. "But now, I think you should be my best friend."

"It would be my pleasure," I said and curled my arm under my pillow. It was nice to have one and I wasn't taking anything for granted, not even flat pillows with ugly chenille shams. "I don't have any girlfriends."

"Really?" She looked confused. "Why not?"

I shrugged. "I guess I've just been too busy with my plan for the future. I spent the past few years hanging out with kids and before that, I was in the Army and moved around a lot. I made some pretty good guy friends, but they got married and had kids and we just don't talk that much anymore."

"That's kind of sad." Bella's head eased into her pillow.

"It kind of is, isn't it?"

"Maybe you could be friends with Ryan?"

I exhaled loudly. I hadn't thought about him for a whole two hours, but she managed to bring him right back to the center of my thoughts. "I don't think Ryan is even his real name. I don't think I'll ever see him again."

"That's kind of sad," she said sweetly, with a smile.

"Yes it is." I closed my eyes. "So, Claude worked for Interpol, huh?"

"Yeah, Gammy says he was a really cool guy, handsome and sort of cocky...I think that's what she said." She blushed slightly. "Is that a bad word?"

"No. It just means confident, arrogant, self assured."

"Oh," she said. "So I could call you cocky."

Laughter erupted from my lips. "I guess so."

I slept incredibly well for being in a strange country surrounded by ugly flowered wallpaper. I think I woke up twice during the night, hoping to find Tums in the bathroom. I don't think my body was enjoying my huge meal as well as my taste buds had, but over all, it was a successful night's sleep. My dreams were erratic and cloaked with violence. I guess it was my subconscious letting me know that I was human and reminding me that I had killed people. I rolled over to see Bella still sleeping and then turned to hear a light knock on the door.

"*What?*" I screamed, because I'm a bear and that's what bears do.

"Café?"

Okay. Captors who bring me coffee? Perhaps we were just on holiday. Perhaps that was Roald's idea of thanking me. He was forcing me to take a vacation.

Maybe not.

Bifocal Man opened the door, slid over a platter of coffee, cream, and sugar towards me as if I were a tiger at the zoo. He kept his eyes on me and then slid back out the door. Very strange man.

They hadn't poisoned us the previous night with dinner, so I took a chance and poured myself some coffee, stirred in a couple drops of cream and brought it to my lips. "Umm. Good stuff." I smiled to myself, and then took an hour-long bath before Bella woke up. She padded into the bathroom half-asleep and made herself comfortable under the shower spray.

I took the opportunity to look under the bed, rake my hands across the wall, dig around in the drawers, and closet to find anything that might help me, a nail, a screw, a machine gun.

Bifocal Man had been very adamant about retrieving our utensils the previous night after dinner. He counted the forks, the knives and even demanded that I give him back the spoon that I wanted to keep as a souvenir. I didn't really want it as a souvenir, I wanted to dig a hole through the wall and escape just as Andy Dufresne did to escape from Shawshank.

The morning went by quickly. We played 'go fish' with a deck of cards we found next to the Holy Bible. I should have been reading the Bible to repent for my sins, but 'go fish' was more fun and the Bible wasn't in English. I suppose that's no excuse, I could have had Bella read it to me, but again, cards were more entertaining. Bella beat me three-hands-to-one before Bifocal Man came back and asked us if we wanted to accompany him to the dining area for lunch, or if we preferred to eat in the room. *Hello?*

We were marched down the hall by Bifocal Man and when we entered the dining area, there were three different men in trench coats sipping tea at a table. No one else was around. I was positive that the hotel was open just for us or perhaps it wasn't a hotel at all. It was probably a safe house, of sorts, not that I felt safe or anything.

"Good afternoon." He was definitely French. The tallest of the men sat down at our table. "You look well." He nodded at Annabelle and I did not appreciate how he was looking at her.

I slapped my hand around his wrist and, of course, that prompted the other men to draw their concealed weapons. I removed my hand and scowled. "Who are you and what do you want?"

He stared at me and smiled. "Lunch?"

There are certain things I hate more than others and being ignored is high up on my list. I'd felt ignored most of my life and I despised it. Right then I decided that, if or when I got my hands on a gun, I was going to shoot that scumbag first.

He stood up and gestured to the wait staff. They brought club sandwiches, with big chunky-style French fries and tarter sauce.

I looked up from my soda and noticed the color run completely from Bella's face.

"What is it?" I half-expected to see an eyeball in her Pepsi.

"This." She pushed her plate toward me. I saw nothing wrong with it, no hissing cockroach crawling around, and no long black hair hanging from her sandwich. She began quietly weeping into her hands.

I moved closer and wrapped my arm around her shoulder. "What's wrong?" I asked. Stupid question, I know.

"This is my favorite." She wiped her eyes and dipped a fry into the tarter sauce. "This is my favorite food. I always order this. Even the fries are the big ones that I like and this is Pepsi, not Coke. I hate Coke and this is Pepsi." She was becoming frantic, frenzied and disturbingly loud. "And the tarter sauce. How do they know?" she screamed loudly.

I looked around at the men who were staring at us. "Shhh," I said quietly. "It's okay. Calm down."

"I can't. I can't calm down. How do they know?"

I shook my head back and forth with tight lips. This was stranger than I thought. It was very odd that whoever had orchestrated this little kidnapping had done their homework and provided Bella with her favorite food. I looked around the table and saw not one shred of evidence that they knew my favorite food. There was no Diet Pepsi, no beef jerky and no peanut butter and jelly. Once again, I felt neglected. Sad, isn't it?

I patted her hand and urged her just to fill up. She took a couple of bites and once the men relaxed and sat back down, she began eating slower and chewing very carefully. I could tell by the look on her face that she was concentrating on listening to their conversation.

"What are they saying?" I asked through clenched teeth, just in case one of them read lips.

"I could only make out part of it. Something to do with what they were going to do after this was over."

Great. After what was over, our execution, our sale to Black Market female slave traders, what?

"Bifocal Man wants to go to Italy with his wife." Bella took a couple more French fries and sipped more Pepsi. At least she was enjoying her lunch. "That new guy wants to go to the States to see a NASCAR race."

Great. Our captors were planning their vacations. I needed a vacation. Hell, I hadn't had a vacation in four years. I vowed at that moment that if I survived and was not sold to slave traders that I was going to take a nice, long Hawaiian vacation, with new clothes and everything. That is what I was going to do.

Bella brought me back to the present when she started choking. I slapped her back a couple of times. She took a sip of Pepsi and finished wheezing. "They just said that once *they* get here in two days, they won't need you anymore. You will be..."

"What?" I practically shouted. "I am going to be... what?"

"I don't know how to translate it... Done? Ended? Over?" she rattled off a couple of attempts at translating what she had heard.

My heart dropped into my stomach. Why did I feel that being *ended* was not a good thing?

Bella listened more intently. Her breathing became ragged, her face paled again and she began weeping. "Remember the man from Greece, the guy you said smelled like pee?"

How could I forget the French guy who smelled like pee? "What about him?"

"What was his name?"

I shook my head. I had never been very good with names, but when Bella said it aloud, I clearly matched it with his bad teeth.

"DuLucere? Right?"

"Right." That made me very nervous, very, very nervous. DuLucere had sold us out to the bad dudes. Hell, I didn't even know who this DuLucere guy was and he had sold out a child. "What about him?"

"I didn't catch all of it, I just heard his name and something to do with what he said he wanted done with us."

Ah, hell.

Some people prefer to hire psychics and palm readers to tell them their futures, who they will fall in love with and when they are going to die. I don't happen to be one of those people. I don't want to know when and how I'm going to die. I prefer to keep that as a cosmic mystery, one that I personally don't look forward to.

I clamped my hand down over Bella's and scowled. "Stop listening. I don't want to know how they are going to *end* me and you shouldn't hear it either. You're only a kid."

"But..."

"But nothing," I said sternly and waved my hand to interrupt the scumbags. "Can I have more fries please?" Suddenly, when I knew I was going to die shortly, I didn't care so much about transfats and cholesterol.

After lunch, the tall lanky man brought out a package of double stuff Oreos and Bella started crying again. I myself never have a problem with cookies, so I picked them up and brought them with us for later. We were once again marched down the hall with high hopes of getting to do this again sometime. I actually had confidence that if we were lucky enough to eat in the dining room, I could make a plan. I could make a move to get a gun and then I would get us out of there. I had to get us out of there because in two days I was going to be ended...finito...finished...*dead!*

"What are you thinking about?" I asked Bella over the sound of CNN. There still were no reports of us going missing. No more information about how Annabelle Squire had been alive and then disappeared again.

"I was just thinking that maybe we could get out of here. I know how to speak Armenian. I'm not perfect, but I could find someone to help us on the streets."

She was thinking like me. I guess she didn't enjoy the idea of me being ended either.

I pushed up from my prone position and popped another Oreo into my mouth.

"Okay." I got serious and tried to think. Thinking had become extremely difficult because I didn't have a gun. I needed a gun. "Dinner. What if they bring us back down for dinner, do you think that you could translate every sign that you see in the dining room? You know, like exit signs—restrooms—employees only—stuff like that?"

"Sure." She nodded and I felt like a member of the Mission Impossible team.

For the next hour or two, I drew the dining area, the exit that they had taken us to, the floor number, which was three. It was odd to me to have a dining area on the third floor of a hotel. I knew the hotel had five floors because there were five little buttons that lit up when we were on the elevator after lunch. I knew that we were on the second floor and that we didn't have much time. I knew that Bella clearly heard 'two days,' but I preferred to give myself a day's head start from the bad people who were coming to *end* me. If dinner went well tonight and we got all the information we needed, then first thing in the morning, we could possibly be home free or at least out of the hotel. Saying we'd be home free in the middle of Armenia would be a great exaggeration. We would still have a long way to go, but I was thinking baby steps.

"What's that?" Bella looked over my shoulder at the little heart I was doodling. I scribbled it out quickly and she grinned and smacked me with a pillow. It had been a long time since I had a pillow fight, so I smacked her right back and giggled like a twelve-year-old. "You're in *love*," she cooed like a girl, and jumped around holding the map and made kissing noises. "S.A.M. Who does that stand for?"

I blushed and plopped my head back onto the pillow. "None of your business."

"Charlie? Do you have a boyfriend?"

"No," I said. Now was not the time to be talking about boys and French-kissing. I wasn't about to play truth or dare. "I don't have a boyfriend. Boys are gross."

"What's it like to kiss a boy?"

"Yucky. Don't do it until you're twenty-one. Promise me."

I could tell by the shameless grin on her face that she couldn't wait to kiss a boy and my little lame attempt at making it sound uninteresting failed miserably.

"When I get home, I'm going to call Gary Walker and I'm going to kiss him."

"When I get home, I'm going to go to Hawaii."

"Oh, I'm going to Disneyworld," Bella said and I smiled.

"That sounds like a perfect idea."

"With Dad and Mom...." She looked out the window and sighed. "Why do parents get divorced? Why can't they just be happy?"

"I hate to say it, but I don't think that a lot of people in Hollywood are truly happy. I think they run around like selfish assholes, milk the media attention for as long as they can, and then break up and start all over with someone else."

"Is that what you think my mom did?"

Wow, I never thought I'd be having that conversation. How was I to answer that one?

"I don't know. I've never met your mom."

"A couple years ago, she ran off with my dad's old assistant. They went to the Bahamas and when they got back, my dad cried and screamed a lot and I thought everything was going to be okay."

Hussy--hussy--slut--whore. I didn't respect that tramp, Nicole; not one bit.

"I'm sorry, Bella. I know this is hard on you, but remember, they both love you very much and I'm sure they want what's best for you." I lied. Nicole Harrison wants what was best for herself and her career.

"She's a selfish bitch," Bella said, then burst into tears and ran for the bathroom. I guess she read my mind.

We changed into new clothes for dinner. I had only the clothes on my back, a new shirt, and one sundress, but only one pair of underwear. Next time, I will remember to pack extra undies in case I ever got kidnapped again.

Bella's eyes were still puffy and red from her crying bout, so I tried to lighten the mood.

"Want to play screenwriters again?"

"Okay," Bella got serious and crossed her legs Indian-style on the bed. "We're going to get saved by Jason Bourne. I don't know how, but I feel like he's watching through my window, so I write him a note and tape it to the glass, then when we eat dinner, he comes in and kicks everyone's ass. Then he kisses me because you are too busy kissing Cute French guy, who turns out to be his long lost brother."

"Ewww," I scoffed dramatically. "As if?" I giggled and felt truly sad that I hadn't taken the time to have friends, have sleepovers, and do all those fun, girly things that I had passed up. I sure missed out as a child. I wasn't normal. I was always so busy trying to prove that I was better than boys were that I never enjoyed being a girl, but I *was* a girl. I hated dirt, I hated blood, and I hated fish guts. Why couldn't I have just been normal in other areas? Then again, if I had grown up to be normal, we wouldn't have been alive right then. Funny how life turns out.

"Okay, I like the Jason Bourne twist, but let's, just for fun, say that he kisses me at the end because you aren't old enough to kiss." That earned me a swift smack in the face with the pillow.

We laughed, hugged and then made up a secret handshake before we set out on our mission.

I picked up the phone and got the weird guy again.

"Vat you need?"

"Are we having dinner in our room this evening?"

I heard scuffling, some shouting and then he came back on the line. "No," he said and hung up. I tucked the map I drew under the mattress and got ready. Deep breath in. Deep breath out.

There was a knock at the door, and then a new guy entered. New guy was sort of cute for a scumbag. He, too, sounded French and all I could decipher from his rapid ranting was... "Dinner?" He cuffed Bella and me together and marched us down the long corridor. I saw Bella's eyes glance in every direction. She was clearly concentrating hard on memorizing and translating as much as she could. I kept quiet and didn't make a stink, even when Frenchy stuck his hand on my ass. It might have been an accident when he reached for the elevator button, but then again, he did look happy about it. I scowled, but behaved. If all went well we would be out of there by the next afternoon and my ass would be safe from strange French dudes with hairy hands.

Dinner that night was steamed fish of some sort, baby carrots and some gunk that looked like rice, but I didn't want to make hasty assumptions, so I left it alone. Bella spoke under her breath with food in her mouth as not to draw any attention to herself.

"Exit." She nodded with her head while sipping milk. "Banquet hall, dance hall and gift shop," she said while I sipped milk. "I can only read half the sign behind me, but the first part translates to 'equipment' I think."

"Broom closet? Maintenance?"

"Probably."

She was good; I had to give her that.

"That cute one thinks you're hot."

"Really?" I perked up. "Maybe he will have a change of heart and let me go." I looked over at Frenchy. He was smiling at me, but had a gun in his hand, so I dismissed that thought for... *I had better block our door tonight.*

I shivered and finished my roll. "What else did they say?"

"The older tall one, who just shook his head, said 'it's a damn shame...'"

Great, they were talking about the end of me again.

"Says that he'd like to have a little of that before you disappear," she continued, and I started choking that time. I had just inhaled a large chunk of bread.

"Stop it." I wheezed. "Stop listening."

"No," Bella said. "He says your ass is sweet like...."

I put my hands over my ears at that point and sent her a glare. She was smiling and stuck her tongue out at me. What can I say; we were both mature beyond our years.

"Now they are talking about football...or soccer I guess," she said as she pulled my hands off my ears. "So, did we get it all?"

"I think so." I looked around and wondered where the stairwell was. I hadn't seen a stairwell yet. There had to be a stairwell.

I waved my hand at the men and watched Frenchy hike up his black trousers and head my way.

"Do you think we could take a walk...I mean, just around the hotel? I feel like I ate way too much and I don't want to get fat." I batted my eyelashes.

He grinned and gave me a thorough inspection before shaking his head and whistling.

I suppressed the urge to ram my fork into his thigh and smiled sweetly. "Pretty please?"

He looked over at his counterparts, shrugged, said a few choice words in French and extended his hand.

For a second I thought he was just going to hold my hand, but no. He handcuffed me and then did the same to Bella. This time we each had our own pair and they then shackled us with our hands behind our backs. I think he just did it to get a better look at *my rack*. But what do I know?

We passed three more signs and I saw Bella's brows scrunch together as she translated the more difficult one in her head. I counted the steps back to the elevator and then counted how long it took to go down one floor. It was almost forty-five seconds later that the door re-opened and we stepped onto the second floor. Forty-three steps later, we were back at our room. I paused and looked up and down the hall before stepping inside. Once we were inside, he took the cuffs off, gave me a wink and was gone.

I barfed up my dinner, and then barricaded the door with the dresser.

Chapter Ten

The next morning I felt much better. I had survived the night without being violated by Frenchy. I pushed the dresser back into normal position then I pulled the map out from under the mattress and went to work. My coffee and Annabelle's orange juice arrived at eight on the dot. Bifocal Man was back. The bags under his eyes weren't as pronounced, so he probably had gotten some sleep on his night off.

I glared fiercely at him when he slunk back out the door and then finished with my work.

"Stairwell was where again?"

"I think you said twenty three paces past the elevator." Bella sat up and helped me with the details.

"Thanks," I said with a genuine smile, and then held her hand tightly. "I want you to promise me that if something happens to me, you will just run. Run like you've never run before and get the hell out. Don't look back." I squeezed her hand. "Promise me."

All she did was nod. What more could she say? She was a kid for Christ's sake, and this wasn't going to be easy. I knew she was going to have to see blood. She was possibly going to witness me killing someone and I feared that things between us would never again be the same.

"And don't look."

"What do you mean?"

"Close your eyes."

"How can I run and close my eyes at the same time?" She almost sounded like her usual self. Snotty and pretentious and well—like a twelve-year-old.

"Never mind, just stay put like we practiced and then run if something bad happens."

"*O-kay!*"

I took a long shower and reined in the surge of adrenaline that was causing my limbs to shake violently. I put on my khaki shorts, blue tank top, and didn't bother with my hair.

"Let's go over it again," I demanded once we were both dressed. "What is the cue?"

"You are going to tuck your hair behind your ear and then I'm going to pass out."

"Okay, show me again."

Bella did her best dramatic performance and fell backwards onto the bed.

"Now, there isn't going to be a bed and I don't want you to give yourself a concussion, so be careful when you fall onto the floor. Go down smoothly, but roll your eyes back like this."

I did my best imitation of myself passing out and Bella laughed.

"You did that in the airplane...in Kenya. It was gross."

I rolled my eyes and grinned to keep the mood light.

"Okay, so when you are down on the ground, what do you do next?"

"I keep my eyes shut the whole time."

"I'll do the rest and don't be scared."

"Do I get a gun?"

My head snapped around so fast I got the spins. "What?"

"Do I get a gun? I could help you."

"No, you don't get a gun."

Breakfast that morning consisted of scrambled eggs with green onions, sausage patties and English muffins. I looked around the room and to my surprise; only two men were stationed nearby, sipping on lattes and laughing.

"I love you," I said to Bella as I finished my juice. "I really do."

"I love you, too," she said without a smile, because there wasn't much to smile about that morning. We were about to go up against impossible odds and neither of us particularly wanted to.

"S.A.M.," I said with a sappy grin. "It stands for Secret Agent Man."

"I knew it." She giggled helplessly.

Two minutes later, Bella stood up and dramatically said she didn't feel good. I stood up with a gasp, knocking my chair over in the process. I saw both men approaching us from the corner of my eye, so I tucked my hair behind my ear and Bella gave an award winning performance if I do say so myself. She went down with a thud and had her eyes rolling back into her head.

I was proud.

I was also quick. Bifocal Man was the first to lean over her body and when he did, I pulled the gun from his hip and took a couple steps back.

"Drop it," I said to the tall French guy and leveled the gun on his chest.

He hesitated, looked around for help and then did what I told him to do. The gun dropped from his grasp and I demanded that he kick it to me. He did and I kept my gun trained on him while I picked it up.

Bifocal Man was speechless and trembling. He started muttering something in dumb-shit. Bella perked up and moved away from him.

"What's he saying?"

"Something about you not knowing what the hell you are doing."

"Oh yeah?" I wanted to blow his head off, but I didn't want to get blood on Bella, so I moved back and glanced around before I made a move for the door.

I should have known that I wouldn't be lucky enough to get away with such a diabolical plan. I grabbed Bella's hand, moved back three or four steps and felt a shooting pain in my lower back.

It all went black after that.

Under ordinary circumstances, waking up alone in bed, face down in a puddle of my own drool didn't bother me, but when I woke up and all I heard was the dripping faucet in the bathroom, I was mortified. The pain in my lower back was unbearable. It felt as if a heavy-weight boxer had punched me in the kidney. My face also hurt; mostly my left upper cheek. I couldn't move my hands for some reason and I could taste blood.

That's never a good sign, but I was alive, at least for the time being. I struggled to sit up and when I realized they had cuffed my hands tightly behind my back, I rolled a couple of times until I fell off the bed. I lay there, cried for a couple of minutes, then cussed, and screamed at God. For the first time in my life, I actually considered myself lucky. At that very moment, I considered myself lucky just to be alive. The moment didn't last long but it was nice while it lasted.

I knew I wasn't in my old room because the horrible floral wallpaper was different and the chenille bedspread was brown instead of white. I screamed out for Bella, but she didn't answer. This was it. The beginning of the end. I just wanted the pain to go away.

I got myself together and made it into the bathroom. It looked as if someone had beat up my face pretty badly. I guessed no one had told the French that they weren't supposed to hit women. Not that it mattered. I didn't think good manners even mattered at that stage in the game. My nose had been bloodied but all that was left was a couple dark lines of dried blood on my upper lip. My left eye had a monster bruise around it, and I felt as if I was back in the Army again.

I really couldn't move around much with my hands the way they were. So I laid down on the floor, did a couple of jiggles, heard a popping sound in my elbow that reminded me that I wasn't twenty anymore and then I finally rolled my butt over my handcuffed hands and ended up with my hands in front of my body. Much better.

I cleaned myself up the best I could and sat down on the bed because my head throbbed and I had the spins. I had never been tranqued before, but I assumed that was what had happened to me because I felt hung over and miserable.

They foiled my plan and Bella was God knows where. I flipped my wrist and looked at the time.

"That can't be." I shook my wrist to make sure it was working. My watch said eleven thirty and that meant that I had been out either for half an hour, or twenty-four-and-a-half hours. I believed the latter because I was stiff and sore and my bruises looked a day old at least.

At that point, I lost all control and started screaming. I didn't think about the pain that my body would be in the next day because I would be dead according to what we overheard at lunch two days before, so I rammed my shoulder against the door over and over again until I collapsed on the floor. No one can fully understand what goes through a person's mind when she thinks she is going to die, but I had new appreciation for my life.

My knees were shaking; I had splinters in my butt and a gnawing morbid feeling in my gut. Unlucky wasn't the word that I would use to describe myself anymore. It would be more fitting to say that I have a curse. Cursed is a good word for me. The tears fell as I laid my head on the hardwood floor and thought about Bella. I'd never felt such a protective feeling for anyone in my life. It was odd. I guess it's because I'm the youngest, so I never had anyone to watch over when I was a kid. Both my brothers did a good job of watching over me. I think Josh was a bit more over-protective than Dave was because Dave told his archrival that he could invite me to the prom. What kind of shit was that? I think Dave had a sick sense of humor and thought it would be funny to watch me beat up the prick when he tried something on the dance floor. I was a bit smarter than that and told the guy to go to hell the day he asked me. I skipped all the proms. I did take my best friend Alan to Sadie Hawkins three years in a row, but no one ever asked me to go to formal affairs.

I started thinking about Bella again and I really wanted her to be okay. It sickened me to think that some twisted fascist politician was using her to make things go his way. I assumed that was what was going on anyway. I still had no idea and right then it didn't matter. I needed to get up, brush myself off and get the heck out of there before they came for me.

I made it into a sitting position before I heard two sets of footsteps approaching my door. Come hell or high water, I was not going down without a fight, so I quickly scrambled to my feet and stood up behind the door. Who ever they were, they were going to get a heck of a surprise when they came in.

I watched the doorknob turn slowly. My heartbeat was so loud against my rib cage that I had a hard time hearing anything other than the pitter-patter of my frightened and overworked heart. The doorknob moved slowly. Perhaps the executioners were just as hesitant as I was about my death. Who knew at that point? My only hope was that cute French guy had decided he wanted me to be the mother of his children and thus couldn't sit back and watch me die.

Okay, I know, I was grasping at straws, but hell, I was scared out of my mind.

The door finally opened a crack and when it opened all the way, I bent my head like a bull, barreled at the man in black, and knocked him on his ass. He scrambled up and shoved me against the wall before I could hit the second guy. I felt hot breath on the back of my neck and it stunk like....cat urine and musk.

Frightened, sure, I almost lost bladder control, but I was also a survivor.

He turned me around and stepped backward. "Miss Ford."

I spit on his face.

He wiped it off with the back of his hand and chuckled. "You remember me then?"

I didn't say a word. I just glared. I had nothing to say to the man other than fuck off and die, but I figured that wouldn't go over too well and I wanted a quick and painless death, not slow painful torture.

Cute French guy straightened his overcoat and calmed his nerves by raking a comb through his thick black hair a couple of times. He had too much hair and to be honest, he seemed a bit vain for my tastes.

"Sit. Please." Smelly guy helped me to the bed. I hesitated, and then I sat down to save my energy for when I got to break his neck like a twig. I doubted that I could do it, but I sure as hell was looking forward to trying.

"Where's Bella?" My voice cracked when I said it. "What did you do with her, you..." My blood boiled, my jaw tightened with indignation but I couldn't think of a word strong enough to describe how much I hated that man.

"The girl is gone and that's all you need to know."

"Where is she?" I screamed again, and connected my hands with his nose. This prompted a trickle of blood to seep down his lip and I closed my eyes a split second before Frenchy had me pinned to the bed. I kicked and squirmed, then resigned my fight when I realized that he was enjoying me squirm. *Pervert.*

"I'm sure Mr. Munson will be pleased at how concerned you are for the safety of his little girl. You must be quite a wonderful nanny...," his eyes narrowed on mine. "among other things."

I don't know why it made me nervous, but it did. It was the way he said it and the look in his eyes when he did.

"I'm sorry that this has to be goodbye," he said.

I've always hated goodbyes.

"Wait," I kicked, screamed, and connected a kick to Frenchy's groin. He let go of his strangle hold on me and I sat up. "Please, just tell me where she is."

"I cannot."

He ever so politely bowed, curled a finger into his mustache and left me alone with Frenchy. Great. Cute guy was going to be the last person I saw before I died. I would have preferred to have an ugly executioner. It was somewhat unnerving to look into his crystal blue eyes and imagine him putting a bullet in my brain. He was too cute, not too cute to kick again, but too cute to be a cold-blooded killer. The second kick got him pretty good and had him grunting in pain. I left him breathless on the floor and I had gotten to the door when Bifocal Man grabbed me by the upper arm and pulled me into the hall.

The two men exchanged some banter, a couple of laughs, and lots of *oh-la-las* that I didn't appreciate.

"Let me go," I shouted when they lifted me into the air. I always used to make fun of women in movies, who kicked and screamed and shouted, 'let me go,' but here I was doing it. Like it was going to help.

The funny thing was that I absolutely, without a doubt, hated people lifting me into the air. I prefer to have my feet planted firmly on the ground. "Where's the girl?" I shouted and did my best to flail and writhe and then when I went limp, I fell through their grasp and hit the floor with a thud.

"Dammit !" I shouted, because then my knees and hip ached as badly as my cheek and kidney. "Just tell me what he did with her?" Dead weight is a lot harder to carry so I continued to act like an invalid.

Ignored again.

They said nothing and lifted me up. That time Frenchy tossed me over his shoulder like a sack of potatoes. We made it down the hall and almost to the elevator when I heard more voices. These voices weren't French; they were something that I didn't recognize.

Both my captors drew their guns quickly and shuffled me into a banquet room. The lights were off; old chafing dishes muddled the floor as well as chairs overturned onto the dusty tables. It felt sinister and eerie and well, a lot like a scary movie where someone chops the heroine into little pieces and stuffs her behind the walls.

"Shhh," Frenchy pressed tightly against my body so that I couldn't move and he and Bifocal Man looked wide-eyed at each other as they listened intently to the voices and footsteps coming down the hall.

I, of course, couldn't just sit there with my mouth shut. I bit into the hand that was covering my mouth and let out a yelp before Bifocal Man shoved his gun into my throat.

I'm sorry, but at that point, when I knew I was walking toward my execution, I could have cared less that he rammed a gun into my throat. I started to scream again and Bifocal Man whipped me around to face him and covered my mouth with his hand.

"Do you vant to die?"

I stared blankly at the man. What kind of a question was that? It was the second time in a week that someone had asked me that question and I didn't appreciate it. Besides, it was sort of moot point because they obviously already had designed and premeditated my death and furthermore, they probably already knew in which river they were going to toss my body.

"Those men vill kill you."

As opposed to the two dudes who were holding me captive in the ugly burgundy-colored banquet hall? I was beyond confused. I bit down and screamed as loud as I could.

Frenchy growled and took two shots, splintering the wooden door and we took off running. I dropped down like a limp noodle until Frenchy snagged me up and tossed me over his shoulder again. We ran down, up, and through the halls. Frenchy was in good shape. He only dropped me once when I covered his eyes with my hands and we smacked into a wall. We both fell like lead bricks and boy I was tired of him dropping me.

I swear to God, Bifocal Man almost shot me immediately. I could clearly see the rage in his eyes when he grabbed me and tossed me over his shoulder.

Shouting resounded from the hallway. I heard more shots fired and I thought for sure my time had come. We made it down three flights of stairs and into the parking garage.

Frenchy caught his breath and then tossed me up against a wall and spit at me while he insulted me in French. I think he was angry, but he could have been asking me on a date for all I knew.

With a loud screech, a big black sedan with tinted windows pulled up. It surprised Frenchy when it smashed into him and left him perched on the hood, gasping for breath and grabbing his broken shin. He cried out in pain and I took Bifocal Man by surprise with an uppercut to the chin. He immediately started bleeding because I think the cuffs must have gashed into his skin. I tried not to look. I grabbed the gun that had fallen from Frenchy's hand and narrowed in on Bifocal Man when he finally shook off the hit I gave him.

"Don't do zis. You don't understand. Ve are Interpol," he said.

The driver of the black sedan got out and pointed his gun at Frenchy.

I was confused. I felt frazzled and I didn't know what to do. I tried to think about what Secret Agent Man had said to me in Africa and about what Brick had said to me in Bosnia. Actually, nothing helped, I wasn't meant to choose who lives and who dies. Just give me a target far away and tell me to shoot. That was my expertise. I hated this up close and personal crap.

The man holding the gun to Frenchy got out and gave me a nod. "Thanks, Miss Ford, we'll take it from here."

Okay, so I was caught up in something sinister, but my only hope of getting to Bella stood with Frenchy and Bifocal Man so I was more inclined to believe them over the new guy who did an awful job trying to sound American. It was almost as bad as Kevin Costner trying to sound like Robin Hood in that Prince of Thieves movie.

The driver moved around and pulled out a walkie-talkie. I had enough foresight to realize that was a bad sign.

"Don't." I moved my gun over and pointed it at him. "Don't do it. Drop it," I shouted and he did.

He dropped the gun and the walkie-talkie, and sent me an evil glare, which I actually appreciated. I didn't want to kill someone who was smiling at me. My brain throbbed, as it never had before. "Where's the girl?"

"Ve don't know!"

So, Frenchy does speak English after all. "Please, listen to us. We are Interpol. You must trust us," he gasped breathlessly. "Just think about it."

Hmm. Trust. Then again, my gut was telling me that Frenchy and Bifocal Man were telling me the truth. There were many indications that led me to believe him. Like the fact that they tranqued me instead of killing me, and the fact that they fed us well and let us have Oreos for dessert.

I knew I didn't have much time to stand around and talk about this all day. I knew that I had already hesitated too long and Brick's husky voice broke into my train of thought. I really despised the memory of his voice, but there it was again. Yelling at me in my head that I hesitate and try to rationalize too much.

I had pretty much made up my mind, but when the driver of the sedan made a move for a second gun, I didn't hesitate and I shot him twice in the chest.

Bifocal Man looked relieved, grabbed Frenchy off the hood, and struggled to get him into the car while I tried to make sense of it all. Nothing about my life made sense anymore, but I thought I just made the right decision.

I cleaned out the driver. Took his wallet, his guns, his walkie-talkie, and kept my eyes from looking at the dark spot on his chest that was growing larger by the second. The last thing I needed right then, was to pass out and lose all composure in front of the Interpol dudes. If, in fact, they were who they said they were. I had many questions and not much time according to the shouts that sounded closer and closer with every breath I took. Bifocal Man grabbed my arm, tossed me into the passenger seat before he peeled out of the garage, and rammed the barricade that blocked the entrance to the underground parking garage.

The first few minutes, I just remained quiet and thought about what had transpired, then I started getting angry and not to mention scared. I raised my gun and pointed it at Bifocal Man as he veered through traffic in an urban part of Armenia. Again, I had no idea where anything was, or where he was taking me, but that time I could think and I felt better because I had a gun.

"Okay, so who are you and where is the girl?"

Bifocal Man drew in a deep breath, kept his eyes on the road and slowed to blend in with traffic. "Inspector Russo and that is Inspector Bellavia."

I looked back at Bellavia. He was white as a ghost and clearly in horrible pain. "We should get him to a doctor," I said. "By the way, who hit me in the face?"

"You fell and hit your head on the table after you were immobilized."

That was a nice way of saying that I was shot in the back with a tranquilizer gun as if I really were a great big bear.

"Honest," Bellavia gasped from the backseat.

"Okay, okay." I was starting to get a clear picture. I dropped the gun into my lap, but kept my hand on the trigger just in case my gut was trying to outsmart me. I had so many questions. "So DuLucere is Interpol?"

"Yah, he's head of Eastern Europe division."

"Why did he snatch Bella and me then? Why not help us get safely back to the States?"

They both shrugged. "Ve vere told to take you and the girl to the safe house and wait for instructions. Zat's all ve know," Bifocal Man replied, and I believed him. *What else is new?*

I dropped my head back on the seat and took a couple of deep breaths. I thought we were past the worst of it, and I thought they did, too. Russo and Bellavia remained calm until another sedan that looked identical to the one we were driving almost forced us off the road.

"*Merde*," Bellavia shouted, and rolled down the window just enough to begin shooting out the side. I think he might have hit one of their tires because the car lurched forward and bashed into my side once again. I think I screamed like a girl a couple of times, but I was scared and convinced more than ever that these bad guys meant business.

Bellavia kept firing away until his weapon emptied; he cursed some more in French and yelled something at Bifocal Man. Bifocal Man nodded and turned sharply, smashing the two vehicles together. I screamed some more and then ducked when I saw a gun pointed directly at me. The bullet bounced off the window and I felt invincible for a couple of minutes. It was somewhat cool. I almost flipped them the bird, but I had manners.

"Where's the girl?" I shouted between screams. "Who has her now?"

"Ve don't know. DuLucere took her after we immobilized you yesterday."

He did his best to drive and calm me down. I don't think he was lying at that point.

I tossed my gun back to Bellavia because I was too afraid to crack open my window. I didn't want to take a chance that an errant bullet would find it's way into my head.

He took the gun, did some more very creative cursing that sounded intriguingly sexy. If we were in bed and a car full of fascist thugs was not chasing us down, I might have felt warm and gooey.

Forget warm and gooey. I stared straight ahead at the brick median that was in our path.

I clearly remember saying, "Look out!"

When I opened my eyes, I was hanging upside down. The pressure in my head was tremendously agonizing. I turned slightly to the left and surveyed the damage. Bellavia was unconscious in back and, thank God, I had worn my seatbelt because he looked mangled. He moved slightly just as I unbuckled and dropped onto the shattered glass, so I was sure he wasn't dead.

To my sheer delight, the other car hadn't been as lucky as we had been and was already up in flames on the other side of the median. I managed to get out with only a few minor cuts on my hands. I was sure my head was bleeding but there was no way was I going to do something as stupid as try to look in a mirror. I heard some screeches, some sirens and then I crawled around the other side to help Russo since there was no way I could pull Bellavia from the back without the benefit of a hacksaw or those Jaws of Life things that I see firefighters use.

Bifocal Man was actually somewhat handsome without his glasses and that God-awful scowl that he always directed at me.

"Come on." I grabbed his hand and tried to wake him. "Russo." I shook him and his eyes fluttered open. "Hey," I said with a smile. "Thanks for all that coffee you brought me."

He tried to smile. The sirens got louder and he closed his eyes. "Hey," I yelled and slapped his cheeks until he opened them again. I was oblivious to the blood because I focused solely on his eyes. "Aren't you supposed to be taking your wife to Italy?" I asked with a heartfelt whimper, and kept my emotions in check. *Maybe I should stay home and raise babies.*

"Tuscany," he moaned and then tried to smile.

"Send me a postcard." I grinned, and firefighters, paramedics, and Armenian police officers shuffled me out of the way. The entire debacle had my mind reeling and not to mention throbbing. Bystanders were shouting, cops were yelling at firefighters and everyone were just talking too damn loud.

The chaos that ensued was nothing short of a circus. Television crews had shown up, the paramedics bandaged my head and all I could think of was Bella.

Two men with long overcoats flashed their identification and had me by the upper arms before I had time to realize what was happening. They pulled me from the back of the ambulance. I kicked and screamed as loud as I could but again, they were stronger and taller and my feet couldn't reach the ground. The second car with the bona fide bad dudes in it let out a high pitch squeal right before it blew up and jumped ten feet into the air. The screams from the crowd didn't help in my effort to draw attention to my kidnapping. Nothing helped me.

I wore a shroud again. Great. I had just escaped the bad guys, lived through a potentially serious car accident and this was the thanks I got. I could hear the hum of an engine. I could feel the bumps of the road, and I could smell really bad cigars. I coughed a couple of times under my shroud and tried to wriggle enough to see anything. All I could see was my scraped up knees and my shackled hands that were in my lap.

The journey to Where-Ever-Land was long, eerily quiet and tiresome. Mostly tiresome because I hadn't had any food and I really wanted to go home. Mostly I wanted to see Bella, but I didn't think that was going to happen. I hoped that she was safe and I prayed that Bellavia and Russo were on the level, but I knew nothing.

My head throbbed because I most likely had a concussion from the car accident. Add that to my other long list of ailments and I was just one big exposed boo boo. No one said a word on the way to Where-Ever-Land and that had me thinking *bad dudes* again.

When the vehicle finally stopped, I smelled the air and I didn't smell cat piss so I ruled out Interpol. I didn't smell cheap cologne, so that ruled out Americans, but I did smell cow manure. That could mean anyone at that point. Perhaps Old McDonald himself had joined the International ring of terrorists. Who the hell knows?

I blew out a breath and tried to rein in my emotions but it was hard. I was so tired that my hair felt heavy. Heavy, like there was a giant gorilla sitting on my head. I could barely move and they had to carry my lifeless body into what I was assuming was a barn because it reeked so badly of cow dung and moldy alfalfa.

"Miss Ford," an eerie voice bellowed in my ear. He sounded obviously foreign, but not French.

It was really starting to bother me that these mean and nasty Europeans knew my name. I didn't like it at all. In fact, I used to wait tables at a little place in Westport, and it bothered me when customers that I didn't know, called my name. And they just wanted more ketchup. Imagine what these guys might want.

I shuddered and didn't want to think about that. I was just concentrating on holding my breath.

"I think I'm going to be sick," I said, and then I was. I think it was a combination of fear, the stench of manure and a horrible concussion. Even shrouded, I could already tell that I had double vision. "I think I have a concussion," I said.

Like it mattered to them.

I heard some voices, all in that strange accent that I couldn't put my finger on. Men scurried around me, then someone lifted the shroud and I *was* in a barn.

One man walked toward me holding my bag. *My bag?* What in hell was he doing with my bag and what the hell? I glared and realized that the last time I saw my bag was at the safe house. I hoped he wasn't angry with me for killing one of his men.

"Charlie Ford. Nice to meet you. You have something ve vant."

The barn spun around, little stars danced in my peripheral vision and I went numb all over. I passed out, or they immobilized me again. I couldn't tell at that point.

The walls were white, the ceiling was white and the man beside me was dressed all in white. White everything. I hadn't seen that much white since my mother had redecorated the front room and then forbade us kids to set foot in it for three years. Three years, we could not go into the living room. In fact, I don't even think my mother set foot in that room. I hated white, white was sterile and droll and so tranquil. For a moment, I thought I was dead. That was until something sharp jabbed into my arm and I felt fuzzy, warm and tingly. I didn't feel dead anymore, I felt high.

"H-e-y." I grinned, or at least I think I grinned. I felt good. I'd never done drugs in my life, but I did enjoy the gas mask at the dentist office back when I had my wisdom teeth pulled. I felt rather tingly and very free. "Who're you?"

Some man that I recognized stepped into view. I wasn't sure where I recognized him from until he spoke. "Hello again, Miss Ford. Did you have a nice rest?" He was the same asshole from the barn. He was dressed a little differently, but same accent and same beady eyes. He looked like a rat. I hate rats.

"I feel wonderful. My head hurts though and so does my back. I think I may have broken my little finger. I'm not very nice to my brothers. My eye hurts, I have a crick in my side and I need to ...you know...pee." I could tell I was high because then there were three rats. I began singing and I never sing. I have a horrible voice that sounds like cats shrieking when they mate. "Three blind mice; see how they run... Oh, I forget the rest."

"Miss Ford," he said sternly and lifted my hand up. I think he was trying to cop a feel, or feel for a pulse.

"What, Mr. Rat?"

Chuckles broke out and then it was silent.

"Where is Claude Munson?"

Oh, my God! My eyes popped open. They felt very heavy. I tried to blink a couple of times but it was hard. My eyes were starting to loose their moisture. Oh, my God! Back to my dilemma at hand. I reminded myself that my dry eyes were the least of my problems.

Truth serum, oh shit. My mind reeled through the fog and I tried to shut up, I really, really did.

"I dunno."

"The girl? Where is the girl?"

"I dunno. She was there, and we had Oreos and Pepsi and then we made a plan and I had this map and then I held her hand. I had her hand, right here in mine." I stared at my left hand and held it up against the light. There were two of them. Two left hands. "I had her hand and then I felt this pain and then it went black and then I think that I peed my pants and I woke up alone. She wasn't there, but I could hear the water dripping, and then I got up and she wasn't there...did I mention that I have to....you know....pee?"

Many harsh words resounded in the room, and then he got in my face and glared at me with his beady eyes.

"Do you even know who you are dealing with? Where is the girl?"

"You look like a rat," I said with crossed eyes. "Templeton," I giggled. "You're Templeton the rat."

A doctor was now in my face with a penlight in my eyes, this time and he asked me some questions. This man sounded like he spoke dumb-shit too. Kind of like Bifocal Man.

"At hotel, who vas coming for girl?"

"The executioner was coming for me," I said with wide eyes. "I don't know who got Bella... I thought I just told you that. Now leave me the hell alone. You're pissing me off and I want to sleep." I closed my eyes and steadied my breathing. I felt sick to my stomach, as if I was going to vomit again. "Hey." I grabbed The Rat by the jacket lapel as he tried to move away. "I feel like I'm going to be...."

Let's just say, there was a lot more shouting and the room quickly cleared.

I did get some sleep and when I woke up eight hours later, I had the worst hangover in the history of hangovers. That and I felt sure I had a concussion. My head was clear then. I knew I was in serious shit, and I knew what I had to do.

I climbed from the bed, quickly tried to open the door. I knew it was too much to ask that the bad dudes had forgotten to lock me in, but there's always a chance, especially since they had all exited so quickly to escape my projectile vomiting. I went through the drawers two at a time and found what I was looking for. It wasn't as big as I had hoped but I was sure that it could inflict damage if I used it correctly. I carefully climbed back under the sheet, and waited. I waited and waited for what seemed like hours before I heard lots of shouting, many loud bangs that sounded like firecrackers and then men in black uniforms with gear similar to what I used to wear took over my room . They all wore masks and when I sat up to try to scream, someone put a mask around my head and yet another one of my captors carried me out over his shoulder. I could feel the cold air on my buttocks because I was wearing a horrible hospital gown with no back. Did they really make those just to humiliate people, or was there a plausible reason for the design?

I tell you, I was starting to think that this was supposed to be my life. My life as a *kidnap-ee.* I think I'll write a book.

The cloud of gas was thick and made it hard for me to see, but when we reached the cool air of the great outdoors and I saw yet another scary looking black SUV with tinted windows, I panicked.

I wish that I had known for certain if my captor was a good guy or a bad guy because then I would have felt a little better about my decision to shove the scalpel I had found into the shoulder of the man carrying me. I dug it in deep too.

I was dropped to the ground...again...as he screamed out in pain and surprise.

I took off running as fast as I could go, my ass hanging out for the world to see. I didn't care. The pavement was cool under my bare feet and my breathing was hard to control. The funny thing was, was that I felt like I had made great strides. I felt like I had run at least fifty yards, so when someone tackled me to the ground not more than twenty feet in front of the SUV, I was shocked. My lungs burned, my muscles ached and I had only run twenty feet. Amazing.

"Fuck you," I screamed loudly and wriggled, writhed and was finally subdued and handcuffed with some plastic baggy ties. "Get off me," I shouted again, screamed out in terror, and was finally tossed into the vehicle. I was no longer playing the invalid card and dug in deep with my toes as someone lifted my legs into the backseat. I kept a good hold on the door and the doorjamb and realized that I was spread eagle in an unattractive position, still wearing nothing beneath my gown. Oh well, I was surely going to die soon anyway. Embarrassment meant nothing at that point. I remained kicking and screaming until my voice gave out.

I gave up trying to move in the SUV because I wore handcuffs and there were six serious looking soldiers sitting beside me, each of them staring out the window, trying not to notice the big hole in my gown. My nipple was hanging out there for all to see, as was my ass and I do have to say that leather is somewhat nice on the bare buttocks.

The man I had stabbed was in front mumbling under his breath and although I wasn't positive, I was sure that he said the word, "Bitch."

"You're *American*?" I screamed out and started writhing again. I managed a good swift kick to the chest of the man across from me and I was sure he was laughing when he grabbed my legs and held them tightly together at the knees. "You stupid assholes. Why didn't you tell me? You jerks," I shrieked at him with strained vocal chords. I managed to get a few good insults before they gagged me. It was probably a good thing too because I had a lot more that I wanted to say.

The drive was nice once I calmed down and felt good that I was most certainly in good hands. I don't know why they hadn't identified themselves, but I was sure that each and every one of them would deny any of this happening if it ever came down to a congressional hearing. I'd heard stories about these guys, and according to the U.S., they probably don't even exist. We pulled to a stop in front of an old building. A large, garage-type panel opened up and we drove in. The vehicle stopped and when I got out, I smelled cat pee.

"You stupid fucker," I yelled at DuLucere and tried to wiggle free to get at him. "Where is she?" I kicked and shrieked and made an ass out of myself before they once again lifted me off my feet and carried me into a room with bright lights, a steel table and a couple cups of coffee.

DuLucere did the gentlemanly thing and wrapped his jacket around my shoulders, to cover my ass along with my breast. It still didn't make up for what he had done, but I was happy that the soldiers were no longer gawking at my nipple.

"Thank you," I said and went inside, took a seat and cried. I cried so hard and so long that I needed an entire box of Kleenex, but it didn't do any good because my tied hands were still behind me. "Is she alright?" I sniffed loudly and sucked back the last of my tears.

"Are you alright?" DuLucere asked me and then lit up a cigarette. I couldn't believe that he didn't even have the courtesy to un-cuff me before killing me with his second-hand smoke.

"No, I'm not," I screamed and coughed because I hate smoke. "I have a concussion, a bruised back, a black eye, and I'm worried about Bella."

"Can you tell me exactly what they said to you? Every detail could make a difference. Do you remember names, faces, any marks they might have had?"

I took the Fifth and sat there biting my bottom lip. If he wanted answers, he was just going to have to drug me the way the bad guys did.

I shook my head, held it high and bravely sucked back more tears. I couldn't believe that they were treating me like a criminal. Where's the hospitality?

DuLucere finished his cigarette, tossed the butt on the floor and left the room. The damn man didn't even have the courtesy to put it out all the way. I stood up and tried to maneuver the chair leg over to smother the butt. After it was properly extinguished, I did the unthinkable and laid down on the floor, wiggled my bare ass against the dirty floor and shimmied myself into having my hands in front of my body. When I got up, I noticed the tiny camera in the corner pointed straight at me. I looked around. There was no big two-way mirror like in the movies.

    I stuck my tongue out at the camera and flipped it the bird. "Did you have a nice show?" I shouted, because I had just exposed my most private parts to a camera and on the other end of that camera were certainly at least six men. Oh well. I couldn't think of one thing that could be more humiliating. I was spent. They had done everything under the sun to me. If it was possible, it had happened to me, and nothing, I mean nothing could surprise me then.

    I was wrong.

Chapter Eleven

I figured the worst was over. I knew that I was in good hands since Interpol had me in custody. I felt good that I had heard an American soldier call me a bitch, but absolutely nothing felt good about sitting in that brightly lit room with my hands tied together with plastic tie strings. The chair I was sitting on was cold as steel against my bare bottom. I had no shoes on, and I had no passport. The bad guys had my bag. *The bag?* The bag that had gotten me this far, but the worst part about sitting alone in that room was that I was alone. Bella was God knows where, and I was alone.

I didn't look up when I heard the creaking sound of the door opening and for a minute, I was happy that DuLucere was back. I just wanted to go home and I was ready to tell my story.

I looked up and swallowed hard. It wasn't DuLucere who had come back; it was Secret Agent Man.

I think my jaw dropped into my lap and I know my heart jumped into my throat and I most definitely was glad to see a friendly face.

"Miss Ford," he sat down as if he didn't know me at all. He looked me up and down without regard and then stood up and went back out.

The door opened a few minutes later and a soldier wrapped a blanket around me and handed me a cup of hot coffee.

I held the coffee up to my lips and sipped it carefully because it was hot and my lips had cuts in several different places. It's a good thing that I wasn't one of those vain women who cared what they looked like. I was sure I looked like a train wreck.

My heart raced. I felt reprieve. That was until he spoke to me in that *Secret Agent Man* tone and suddenly sounded like all the rest of them.

"Can I call you Charlie?"

I sucked back my tears because there was no way I was going to bawl like a baby in front of Ryan. I glared hard, did my best impersonation of a prisoner of war, and pretended he was the enemy instead of the man I'd been fantasizing about in the shower.

"Who's Charlie?" I snapped because I was angry, hurt and feeling my true grit.

"Okay," he said hastily. "Miss Ford it is."

"My name is Natasha," I barked and held back the tears.

I think he almost smiled, but he held back and frowned instead. "Natasha?"

"Natasha."

"Fine." He blew out his breath and stood up. I could see the monstrosity of a brace on his foot and a cane by his left hand. He looked almost as exhausted as I felt, but I held back my sympathetic feelings and concentrated on my hands, still shackled in my lap. "Mr. DuLucere tells me that you are hesitant about helping us out."

I kept my lips pursed tightly together and glared into his eyes, begging him to cut the crap and give me a hug for fucks sake.

"*Natasha,*" he yelled and I noticed a new tension in his jaw that I hadn't seen since he snapped that man's neck in the tent in Africa. Even if I had wanted to speak at that time,

I couldn't have. I just glared and felt one tiny tear seep out. I held up my hands to wipe it dry.

"Can you take these off me please?" I asked.

He shook his head with a scowl. "You tried to kill one of my men, Charlie."

Oh--that was so unfair.

"I said my name's Natasha," I barked, and my voice cracked due to the tears I was so desperately trying to hold back. I don't think anything I could have said would have made a difference. These people weren't like the rest of us. They lived by a different code and spoke a different language. "Who *are* you?"

I swore to myself that if he said Ryan, or Duane or Vince I was going to ram the top of my head right into his diagram.

"You can call me Duane."

I am a woman of my word, even if my word is just something I tell myself, so I swiftly jumped up, knowing full well that with that giant brace on, he would not be able to move fast enough, and I bent my head like a ram and crashed right into his body before he knew what hit him. Ryan staggered backwards and landed on his ass. I enjoyed it tremendously.

The room, of course, filled with men and they lifted me off my feet, thrashing and screaming like a delusional mental patient.

"You asshole," I screamed and then I was cuffed to the metal chair, my blanket was on the floor, my boob was hanging out and I had spilled my cup of coffee. Damn, it was actually good coffee, too.

Ryan dusted himself off and didn't look too happy with me. In fact, he looked livid and a bit disappointed that I would take my rage out on him. "Maybe we should do this tomorrow, after you've calmed down a bit."

"*Calmed down?*" I literally spat and wiggled in my seat. "Fuck you. Do you have any idea what in hell has happened to me in the past few days? Do you? I've been through hell and you have the fucking nerve to tell me to calm the fuck down!" I took a well-needed breath. "Fuck you."

Ryan remained docile. He really had the stealth and poise of a panther. He looked me straight in the eye and sent me a message that he meant business.

"What can you tell us about Claude Munson?"

I remained silent and glared hard. I meant business, too.

"Did you hear or see anything that might help us out?"

"Fuck. You," I grumbled one more time. That was all I had left.

After a few minutes of staring into my lap, I heard the door creak open and two soldiers escorted another man inside. This man was a bit older than Ryan was, but seemed to be a rung below Ryan on the ladder of assholes. He was dressed like Ryan, in jeans and a long-sleeved oxford. Only Ryan made it all look good. He still managed to make my blood boil, but he also made it travel to my sensitive spots, and right then was not the time for me to be looking at Ryan with warm-fuzzy feelings.

This man dropped a manila file down in front of Ryan and sent me a nice head nod. Ryan opened it. He flipped through the pages; he gave me a smirk a couple of times, and took his time reading it. He kicked his feet up onto the table and then turned to me after he was finished. He closed the file and my curiosity piqued.

"Natasha, was it?" That time his eyes had softened, but I still wasn't in the mood to play his games. I nodded in lieu of an answer. "Natasha what?" he asked, and I thought very hard to come up with a good spy gal name. I stared at the concrete block wall behind his head, started with Anderson, and ended up with...

"Lewinsky."

He laughed under his breath, dropped his feet to the floor and leaned forward across the table. I could smell him then since he was so close. I would have given anything for that hug.

"Any relation to...."

"Distant cousin." I cut him off and turned to hide my amusement. When I was serious again, I narrowed my eyes on him. "What happened to your leg?"

There was that spark in his eye that I missed so much. "I tripped." He almost smiled and I laughed. I laughed because it was so good to see him. I laughed because my life sucked and I laughed because I was hysterical. The laughter quickly turned to tears; he motioned to the camera and a soldier came in.

"Untie her restraint please," Ryan said and the soldier untied my hands from the chair, then stilled and looked at Ryan over his shoulder. It was probably already common knowledge that I had dug a scalpel into another soldier's shoulder.

"Both, sir?"

"No." Ryan narrowed his eyes on me. "Just the one."

I guess that was better than nothing. "Thank you." I grabbed a tissue and blotted my red eyes, with my hands still snuggly bound together.

"Sector 72G, huh?" Ryan said intriguingly.

I stared at him for a good three minutes.

He tapped his fingers on the file and stood up. "Fort Benning, Georgia." With palms planted firmly on the table, he bent forward in a hostile manner and stared me down.

"What do you want from me?" I asked through clenched teeth.

"Why won't you just talk to me, Charlie?"

"I am talking, but no one is listening," I shouted and stood up to get into his face that time. The chair banged against the floor and bounced on the concrete a few times before I finally spoke. "I want to know where Bella is and I want to know *Now!* I slammed my hands down and grabbed my file. "This is mine."

He tried to grab it back, but I, too, can be fast.

"This is private," I yelled at him and not even for a second did I want Secret Agent Man to know anything about my past. As far as I was concerned, he had no right to be looking at my military record. I was just an ordinary citizen trying to make a decent living as a nanny for Christ sake.

"Charlie, cut the bullshit."

Clearly, he felt stressed again because he was raking his hand through his hair. I didn't care though. No one could possibly understand my state of mind during that time, and keeping my cool had flown out the window the previous week when I shot and killed a number of men.

"*Duane.* You tell DuLucere to level with me about Bella and I will tell you everything you want to know."

I think that amused him because one corner of his mouth perked up.

"Even the reason you quit?"

I think I paled slightly. I know my breathing grew ragged and I felt my knees buckle. No one outside of my unit knew why I quit and I wasn't keen on the idea of talking about it nearly four years later.

"That's personal."

He cocked a brow, but then let it go. "Some other time then," he said as he conceded. "I'll talk to Inspector DuLucere."

I think he looked at my boob.

"Can I get you anything?"

I looked down at myself and shrugged. "Clothes would be nice."

"Got it."

For some reason, I rather hoped that he'd give me the shirt off his back, but that didn't happen. He did return with some black sweats pants, a U.S. Navy sweatshirt and a pair of shoes that were two sizes too big. It was the thought that counted.

"Thanks."

"My job is done then." He grinned and went to leave.

"Sir." I grabbed his wrist. I'm surprised that the room didn't fill with bad asses again, but it didn't. "Is she okay?"

"I don't know, Charlie. I honestly don't know."

DuLucere came back after Ryan left and after a hot turkey sandwich, a bag of potato chips and an entire cup of coffee, I started asking questions.

"Why did this happen? Why did you have us removed from Athens?"

He blew out his breath then lit a cigarette because he hadn't inhaled toxins for about thirty seconds. His eyes looked tired. My guess was that he was sixty going on eighty.

"When I walked into that conference room at the embassy in Athens, I knew that all hell would break loose if Claude's enemies found out about Annabelle, so I took it upon myself to initiate a preemptive strike of sorts."

"So, you had us moved to protect us from his enemies?"

"Yes, in so many words."

"What aren't you telling me?"

"There are forces here in Eastern Europe that have been working and strategizing for years. Years longer than I have even lived. Let's just say that I owed a very good friend a very big favor."

Interpol? I just then put two and two together and my guess would be that Claude and Christian DuLucere went way back. Back to the days when Claude was working for Interpol. Somehow, my questions remained unanswered, but I had bigger things on my mind.

"So, where is Annabelle now and what were you planning on doing to me?"

He laughed and sat down, reached out and placed his hand over mine in a comforting way. "Miss Ford. My men never meant any harm. I was the only one privy to your background, so I asked them to take extra precautions, but not to harm you or the girl. My men didn't know anything about you and Annabelle, they were just following orders."

"So, you weren't going to have me...." I winced "eliminated?"

He chuckled again. "Non, my dear. We were simply going to make sure you made it home to the States once Bella was safe, and we no longer needed you to look after her."

I let out the breath I had been holding and felt bad that I had kneed cute French guy in the groin and had given DuLucere a bloody nose and, of course, all the horrible things I said and did to Bifocal Man.

"I'm sorry if I was trouble. I'm just really worried about her."

"She's safe, Miss Ford. I guarantee it."

When we finished talking about the bad guys who drugged me and tried to make me talk, I looked through some photos and could only pull one guy out of a black and white surveillance photograph and that man was the Rat. I could not and would not ever be able to forget his face.

It amazed me that things were so formal and choreographed. These people took everything so seriously. I did get to make an apology to the soldier I wounded with the scalpel. He understood that I felt traumatized and gave me a firm handshake, before grinning and telling me that I had a nice ass.

I actually liked the compliment at that time. I asked him to send in Duane and he looked at me with a funny expression.

"Duane?" I said again.

"I don't know who you mean, ma'am."

Here we go again. "The man, the man who was wearing the cast?"

"Oh him," he said and I was sad again. "He's gone, ma'am."

"Oh," I said without expression and sank back down in my seat, feeling sorry for myself as I thought about how much I wanted to tell him that I was sorry. I hadn't been myself lately. I'm a bear. I know that, but not always. Most of the time I can be quite pleasant. I can sit in a room and actually not go for the jugular when I get irritated. I wanted him to know that I was nice. I was normal...well...sort of normal and that I'd like to share a meal with him sometime; preferably not one that we had to catch ourselves and dangle over the fire in the middle of hell. I'd like to take him to Henry's in Westport. They make a mean Steak Diane at Henry's, but I never get to order it because Steak Diane is a meal for two and I never date. I wanted a date; a date with Ryan. *I'm a woman,* I wanted to shout. I'm a woman, and I'm not ashamed of it anymore.

A few minutes later, the door opened and a man dressed in a sharp suit sashayed in and dropped his briefcase on the table. Visitors at that time were just icing on my happy little cake that I called my life. I figured that this man was the key to my ticket home. That man looked like a lawyer.

I was wrong again. If I had learned anything about myself in the past ten days or so, it was that I make too many assumptions.

"Miss Charlene Ignatius Ford," he said sternly and took a seat in front of me. "Let's talk."

On the airplane ride home, I thought about many things. I thought about Bella, Ryan, the man in the Armani suit and I tried not to think about why I quit Sector 72G. It had been a long healing process for me to deal with what happened that day and I still wasn't ready to talk about it. Perhaps I never will be and I was somewhat glad that I'd never see Ryan-Duane-Vince again, because I didn't even want to tell him it was over. I think I've learned from my mistakes and was past it. I wanted to move on with my life.

I stared out the window and tears rolled down my cheeks when I saw the twinkling lights of the runway at LaGuardia International Airport. When we touched down and I felt the first little jolt caused by the wheels hitting the runway, I eased back in my seat, closed my eyes, and said a prayer to God. The only thing I had was a letter from the U.S. Embassy in Armenia saying that I was a U.S. citizen and nothing else, not a driver's license, not a credit card. Nothing but the U.S. Navy sweatshirt that I was wearing and the giant tennis shoes that some poor SEAL donated to me in Northern Armenia.

I sort of felt like a traitor, wearing a Navy SEAL sweatshirt and all, but it didn't matter then. What mattered was that I was home. Home. On American soil.

I hadn't slept on the long flight home, so I couldn't wait to curl up in bed and slip into my pajamas.

"Yoohoo." I heard his cat call before I even started looking around. "Charlie," Gregory shouted from behind a crowd of people. Even at ten o'clock at night, the airport was full of international travelers, domestic travelers and even some drunks who just like to frequent the airport lounges.

I wouldn't say that Gregory and I are even friends really, I mean I hardly know the man, but I was damned happy to see him and even happier when he pulled me into his arms and gave me a big giant gay-man bear hug. He rocked me back and forth and wept into my hair as if he were my mother. "How are you?"

"Overwrought." That was the best word I could come up with to encompass how I was. Then I added another. "Elated." And I smiled.

I slept the entire way to Greenwich, which was only about a half an hour without traffic and that night there was none. The giant wrought-iron gates opened up and Gregory parked in the fourth garage bay. It seemed so strange for me to be returning home without Bella, but it didn't feel right for me to return home to Oregon without seeing for myself that she had made it home safely. I still had no idea when that was going to happen, but I hoped for sooner, and not later.

"*Oh God*," I groaned at the giant plate of peanut butter and jelly sandwiches that Gregory had been kind enough to make me. "You're my hero," I gushed and sat down at the counter. I ate three sandwiches before I even felt the need for a hot bath.

"Do you think he'd mind if I used his bathtub?" I asked Gregory, because I wanted to ease myself into the giant tub. The tub seats five grown-ups, but it was in Roald's private bathroom so I felt strange about it.

"Are you kidding? The man can't stop gushing about you. I think he'd give you anything you want at this point. Go on up. He's still out of town anyway."

It took me a minute to retrieve my things from my quarters. I still couldn't believe all the things that had happened to me. I wanted to write it all down so I wouldn't forget any details. I wanted to remember what burned figs smelled like and I wanted to remember the way that Bella looked at me when she finally realized that I wasn't just another bimbo out to marry her father. I wanted to remember it all. Well, I'm exaggerating a bit there. I would rather forget some parts. The bruise around my eye still told a gruesome story and the puncture mark on my lower back was still sore from where they hit me with a tranquilizer. I still couldn't believe that they had drugged me like a wild animal.

I'm not that bad, am I?

I peeled off my clothes and slid under the bubbles. Gregory let me use his own private stash of lavender bath beads. I love lavender. Lavender makes me want to sleep. I'd like to sleep for the next week if that is possible.

I had just closed my eyes when I heard the light knock on the door.

"Can I come in?" Gregory stuck his head in and handed me a well-needed martini: an apple one with a cherry floating in it. He had one too, and had a look in his eye as if he wanted the juicy stuff.

"You first. What's been going on here?" I took a sip and felt the alcohol warm my veins.

"Well..." He began and went on and on about how Roald and Nicole were all set to fly over to Athens in Steven Spielberg's jet, but then they got a phone call from Gammy saying not to bother because Bella had been moved somewhere safe for the time being.

Then I got it. Gammy was privy to the deal, too, and therefore filled our captors in about what kind of food Bella liked. It was Gammy, and Gammy probably had her. I felt a bit better about things after Gregory went on and on about the phone calls, the letters from fans, and how everyone from Barbara Walters to Connie Chung wanted interviews once she returned. After three martinis, he finally fell silent, winded.

"Nicole is doing her best to kiss his ass with all the publicity and all. She wants to move back in and start over..." He rolled his eyes, as did I. "She's such a skeezer."

"Nice." I laid my head back. "What's a skeezer?"

"I dunno," he slurred and dipped his bare toes into the water. A cross between a slut, a skank and a tease maybe?"

I laughed hard and it felt good to laugh. I decided I needed friends after all. Friends make the world a brighter place.

"Can we finish this tomorrow? I'm exhausted."

"Sure. As long as you tell me *everything*," he gushed dramatically.

"Sure." I lied. No one needed to know everything. Some things are just better left in the closet.

I slept in Bella's room because I wanted to and she wasn't there to kick me out of her space. Photo spreads of Justin Timberlake covered the ceiling above her bed. I had a strange feeling that he was watching me while I slept so I turned over and thought of Ryan. How pissy he would get with me when I watched him sleep. How did he know? Was he that good of a spy that he just knew?

I closed my eyes and tried to dream of Ryan. I dreamed of Bella instead.

Morning came quickly. At least it seemed that way to me. I guess I hadn't slept as well as I thought I would, being home and all. Gregory had taken the dogs to the vet, so I had the house to myself. I made pancakes with real maple syrup and scrounged around for bacon. There was none, so I cut up some ham steak into strips and pretended it was bacon. If it looks like a pig and smells like a pig—it's bacon.

I didn't know what to do with myself after cleaning up and soaking in Roald's tub for an hour and a half, so I went to my lonely cottage and noticed my machine was blinking. I pushed the button and there were fifteen calls from my dad.

I wept like a baby, sitting there on my bed, staring at the machine as my father left message after message. Most of them were short and sweet. "Call me...I love you, Charlie."

Others were a bit longer. "I got your letter sweetheart and I...well, I don't know what to say, really...I guess I'd just like to say I'm sorry, baby. I'm so proud of you and I'm sorry."

"Wow," I said aloud after the last one. He actually said he was proud of me and I hadn't even broken the news to him that I almost have a master's degree. Holy shit. I grappled for the phone and dialed him at home, no such luck. I tried his office and again, I just hung up because I didn't want to leave a message.

Without even realizing it, I had changed the course of my relationship with my father forever. I knew that things might not ever be perfect between us, but I somehow had made him hear what I had to say and somehow that made him proud. That's all I could ever ask for.

I had been through so much shit the last couple of weeks that just having a father who was alive and healthy was just about good enough for me. Don't get me wrong, I loved hearing him say he was proud of me and that he loves me, but somehow my zany fiasco abroad had changed the way I looked at everything and I wasn't going to sweat the small stuff anymore.

Things were looking up for me and I know now that I will never look across the street or turn on the TV and think that the grass is always greener. 'Cause it's not. I'm happy with who I am and I'm happy and I'm grateful for what I have. *It's a whole new me.*

Chapter Twelve

That night, I had just finished the dishes when I heard laughter coming from the garage. Female laughter.

I wiped my hands dry on the dishtowel hanging by the oven and prayed it was Bella.

When she walked in, my smile faded and I felt completely demolished because I had gotten my hopes up that it was Bella.

"Charlie," Roald grabbed me under the armpits and spun me around in the kitchen, hugging me so hard that I struggled for breath. "How's my hero?" His voice was boisterous and gleeful. "When did you get back?" He looked me up and down and carefully touched my battered cheekbone.

"Last night." I said, and extended my hand to Bella's mother. "I'm Charlie Ford. It's nice to finally meet you."

She smiled that fake actress smile and shook my hand, then helped herself to a bottle of Perrier from the fridge. I don't know why I took offense to her doing that, but I did.

"We just can't thank you enough for all that you did," she said, then smiled at Roald. "We should get ready, the gala starts in an hour." She walked past me and into the foyer.

Roald stood speechless and then gave me another hug. "I spoke to my mother this morning. Bella should be home in a few days. What do you think we should do for a welcome home party?"

"Whatever you do, invite Justin Timberlake." I grinned and he slugged me in the shoulder, pulled me into his burly arms and began weeping against my hair.

Now that is the strangest thing that has ever happened to me. His estranged wife was changing her clothes and he was weeping into *my* hair.

"I don't think I can ever repay you or thank you enough. I want to hear everything." He sat down and wiped his eyes. "Bella told me that you were a real hero."

"Ah shucks," I said playfully, and then realized that he wasn't kidding. "I had help. There was this guy, I don't know who he was, but he got us safely out of there. I didn't do anything that you wouldn't have done yourself. She's a wonderful girl and she deserves the best."

"I will give it to her." His eyes lit up. "A party, yah! A big one with all her friends and I'll invite that boy..."

I had to cut him off at this point. I'd like to think that I got to know Bella pretty well over the past couple of weeks. "Roald. Stop." I shook my head. "All Bella wants is you. She needs her father to pay attention to her. To see her and to know what she is doing. Don't take her for granted..." This time I cried. "She's a very brave and special girl and she has so much going for her. Please don't ignore her."

I had said my piece and it was time for me to shut up. "Please don't ignore her." Okay, so I can't shut up. I was on a roll and he was still listening. I continued and spilled my guts about everything that I thought pertained to their relationship and how she felt about him being gone all the time and I think he was happy that I told him. I know it was good for him to hear.

"Charlie?"

"Yes," I said and turned to look at him.

"I'm really sorry if I offended you before we left for Africa. I was pretty drunk and I'm truly sorry."

"History," I chuckled and waved goodnight.

My morning started like any ordinary morning. I got up, took a three-hour shower, ate more pancakes, a couple of peanut butter and jelly sandwiches and let Gregory convince me to try Espresso. He made me a triple shot mocha, and let me just say I felt wired.

I went into Westport for a couple of new outfits and a new bag. The mall was full of teenagers and that made me think of Bella. I stopped by the DMV, posed for a new driver's license and that made me think of Bella and how excited she was that I let her drive in the savanna. I mean how cool was I? I think I must be the world's greatest nanny.

I went to the bank and canceled my checking account and MasterCard. I felt so violated by the thought of some international criminal holding onto my identification that I was somewhat inclined to change my name.

I didn't. I refused to give into the fear and decided to buy a gun instead.

"What exactly are you looking for?"

"Small, sleek, easy to handle...You know, a girl's best friend."

The man behind the counter at Gun Town held up a twenty-two with a pearl handle.

"I was thinking more along the lines of a nine millimeter. Black." I glanced over the counter and pointed to the bad boy that I wanted. "That one."

He handed it to me and it was a perfect fit. It molded into the contour of my hand. I never thought that I would buy a gun for personal reasons. I knew someday when I joined the force I would need one, but this was serious. I was about to become a statistic. "Perfect."

"What do you need a gun for?" the man scoffed, and swiveled around to grab the paperwork that I needed to fill out. "You look like such a nice girl."

I had to laugh, because I was a nice girl: a nice girl with grit, gumption and a fear of international spies sneaking up on me in the dead of the night. I was probably being completely paranoid, but my father always taught me it's better to be safe than sorry.

I knew that I had to wait the usual five-day waiting period, so I picked up some pepper spray in the mean time.

When I returned my answering machine was blinking again. I listened to yet another message from my father. I dialed my parents' number.

"Dad." I could hardly talk over the tightening in my chest. I cried. I think he cried, too.

We talked for an hour about everything that I had said in the letter and then he asked me if he could visit sometime.

"Of course," I said happily. I knew he hadn't been back east since he was a kid and he had never once suggested it before.

"We're having a big get together for Josh when they return from Austria next month, do you think you can make it home?"

"Are you kidding? I'll be there." I smiled and listened to him talk about the hospital and about how he might open his own practice so that he and Mom could travel more.

I didn't mention anything about what happened to me overseas. I just didn't feel the need to put him through that and for once, I wasn't so anxious to talk about myself. I knew that I was a good person and I guess now that I was proud of myself and felt good about my life, I didn't need to hear it from him anymore.

Two days later, I reached the front door of the main house just as the limo driver emerged from the driver's side and moved around to let Bella out. To my surprise, a tall gray-haired man was the first to emerge, followed by Gammy, Roald, Nicole and finally Bella.

She ran to me with open arms and hugged me tighter than anyone has ever hugged me my entire life. I felt loved and truly happy to see her. "I'm so glad to see you. I missed you. I missed you and I love you, Charlie," she gushed, and peeled herself off my shoulders to turn around and make the introduction. She let go of me and grabbed her grandfather's hand.

"Pappi, this is Charlie. Charlie, this is my grandfather, Claude Munson."

He was regal. Handsome and smiling happily with his hand wrapped around Bella's much smaller hand. I was surprised to see him.

"Miss Ford." He bowed. Probably some sort of weird European ritual of sorts, but he bowed just the same. "Our entire family will be forever in your debt. I'm so thankful; I don't even know how to begin."

"It's okay. It was nothing." But it felt good just the same.

Bella scoffed and rolled her eyes. "She's amazing and when I grow up, I want to be just like Charlie."

Nothing could have made me smile brighter at that point. It felt nice to feel loved, and it felt nice to finally feel appreciated by a family that I worked for.

Over coffee and muffins a couple hours later, I finally finished telling them about Africa and how brave Bella had been, and then I told them about Armenia and how Bella had been so strong and brave and, of course, she was the hero because I didn't even know where we were.

It was great to see Bella snuggled in beside her father and I finally was able to hear what I wanted to hear once he carried his exhausted daughter up to her room.

"Mr. Munson." I kept my voice calm. "I have so many questions I don't know where to start."

"Charlie," Gemma said cheerfully and patted my hand. "We all appreciate what you did for Bella and I just wanted to apologize for the way things happened at the hotel. DuLucere told me that you received some minor injuries and I'd like to extend my deepest apologies. I never meant for any harm to come to you and I would like you to have this as a token of our appreciation."

She handed me a gold-embossed envelope.

I took it with wide eyes and a tingle in my stomach. No one had ever given me a bonus before. I opened it and gasped.

"Oh, no, you really didn't have to do that," I said, and then smiled because there was a check for a whole lot of money in that envelop.

"Oh, yes. We want you to have it and I hope that your troubles abroad won't deter you from taking care of our sweet Bella. She really has grown quite fond of you," Gemma said.

"She's a wonderful girl, and I'm not going anywhere," I said in memory of our time together. "Are you finally out of hiding? I mean, are things safe for you now?" I asked Claude.

"Things have been taken care of and I am now free to accompany Gemma back to Belgium and resume my life with the European Parliament. As for safe?" He winced slightly. "I don't know if there is such a thing in my line of work. You take the good with the bad and make the best from every situation. It keeps us on our toes." He winked at Gemma.

At that precise moment, I felt my heartbeat quicken and I felt a twinge of loneliness. Gemma and Claude had persevered through assassination attempts, her parents' disapproval, and months and months of being apart from one another yet they still looked wildly in love. Maybe there was something to that. Perhaps love should keep you on your toes.

"I should be getting to sleep, too. Will you be staying for awhile?"

"Just a few days."

"I'm sure Bella would like that."

Roald came down the stairs a minute later. "Bella wants to know if you want to have a sleepover in her room."

"Oh, goody." I jumped up as if my ass was on fire. "Duty calls." I winked and took the stairs two steps at a time.

Life resumed back to normal once Gemma and Claude left for Belgium, but I personally don't think any part of a celebrity's life is quite normal. Roald's entourage was at the house daily now, probably just because he insisted on spending more time at the house with Bella, so they just came to him instead. He was an international superstar after all and I guess that is just what they do.

Roald was more humble about things than Nicole was and he only agreed to meet with the heavy hitters like Barbara Walters and Larry King. Nicole bounced back and forth from coast to coast doing interviews for everyone. Thank goodness Roald had a brain and put his foot down, insisting that Bella would remain out of the spotlight.

Nicole hasn't been back to Greenwich for nearly three weeks.

Roald and Bella spend a lot of time together, which gives me plenty of time to get back into prime physical shape, hone my weapons skills and brush up on my self-defense moves. If anything, I believe that I was meant for something bigger, something better and something that would keep my mind sharp and my adrenaline pumping. I registered for classes at the college, and they are set to start after I return from my vacation at the end of August.

Roald and I sat down over peanut butter sandwiches just last night and coordinated our schedules so that he had three weeks off with Bella during the time that I would be in Hawaii and visiting my family.

Bella was going to get her wish and both Roald and Nicole had promised to set aside a couple of weeks to take her to Disneyworld. After all, we both deserved a good vacation after what we had been through.

While we were shopping in New York City this morning, Bella helped me pick out an entire new wardrobe right down to my sexy new underwear and bras.

"I don't think so. I don't wear thongs," I said haughtily. No amount of humidity and heat would convince me to wear something that was purposefully crammed into my crack. I had a hard enough time trying to extract regular underwear, why would I buy ones made to floss my ass?

"How about these?"

Why did I get the feeling that I was being set up to look sexy?

"Why does it matter? No one will be seeing my underwear." I glanced over my shoulder for the fourth time in ten minutes and stilled. The hair on my neck stood straight on end. I wasn't ordinarily paranoid about someone watching me or even stalking me, and I was somewhat used to media attention, because after all, this was the third high profile celebrity family that I had ever worked for, but today, something just felt off, and I just went with my gut. "Let's just go." I dropped the panties and bras that I had already chosen and took off for the escalator.

I shuffled her out of Bloomingdale's and hailed a cab.

"What was that for?" she asked with wide eyes as the cabbie screeched to a halt near the sidewalk.

"I don't know." I shivered, but wasn't about to tell her that I had a bad feeling that someone had been watching me all day. It was probably just post-traumatic delusions of grandeur, but it felt real. "I just want to go home."

The cab driver circled around and we called Vinny from Bella's cell phone and asked him to meet us at a different location. For all I knew, Vinny was the one who had been watching us. Roald could have the same paranoid delusions that I had and could have easily hired someone to keep an eye on us. That's what I would do if she were my child and someone had abducted her twice in the past month.

Vinny agreed and we met up at Rugliano's Italian Restaurant and jumped from the cab and into the limo. I interrogated Vinny the best I could and asked him many questions about where he had been and if he liked the underwear that Bella was trying to get me to buy. Vinny didn't answer me. Vinny never answers me. I've heard him grunt a couple of times. I've heard him say, "Yeah," three or four times ever since I met him, and that's it. I figured I'd get him with the underwear question, but he had a poker face that you wouldn't believe. I didn't feel any better about the fact that someone had been watching us.

When we returned to Greenwich, I wanted to change into my clothes for the gym and Bella wanted to play makeover.

"Come on," she begged for the third time. "You could be so beautiful."

I didn't think she meant anything by it, so I just smiled. "Thanks, sweetie, but I like the way I look. I'm comfortable in jeans and I don't see what the big deal is."

"The big deal is that it's fun. Paaaaa-lleeease."

"Fine." I opened the door to my little cottage out back of the Munson castle and dropped my bags on the floor. Even though I had passed on panties and bras at Bloomies, I had still made a killing at the Banana Republic sale and had even bought a couple of sundresses at Macy's that made me look like a woman.

I picked up the mail that had been piling up for three weeks and flipped through it while Bella helped herself to my fridge. "Tomorrow we can play dress up, but right now, I have an appointment with my personal trainer and you promised Gregory that you would have tea with him." I had almost finished flipping through the pile when a bright photograph caught my attention. I dropped the remainder of the mail onto the floor and brought it up to my face to study it. "Holy shit," I mumbled under my breath, but Bella has ears like a bat.

"What?" She jumped to my side and looked over my shoulder. "Who's it from?"

I turned the postcard over because I was wondering the same thing.

"That's weird." She plopped down onto the bed.

It's more than weird, I thought. The postcard was completely blank on the other side. The front was a picture of a winery in Tuscany, but the back was blank. Even on the side where my address should have been.

I wasn't paranoid.

A shiver of terror raced across my spine and my breath caught in my throat as I gazed out the window then quickly closed the blinds and sank down on the bed. That postcard had been hand-delivered because there was no address written on it. Was this some sort of sick joke, or was Bifocal Man stalking me?

"I gotta go." I hurriedly got Bella back into the house and then ran back in and got my gun from its safe and tucked it under my front seat. The money that Bella's grandparents had given me had funded my brand new, custom SUV. It was perfect, except I had opted not to get the bulletproof windows. How silly of me.

So, I wasn't completely paranoid. Somehow, a postcard from Tuscany had made it into our mailbox, here in Greenwich, Connecticut, and that made me very nervous. One—because Bifocal Man—I mean Russo—was the only one there when I told him to send me a postcard. And, two—I was positive that someone had been watching me from various locations in New York City earlier today.

When I reached the gym, I had perhaps the best, most satisfying workout of my life. I felt agile and strong and wound *pretty* damn tight. My vacation was still a couple of weeks away, but I was more and more anxious to get away. For good measure, today I stopped by the Westport Gun Club just in case anyone was following me and I spent a couple of hours blasting paper men and pretending that I wasn't scared.

It was almost dark when I returned and Bella and Roald were discussing plans to head to Vermont for the weekend. That meant I was on my own, which would be fine. I would rather have Bella tucked away in the woods than standing next to me when someone kidnapped me again.
"Do you want to come?" Roald asked.
I smiled. "Really?"
"There's plenty of room and it's very pretty up there. We have a spot right on the lake and maybe it would be good to get away. Gregory is coming too."
One big happy family. I couldn't believe that this was happening. My luck was definitely changing for the better. Now I could escape and hide in the woods for a couple of days, rein in my wild imagination and get a handle on my emotions. What more could I ask for?
"Darien Sparks might be coming too." Bella bobbed her brows and giggled.
Darien Sparks was another action star who usually played bad guys. He was Roald's archenemy in the movies, but his best friend in real life. I watched a couple of his movies with Bella one night and she had heard me say once or twice that I thought the guy was cute, and very nicely put together. Now I understood the need for a makeover and sexy underwear.
I narrowed my eyes on the girl with a playful grin. "How long have you known about this?"

"I dunno," she giggled and ran from the room. I chased her through the backyard before I caught her and tickled her silly. We ended up jumping into the pool and laughing about me and Darien sitting in a tree--K-I-S-S-I-N-G.

Wrinkled and tired after playing Marco Polo, she followed me to my room and grabbed a Calistoga from my fridge.

"*You* bought them?" She went to my bed and picked up three pairs of very sexy, very small underwear. I looked over to see what in the heck she was jabbering about, I think my heart stopped beating. My knees buckled out from under me and I grappled for the nightstand with a breathless gasp.

She held up the black and white thongs and sent me a sinister gaze. "Tomorrow we make you gorgeous." She giggled but I still couldn't catch my breath.

I had had no part in the purchase of the underwear and my gun was still in my truck. I felt more violated by this intrusion than I ever did at my yearly doctor exams. It terrified me that someone had snuck into my space and left me such an uncomfortable gift. It would have been a different story if perhaps a box of chocolates or a dozen red roses were lying on my bed—but underwear? What's more private than underwear?

"Can we have a sleepover tonight?" I asked and started packing for Vermont, leaving the thongs right where they were. It didn't even matter what she said, I was moving into the main house for the night and there was nothing that anyone could do to stop me.

I don't think I slept a wink that night. I tossed, turned, and listened to Roald's horrible taste in music until he finally turned off Meatloaf and stumbled up the stairs and silence blanketed the house. I think I actually preferred noise because then all I heard were strange sounds and the loud snoring of Hamlet and Othello. Both dogs were as big as horses. Both Great Danes with magnificent black coats and they both slobbered...*a lot.*

I tried counting sheep, I tried singing theme songs from TV shows, but nothing worked. The strange goings on that had transpired today pre-occupied me and as if things couldn't get worse, I started thinking about Ryan again.

Then I wondered if Ryan was the one stalking me and this was his idea of foreplay. I know, I know, I have thought that before, but perhaps I was right this time. Or perhaps I was just obsessed with sex lately and since I don't get any other form of foreplay I was inventing new scenarios and crossing my fingers that it was Ryan and not an evil guy who wanted revenge for something I did or said whilst I was incarcerated in Eastern Europe.

I tossed and turned again and buried my head in my pillow to try to shut off my brain. No wonder I couldn't sleep. I'm a freak who has to analyze everything to death.

"Morning," I grumbled, and sank down on the barstool across from Gregory. Gregory has perfect skin and exudes energy in the early morning. I hate him. "Coffee?" I mumbled.

"Espresso!" he said a bit too cheerfully. I think he had had too many shots already this morning. "I'm off to shop for Vermont. Is there anything special that you want?"

"Alcohol, and lots of it," I said. "I think Bella is trying to fix me up with Darien and since I think he's hot, I should probably just be drunk all weekend so I can blame all my drooling and stuttering on the booze."

"Good plan. That man is hot."

Gregory usually doesn't sound gay. In fact, if I hadn't known better I would never have guessed that he was. Well, I guess I would now because he just called another man hot, but other than that, he's pretty much a regular Joe.

Two hours later, I finally got enough courage to open the door to my cottage and nothing seemed wrong.

Everything seemed to be in the same place I left it. I finished packing for the weekend, and then met Bella by my Expedition for our trip to make me over.

"Hair?" she asked. "Or nails first?"

"Hair? What's wrong with my hair?"

"Duh." She was such a girl. "It's only one color. You need at least three colors, let's go." She prodded and I jumped up and headed to Gigi's on the north side of town. Gigi used to do Nicole's hair before he accidentally turned it green before an interview. The bitch actually sued him, so he moved his shop from New York into a little strip mall in Greenwich. Bella had known the man since she was three, so she continues to use his services, behind her mom's back, of course.

"Baby girl," Gigi cooed, and Gigi is not gay. He acts gay and sounds gay because that is what his clientele expects, but he's all man and he likes T and A. He's a closet heterosexual.

"Can you do anything with this?" Bella flipped her hand under my chin length hair and took a seat. Sometimes I have a hard time believing that she is only twelve, or...excuse me...almost thirteen, as she likes to say because her birthday is in two weeks. Unfortunately, I will be in Oregon and she will be in Florida, so I have been trying to contrive some sort of celebration before she leaves.

I waited under the hood of the dryer and again had a bad feeling in my gut. Call me completely deranged, but I felt as if everyone was looking at me. They were, because I looked like a model. I couldn't believe what he had done to my face. He waxed my brows for the first time in my life and yeah, it hurt.

He curled and conditioned my lashes and he even tinted my brows and cut some wispy bangs to accentuate my eyes more. Whatever.

What can I say? I walked into Gigi's a regular woman and I emerged a babe. Bella was right; I *can* be beautiful when I want to be. I kept the make-up on and carefully stepped out into the sunshine. I looked around, it seemed safe enough, so we headed to my SUV and went straight home to prepare for what could be the most relaxing weekend of my life.

Vermont was beautiful and relaxing and I didn't feel threatened or paranoid the entire time. Darien ended up bringing a bona fide supermodel with him, so I just got drunk with Gregory a lot, lathered myself with sunscreen and lay on an air mattress the entire weekend. I think I got out of the lake to sleep at night, but I ate, I drank, I read books and felt sorry for myself from the water. Bella actually felt bad for her lame attempt at fixing me up with her dad's best friend. It was fine though. It wouldn't have worked out anyway because I happen to know that I would not feel comfortable dating a man who looks in the mirror ten times an hour. Furthermore, I don't think I could sustain a relationship with a man who doesn't know his ass from a hole in the ground. The man was stupid. Not just dumb. Stupid.

When we returned home, I found everything as it should be. I had no strange underwear on my bed, no G-men hiding in my closet. I just felt that I was home and I was safe.

That was three weeks ago and I can safely say that I think the past is behind me and whoever it was that pulled those little pranks on me, was most certainly out of my life for good and I preferred it that way. It had been a quiet few weeks with not much to do, just a couple of play dates. There was a trip to New Jersey to watch the U.S. Open, a movie premiere or two and school clothes shopping with Bella.

Bella was off with her friends and I had just sat down for a late lunch when the phone rang.

"Hello."

"Did you get my gifts?"

My throat closed up around my vocal chords. I didn't recognize the voice, but it was foreign. "Who is this?"

He didn't answer. I heard a long slow breath exhaled as if someone were thinking real hard...or smoking. "DuLucere?"

I heard laughing and I didn't think it was funny. "Non, it's me, Bellavia."

Cute French guy? I'll kill him.

"You have a lot of nerve, pal!" I shouted and waited for an explanation. At that point, I was undeniably disappointed that my theory was once again incorrect. I guess I had wanted to believe Ryan was the one stalking me and leaving me sexy underwear.

I need therapy.

"Sorry." He fumbled with his words. "Russo asked me to deliver that postcard while I was in the States and I just thought you would look good in those panties. I did not mean anything by it. Really, I did not."

"Haven't you ever heard of a phone? You broke into my house. You scared the crap out of me." I inhaled sharply and regained my composure. The French are weird.

"I did no such thing. The door was open and I slipped the postcard into the mail slot. I tried to reach you many times, but there was always no answer and then you were gone when I came to say hello."

"Oh."

"I did not mean to frighten you, I just thought maybe you wanted to have dinner, but I'm home now, in Paree, so some other time."

"Jesus Christ. Next time call me first—geez." I wiped the sweat from my brow and let out a chuckle. "So, did you get to see NASCAR?"

"How did you know?"

I laughed and leaned back against the counter. I, too, have my ways.

We talked and he apologized repeatedly for what had happened in Armenia. He wished that he could have told me, but he knew nothing about it until it was over. He did admit that he has a huge crush on me and would very much like to see me again. After all, it wasn't everyday that a woman who looked like me could kick his ass.

He informed me that he and Russo survived the crash with only semi-serious injuries. He lost his spleen and they put a rod into his shin to help his leg heal properly. It was nice to hear that everyone was doing well and it was somewhat cool to have an admirer. I'd rather it had been Ryan and not Frenchy, but it was nice just the same.

Chapter Thirteen

My brother, *Dave, The Doctor,* picked me up from the airport on Friday night in Portland, Oregon. Dave looked a lot like Mom and me. Dark hair, slim build and he was a couple inches taller. Dockers were his pants of choice, but they looked good on him, because he's an intellectual. It seemed fitting.

His one-year-old son, Marcus, was already asleep in the back. His wife, Carrie, was cordial and standoffish as always, but then loosened up a bit when I pulled her into my arms for a hug.

"I'm sorry that I've never taken the time to get to know you better." I stepped back and gave her hand a squeeze. It had been awhile since I had seen her, but she looked much thinner, more ashen too.

She looked at me and then threw up on my new shoes.

"She's pregnant," Dave said as an apology and helped me clean up while Carrie continued heaving until there was nothing left. It was a good thing that she had the foresight to weave her long black hair into a French braid.

I looked at her all hunched over and ill and I couldn't believe that I was so anxious to go through all that. Maybe I could put it off for several more years.

I helped her into the minivan and took my seat beside baby Marcus. The entire three-hour drive, I had a wonderful heart-to-heart with my brother and apologized for not keeping in touch and told him that I wanted to do better. I wanted to be a better sister and I knew that I couldn't blame him because he did what Daddy wanted and became a surgeon.

"I did it because I wanted to," he said. "Dad had nothing to do with it and if you hadn't been such a damn rebel all the time, you would have known that all Dad ever wanted was for us to be who we wanted to be. You just didn't listen, Charlie. He wasn't trying to force you into medical school. You just assumed it because you were so hell bent on doing the opposite of whatever he said. I still can't believe you joined the damned Army." He shook his head with a disbelieving scowl. "And why the hell did you stay eight years? Did you really like it, or were you just trying to piss Dad off?"

"I loved it, Dave. I really did."

He looked at me in his rearview mirror. "Then why did you quit?"

I wasn't going to answer honestly, we weren't that close. "I wanted to be a nanny."

"So, are you going to be a nanny forever, or are you going to grow up?"

I could've lied to his face and said yes, but I chose to remain mysterious and shrugged my shoulders.

It was past eleven when we got to my parents' house in Bend and I crept quietly into the house, knowing that my parents weren't night owls and had most likely gone to bed at nine as they always did.

My room was actually clear of all Mom's sewing projects and it was nice to feel welcome. That was perhaps the only time in the past four years that I had come home because they invited me or because I had wanted to. In the past, they were usually forced visits because I had lost my job. Not this time. This time it felt different.

The sun woke me early because the thin curtains were no match for the central Oregon sun. I heard commotion downstairs, some crying by Marcus and, of course, the ruckus of my mother cooking breakfast. I popped up out of bed and raced downstairs.

"Morning," I said with a bright smile. My mother and father were lip-locked in the kitchen standing over the pan of Garden-Sausage. Carrie and Dave were feeding Marcus waffles and trying not to watch the horror of our parents making out. They were always making out. When we were young, we were usually afraid to bring friends over to the house because our parents were sex fiends. Now, I just thought it was romantic and I hoped that someday someone would want to make out with me for forty years.

My father was the first to round the kitchen island and give me a hug. "It's good to see you, Charlie." He pushed me back and gave me a long slow once over. "What did you do to yourself? You look wonderful...and happy."

"I love your hair," my mom gasped. I knew she would notice. She noticed everything. I once didn't come home for a three-year stretch when I was in the Army and the first time she saw me, she noticed every new scar, every scrape, and every bruise. She had asked me if I had an abusive boyfriend. Huh, that was hard to say. I don't think Brick was ever abusive in the way that she meant, but he was a cocky bastard.

"Bella gave me a make-over and said I needed three colors." I rolled my eyes and grabbed a piece of bacon off the counter. "How are you two? Still humping like rabbits?" I grinned at my parents and dodged my brother's noogie. He eventually got me and I let him have his fun.

"Oh, my God! I almost forgot," my mother shouted, ripping off her quilted apron. She was so beautiful and full of life. Her hair was still the color of dark chocolate, probably fake, but it looked natural. She usually keeps out of the sun, so she has a face like a cherub. I hope, when I'm her age, I still know how to live life to its fullest. She disappeared into the dining room and then came back dragging a great big box into the kitchen. "This came for you a couple of days ago. It's from Africa."

"Africa?" I winced. "Hhhhm."

"We heard all about that girl you baby-sit on the news and in the paper. How her father thought she died and then found out she was alive" My father shook his head. "Where were you when all this happened?"

"I was with her."

My father dropped his coffee cup onto the floor and the man was a surgeon, he rarely dropped anything. He had nerves of steel. His hands were shaking. He sat down hard at the kitchen table while Dave ran for a knife to cut open the package, and my mother cleaned up the spill.

"What do you mean, honey. You were with her... where?"

"In Africa," I said, and then noticed how pale my father was. Perhaps this wasn't the time or the place. "It was all just a big misunderstanding. He heard that her plane went down, but it was a different plane. We were just fine."

"But...but...?" my father stuttered, then closed his mouth when Dave finally opened the package and took out a very impressive large gold and ivory tribal mask. Embossed with copper and brass and from the looks of Dave's strained muscles, it was heavy.

"What is it?" My mother tilted her head to the side and watched me read the letter.

I chuckled a couple of times at how sweet the letter was. I even felt tears well up behind my eyes.

"Who's it from?" my father asked, looking much calmer.

"Just a man I met in Africa." I folded the letter and put it in my pocket.

Some things should just remain in the closet.

I walked Ruger after breakfast and held my head high. It was nice to feel appreciated. It was nice to feel acknowledged and it was nice not to feel that twinge of jealously that I had felt my entire life when I was in a room with my two perfect brothers. Mostly, it just felt nice to have family that I loved. My parents' neighborhood looked the same as it always did. Mr. Jenkins was already in his front yard sprinkling fertilizer in his overalls and sun hat. The man loves his lawn. Rick was washing his Porsche, Lewis Riley was playing catch with his son and I was walking Ruger. It was almost as if no time had passed at all since the last time I had been home.

When I arrived back at the house, Dave was sitting on the porch. He grinned and patted the concrete next to him. "Let's talk, little sis."

I squirmed. Dave was never the serious one. Dave was the prankster, the goof off, the clown. I don't think we have ever had a serious talk in our entire lives.

He pulled the letter that I got from Prince Armand out of his pocket.

I narrowed my eyes.

He was also a sneaky bastard.

"You want to explain why the Prince of Gaborone sent you an ancient tribal mask that is probably worth a half-a-million dollars and why he thanked you over and over again for saving his life—and his country for that matter."

I swallowed hard and stared out into the grass. It needed water. I stood up to do something about it and was pulled back down by the strong arm of my big brother.

"What aren't you telling us and why are you keeping it from Mom and Dad? What happened to you in Africa? I saw the news. I know that they thought that little girl was dead for something like six days. Where the hell were you?"

"Jesus, Dave, I don't think you want to hear any of this," I said sternly.

"I do know what's going on in the world, little girl, and I know all about Prince Armand and the uprising in his country when they feared he had been assassinated. I do keep up on my current events. Is what he said true? Did you save his life?"

"Yes and no." I smiled and sat down. I had no idea how to tell my brother what I was about to tell him. How does one blurt out that they'd been trained to do what I do? I thought I'd start with one little confession and hope that my brother, the vascular surgeon, could put two and two together.

"Do you remember when I told Mom and Dad that I joined a special traveling unit during my second four years in the Army?"

He nodded. "Yeah. So what about it?"

"Did you ever wonder why I never talked about it when I came home?"

Dave chuckled and gave me an apologetic smile. "I just figured you couldn't get a word in edgewise because Josh had just signed with the Glousterhawks and I made medical review for the third time. Is there something you aren't telling us?"

Let's see. What *am* I telling them? Oh well, I had to tell someone eventually. It might as well be my big brother.

"I was with a special unit called Sector 72G." I smiled as I said it to lessen the blow. Sector 72G wasn't as well known as the Navy SEALS, but anyone who knows anything about our military, knows about the Army's special tactical unit.

Dave stood and raked his fingers through his thinning, dark hair a couple of times. I wondered if this was something that all men do when they felt stressed or was it something that I was doing to them, because I have never seen so many men play with their hair in my life.

"Jesus, Charlie." He exhaled sharply and sat back down beside me. "Those are some bad-ass soldiers."

I shrugged my shoulders and grinned. "What can I say? I'm a bad-ass." That wasn't as hard as I thought it would be. Perhaps it was time to tell Mom and Dad the truth about my other life.

"Shit. You're serious aren't you?" He looked amazed, even impressed. It took him a moment to speak again. I think I had completely blindsided him and he needed a minute to re-group. Then he grinned. "Do not tell Mom."

Okay, so maybe it could wait. Dave was right. Our mother would flip out, then continuously fret and end up in church five times a week to say endless rosaries to save my soul. "Like I would," I chuckled and then gave him a hug. "Please don't repeat this to anyone and let's keep that letter between the two of us, okay?"

He handed the letter back to me and narrowed his eyes. I could tell by the look in his eyes that he had many more questions than I was prepared to answer.

"Charlie, have you ever killed anyone?"

I glanced back over my shoulder and winked.

Josh and his two children, his wife Julie, and her parents all arrived around five for a barbecue in the backyard. I was already in the pool soaking up the sun on my mother's fancy air mattress and playing with the kids by the time Josh even realized that I was home—but that was just Josh. Josh's world revolved around Josh and Josh alone.

"Hey, little girl." He jumped into the pool and dumped me over, carefully keeping his thick head of *John Elway* hair from getting doused. "How's nanny life treating you?"

"Fine," I said and got comfortable again. "How's retirement treating you?"

"Are you kidding? You haven't heard?" He winked smugly and sat up on the edge of the pool. Josh had muscles everywhere, just like my dad. They looked amazingly alike. "Hey, Dave, why don't you tell little girl here the good news?"

Josh was such an arrogant showboat.

Dave cleared his throat and didn't look amused by his attempt to take over the spotlight. "You tell her, you stupid prick," Dave chided and tossed him a beer, narrowly missing my head.

"Hey, where's mine?" I yelled and held up my hand. A beer flew through the air and I caught it, opened it and had half of it chugged before Josh began again with his little speech.

"I signed with the Bills. Three-year contract. I made it. I made it to the NFL."

"No shit," I yelled out and patted him on the back because that's what he likes.

Ohhh, I so did not ever want to be that blatantly obvious about wanting attention. It made me ill. No wonder Dad always paid attention to him. He asked for it. Hell, he was still asking for it, even at age thirty-eight. "Congratulations."

"Thanks, little girl," he said and then did his best to make me feel small. I should have known better than to let it get the best of me, but old habits die hard. "So, really, how is the nanny job going? Do you have to clean their house too, or do you just baby-sit?" *Classic Josh all the way.*

"I scrub toilets and vacuum and sometimes I do laundry," I lied. "But mostly I just watch TV, eat bonbons and make sure she stays out of trouble."

Dave caught the smirk on my face and burst into laughter. For the first time in our relationship, I felt like I had an ally.

Three hours later, after steaks and chicken had been devoured along with bowls of Mom's famous potato salad, Dave made the big announcement that Carrie was almost three months pregnant and then Josh had the audacity to stand up and propose a toast to himself for finally making it to the NFL. I mean, the man was just a kicker. It's not as if he's the next Kurt Warner, or Tom Brady. He had an ego the size of Texas.

My father took my mother's hand and stood up to propose a toast. "To our family. May we stay healthy and happy and honest with each other." He looked directly at me and gave me a wink. I think he was talking about my letter. I hoped he was talking about my letter.

After another couple of beers, Dave and I snuck out back to smoke cigars. Something we hadn't done since he came back from college one year and got me drunk just to be an ass.

"I want to hear everything that happened in Africa. I really do," he said.

"Okay, but don't say I didn't warn you." I winked and felt a lot braver because of the beer. I started from the beginning and watched his eyes open wide at times. At other times, I thought he might cry, but mostly he just nodded, listened, and dropped his jaw every few minutes.

Who would have thought that my life was that interesting?

I talked and talked, and had just gotten to the part where no one would take our phone calls from Athens when we heard an obviously drunk Josh barrel through the door.

"You guys talking about me again?" he slurred when I shut up and looked up at him from the top step of the deck. Dave and I looked at each other and burst into laughter.

"You're so vain. How does Julie put up with you?" I said playfully, but honestly I meant every word.

Josh sank down on the other side of me and dropped his chin to his chest. "She's leaving me."

Dave and I both stared at him with eyes wide open.

"She came this weekend so Mom and Dad could see the kids, but Monday she's heading back to California with her parents."

I didn't know what to say. I had had no idea but then, again, I never kept in touch. I never asked him how he was, if everything was okay, or if he was even happy. I'm a horrible, horrible sister. "I'm sorry, Josh. I really am. Are you okay?" I wrapped my arm around his shoulder and pulled him close. He dropped his head onto my shoulder and groaned.

"No. I'm not." Then he swiped a tear off his cheek and grinned at me. "Enough about my sad life. What are you two talking about?"

I looked at Dave and decided now was a good time for some good news. "I was just about to tell Dave that I'm two terms away from my master's degree... Ha, ha." I grinned and liked the reaction I got from Dave. Who would have guessed that me getting a college education was more surprising than me killing people? Both my brothers looked dazed and confused.

"Why haven't you told Dad? Why do you still let him torture you like that? Are you sick?" Dave asked.

I shrugged and took a long puff on my cigar. "I've been waiting for the perfect opportunity to knock his socks off."

"So..." Josh prodded with wide eyes. "What's your major?"

"Criminal Justice."

Josh laughed. My arrogant older brother actually laughed at me. I should have expected it. "Yeah right. *Little girl, the cop,*" Josh scoffed and rubbed my scalp with his knuckles. "I just can't see it."

Dave chuckled under his breath, sent me an empathetic glance then raised his beer into the air. "To Charlie, the cop."

"To Charlie," Josh chimed in and I smiled.

My visit with my family was a great one. I was happy to see Josh and more happy to see Dave because it had been a few years. I think I was going to enjoy having Josh back in the States again, and even more excited that I now had a brother in the NFL. I was sure I'd be taking many trips to Buffalo to watch him in action.

We all sat down, had a family chat to discuss his break-up with Julie, and tried to make it somehow better for him.

The man has an overly inflated ego, so I have confidence that he'll bounce back. I know he loves his kids to death, but he's rich. He'll just have to figure out a schedule that works for him during the off-season so they can share custody. I never really liked Julie anyway. Dave's wife was nice, but Julie was one of those ditzy blondes with big boobs and painted on eyebrows.

Dave was amazing. It was nice to have a confidant within my wacky family. We spent the rest of the weekend bitching about Josh and how Dave had felt inferior when they were teenagers, because Josh did everything perfectly. I guess that helped me put things in perspective.

I still didn't tell my dad about my master's or what really happened Africa. I didn't feel the need to overshadow Josh's impending divorce, or Dave's baby on the way.

Dave promised to keep his mouth shut about everything and he gave me his pager number at the hospital and told me to keep in touch. He actually asked me to be the godmother of the baby on the way. I cried. I guess Dave was a good big brother after all. I had to admit it. But then again, Dave also put gum in my hair and put my training bra in the freezer when I was thirteen.

Chapter Fourteen

The next morning, Dave dropped me off in Portland on his way home to Seattle. I thanked him again for such a great weekend and then told Carrie to hang in there and send me a copy of the ultrasound photo so I could be the first to see my godson or goddaughter in the womb.

My flight to Hawaii was the first time that I had ever slept on an airplane in my life and I have been on many planes. I think I chalked it up to God owing me a break or two and I felt that I was in good hands.

Kaui was even prettier and more perfect than I had ever imagined. The best part was that it was all paid for. Everything from my greens fees to my Piña Coladas was being taken care of by Roald Munson.

"Your cabin is just to the left of the pro-shop, number 13," the nice Hawaiian man said from behind the front desk at Kapalua Shores, where I had reserved the honeymoon cabaña just because it was the best and, after all, I deserved the best.

I winced and took the key he handed me. I'm not a superstitious person by any means, but come on. I'm already unlucky in love, in travels and even making toast is a precarious chore for me these days.

I looked into the sky with a smile. My luck had to change someday. Hopefully, a great white shark wouldn't eat me after all I'd been through. Again, I was taking it day-by-day, minute-by-minute and even appreciated the tiny rocks that were poking my toes. Then I had enough and shook my feet a couple of times to release the pebbles from my Birkenstocks.

"Wow," I think I said aloud as I dropped my new luggage full of brand-spanking-new clothes onto the bed. I so deserved this.

The fridge was packed full of bottled water, a couple bottles of select Microbrews. A bottle of champagne, some apples, one orange and the biggest pineapple I have ever seen. On top of the kitchen cabinet was a box of chocolate turtles, a jar of macadamia nuts, a giant bouquet of fresh flowers and a note from Bella and Roald. I smiled and removed the card from its tiny white envelope.

Hope your vacation is as wonderful to you as you have been to us. We appreciate you more than you'll ever know. Love, Roald

And in Bella's cute squiggly writing, she added...

I love you, I'll miss you and I'll bring you home a tee-shirt.

What can I say? It brought me to tears.

After a good cleansing cry and a nice long hot bath, I changed into my sexy sundress and intended to find someone to flirt with. It had been a long time since I'd had a date, a warm kiss goodnight or a hot sexual experience that left me breathless and wanting more. Right then I wanted more. This island had to be jam-packed full of single, horny men, looking for a hot babe in a backless sundress who was willing and able. Well, at least my body was. I wasn't sure that my heart would ever be willing and able, not since my breakup with Brick Miller--asshole extraordinaire--but my body constantly screamed for attention. I'm sure it had something to do with hormones, my sexually peaking years and chemistry and hopefully nothing to do with the fact that I wanted babies someday and time seemed to be ticking away faster everyday.

I actually curled my newly highlighted hair, applied a small amount of eyeliner and rouged my lips. I was a woman on a mission.

After my mission failed miserably, I took a walk along the beach and kicked the sand around with my toes. I thought that I had changed enough over the past few months to get past my horribly stringent expectations of male companionship, but I hadn't changed that much. I still wasn't willing to settle for anything less than perfection in the man department. I didn't want just any man. I wanted a man who kept me on my toes. A man who made them curl with his kisses and a man who made my blood boil with just a glance. I knew who I wanted, and every other slobbering moron that I had met tonight paled miserably in comparison.

The sunset was gorgeous and I stayed and watched every millimeter of the sun as it dipped down into the Pacific Ocean. The colors it made astounded me. I loved the sound of the ocean. The pounding of the waves and the hiss of the salty water as it receded from the shore and fizzled into the sand. The ocean is an amazing thing. It makes me want to go scuba diving, parasailing, snorkeling; to do all those things that I had always been too scared to do. Wow, I wasn't scared anymore. I wanted to see it all, even eels and sharks and jelly fish. I smiled at the darkening sky as I laid my head back in the sand. I really was a new woman.

I was ready for dessert by that time, so I cruised up the sandy dune and back to my cabin. My travel agent was going to get a nice big box of chocolates for hooking me up with such an incredible spot, right on the beach with no one else around. I was sort of secluded and lonely, but the view was the best.

I slid the key into the lock, opened the door and stepped inside. I kicked off my sandals to keep from bringing sand into my perfect cabaña. The dim light from the Tiki torch outside lit up enough of the room for me to notice something move slightly out of the corner of my eye. I hoped it wasn't a giant flying cockroach. I narrowed my eyes on the dark shadow and quickly dismissed my cockroach idea. Bummer, cockroaches were a lot more fun than big scary guys sitting in my comfy chair were.

My heart not only leapt from its correct position under my rib cage, it fluttered rapidly and I flushed all over from terror. Okay, so maybe I did still have a little fear left in me.

"You're a very difficult woman to find, Charlie Ford." His deep voice was husky and tattered. Thank God, he sounded American. My heart flip-flopped again, but in a good way that time. I saw his lean arm ease toward the lamp, and then he clicked it on and sent me the sexiest, most confident smile I had ever seen. He eased forward and leaned so his elbows rested on his knees. He seemed completely relaxed and damned sure of himself. The man definitely had cajones.

I, on the other hand, was expressionless and bamboozled and so far from relaxed it wasn't funny.

He looked so much different than the last time I set eyes on him. His black hair was extremely short, and he'd grown a goatee. His face had healed nicely except for a small scar across his left cheek that was clearly visible in the dim light. I'd never been fond of Hawaiian shirts, but he managed to make one look sexy as hell.

I opened my mouth to speak, but no words would come. It was as if someone had sucked my brains out through my ears and all that remained was undecipherable gibberish.

He just stared at me, willing me to speak and then tried to speed it along by raising one eyebrow and giving me a wink.

"You," I finally shouted because I was that mad he scared me, and that happy to see him. I moved toward him swiftly, unsure if I was going to fall into his arms or smack him in the face.

He jumped up and caught my fist in his hand before it connected with his chin. This man kept me on my toes. He twisted my right arm behind my back and held it tightly against my bare skin.

"Aren't you happy to see me?" he asked.

I whimpered in his grasp. I was so fucking happy to see him, I couldn't see straight, but that didn't change the fact that he deserved a good pop in the mouth. It had been six weeks. Six weeks without a phone call or a postcard to apologize for the interrogation room. Nothing.

His hot mouth closed tightly over mine when I didn't respond to his question. I think at that time my body language told him exactly what he wanted to know. I couldn't get enough of him and when I felt the warmth of his tongue touch mine, I crawled up his body and wrapped my thighs around his hips. I'd never felt so much raw desire for a man before. It was as if I was being sucked into a vortex of sexual need and nothing short of death was going to stop me from crawling into his shorts. Besides, it was very cool to be kissing Secret Agent Man again.

Then again...

I pulled back abruptly and gave him a glare, dropped my bare feet to the tile floor and moved away from the hand that had just clamped onto my erect nipple. I had so many questions.

"Why were you there? Why did you sit there and pretend that you didn't know me? Why?"

"Do we have to do this now?" he asked breathlessly, and moved closer, so close that I felt every hard part of him and he felt good. He began kissing down my neck, across my throat, up to the soft flesh of my ear. He whispered some things that he wanted to do to me.

My knees buckled, my toes curled. I let out a throaty whimper and then pushed him away.

"I don't even know you. I don't know your name. I don't know if you have brothers or sisters, or where you were born." I did slap him this time—in the chest, because he was too cute to slap in the face. He grabbed my hand and pulled me closer; so close that his lips touched mine when he smiled.

"Can we play twenty questions later? I've waited a long time for you Charlie Ford."

Well hell, if that's not a good line—I don't know what is.

I kissed him this time and wrapped my arms around his neck to bring him even closer. I kissed him with passion and tenderness, ran my fingers up and down his neck, into his stubby hair, around his ears, and finally cradled his face in the palms of my hands before coming up for air and then starting all over again. I moaned and shifted against his body before breaking from the kiss again. I brushed his lips with mine and stared into his dark sultry eyes.

"No." I pushed him away playfully and ran from his grasp. I moved to the other side of the bed. "We do this now." Looking over at the bedside table, I let out a giggle. That stack of Belgium chocolate bars wasn't there when I left for dinner. My laughter prodded him to move closer to the bed.

I reached up and held the button of my red sundress between my fingers, teasing him into telling me the truth. "What's your name?" I asked sternly, and tried to keep the smile from spreading across my flushed cheeks. "Real name this time."

This action on my part induced a salacious grin to tug at his lips and then he popped the top button on his denim shorts. "Jack."

"Jack what?" I asked.

He smiled and took two more steps towards the bed. "Jack Edward Sullivan."

I undid one button and let the first strap hang over my chest, exposing the top half of one bare breast. I could see the change in his eyes. He'd seen my breasts before, but not quite like this. I watched his eyes narrow, his brows crease together and his chest rise and fall quicker than normal.

I had him right where I wanted him.

"Where were you born?" I held on tight to the button on the other side, rolling my fingers along the button before slipping it half way through its loop.

He licked his lips. "San Diego."

I let the other strap fall, but my breasts held the dress in place.

I looked down, then back into his eyes, and smiled.

He smiled.

"Here's my driver's license." He grabbed for his wallet and tossed it onto the bed.

I opened it, found his driver's license that had the name Jack Sullivan on it. The address read Baltimore, Maryland. His age was thirty-six. That surprised me, I figured him for about thirty-three. Height: six feet, weight: one hundred and eighty five pounds. I flipped through the credit cards. They all read Jack E. Sullivan, too.

I looked up and caught him taking off his Hawaiian-print shirt. My jaw dropped. I swear his pectorals had grown over the last six weeks. I think I licked my lips and moaned.

"This doesn't mean anything. You could have forged these." I flipped through his money. A couple of twenties, three fives and four ones and then I found.... "What's this for?" I held up the condom and grinned. I suppose I was doing a good job at pretending to be demure, that is until I giggled. "What? Only one?" That didn't last long. Now I was doing a good impression of an insatiable hussy. Oh, well.

He smiled and kicked off his shoes.

When I once said he was quick, I only meant on his feet. In bed, he moved like a sloth. Every minute counted. Each stroke of his hand against my bare skin felt perfectly orchestrated. Every precisely planted kiss meant something special and there was not one damn thing about it that I took for granted. I made love with him as if it was the only time in my life I was going to be lucky enough to do so.

When the intense breathing stopped and I was appreciating my afterglow, Jack rolled onto his side and smiled. "I heard about Bella from my sources at Interpol and I knew you had to be with her." He offered out of nowhere then laid his cheek on my bare breast.

I wasn't even thinking about Armenia. I was thinking how magnificent he was in bed. The past was the past. Okay, so I did appreciate the confession at that point. Hell, I'd just slept with the man. It was nice that he was finally opening up to me.

"How did you find me?"

"I have my ways." Once a Secret Agent Man, always a Secret Agent Man.

"So, it was you who orchestrated my rescue from The Rat?" I asked as I snuggled my arms tighter around the man who had saved my life. More than once, I might add. I inhaled deeply and closed my eyes.

"Uh huh." He nodded and kissed me again with tenderness. I appreciated his caresses because I now knew he had come for me. He was so much more than Secret Agent Man. "I also heard everything about what happened to you and I'm sorry that you got caught up in that mess that had nothing to do with you. DuLucere taped your statement and sent it to me." He actually looked sympathetic to my pain. "I also know that you were paid a visit from one of ours...Doug Lyons."

I popped my head off the pillow. Doug Lyons was the man who had threatened to erase my memory in that damp little room in Armenia. He was also the nice man who gave me a makeshift passport and paid my airfare home. "He's one of yours?"

"Sort of," he said, and began kissing me again with that same lustful yearning.

I knew I'd never get a straight answer out of him, but I was willing to bribe him with sex, repeatedly, until he spilled his guts.

We ended up doing it four more times before cuddling under the covers and finally talking about his family.

"I have two sisters, Robin and Kristina. My parents Edward and Megan are still married. They live in Sacramento." He licked his lips slowly. "If I tell you anymore than that I'll have to kill you." He kissed me again and licked down my stomach to find where he had left that last piece of chocolate.

When he returned, I still couldn't catch my breath, but I was smiling and I felt fine with the fact that I wasn't receiving oxygen.

"Come to work with me, Charlie," he said, then quickly kissed me before my eyes popped out of my skull.

"Uhhhh." I was still recovering from the tongue bath I had just received. "What do you mean?"

"We'd be good together, Charlie."

Okay, so his mind had melted into mush by all the hot sex. He couldn't be serious.

"Are you serious?" I propped up onto my elbow and looked directly into his satisfied dark eyes. I do have to say that it did sound appealing in a weird and freakish kind of way.

"Think about it." He rolled off the bed and left me alone and naked to think about going to work with Secret Agent Man. That sort of thing doesn't happen every day, not to people like me.

"I'm not finished with my master's," I yelled toward the kitchenette. He came back to me with a bottle of champagne and no glasses. "I'm going to be a police detective, I'm going to buy a place in the country, with acres and acres of jackrabbits and I've already bought my dream SUV...."

His kiss was warm and inviting. As was his hand on the back of my neck. "A police woman, Charlie?" His head shook in disapproval. "Come on, honey. You have skills. You have instincts. Your moves need a little bit of work..." he chuckled playfully, and dodged my hand, "but other than that, you're pretty much a shoo-in."

I blinked once or twice and scrunched my brows together. My moves need a little work? If I hadn't been naked, I would have flipped his ass onto the ground and shown him a thing or two. *Oh. Maybe that would be fun with no clothes on.*

The cork bounced off the ceiling.

"I don't even know who you work for." I took the bottle of Dom Perignon that he offered me and sipped carefully, never taking my eyes off his.

One of his eyebrows cocked and bounced up and down dramatically. "I think you know."

"Okay," I scoffed. "So I have an idea."

He bent and nibbled my ear, whispered something intriguing and crawled back into my bed.

I was right. He works for the _ _ _.

Epilogue

Two weeks in Hawaii with Secret Agent Man should be something I do every summer. I think I will add that to my new life's plan. For once, I was considering my options and amending my to-do list.

Jack...I still don't think that's his name, but it fits him now that I have screamed it out in bed a couple hundred times...told me that I had plenty of time to make up my mind about coming to work with him. He still had six months of paperwork to catch up on here in the States and months of physical therapy to get full strength back in his ankle before he could return to the field full time. He informed me of his six surgeries and of how he is convinced that his ankle is now bionic because of all the hardware they had to install to fix it properly.

Time? Time is something I don't have much of these days. Bella and I spend the majority of our free time together when I'm not in school and she's not in school or hanging out with her teenage friends who actually think the Backstreet Boys are cute. Now that she's officially a teenager, it's a completely new ball game, but I do my best to keep her feet planted firmly on the ground so she doesn't end up like her mother.

Roald finally decided not to take Nicole back, for which I congratulated him. I suggested that he find a nice, down-to-earth woman who didn't even go to the movies. He said that he would rather spend his time concentrating on Annabelle and strengthening their relationship. I guess therapy does work. Perhaps I should try it.

Nicole is now dating a rock-star, who can't really sing, but looks good in spandex. She is such a Heather Locklear wannabe.

Jack pops in and out of my life at the most inconvenient times, like this morning when he snuck into my bathroom and I almost shot him in the head. He likes keeping me on my toes and constantly jokes that I can't ever see him coming—which is true. He'll tell me he's off to Britain, I'll actually believe him and then he will sneak into the back of my SUV while I'm at the gym. I swear the man has super-abilities that I can't even fathom.

Finding time for each other is a huge obstacle and it is pushing me in a new direction. My life plan seems to have changed a bit since my time abroad and more importantly, it has changed even more so since my two weeks with Jack in Hawaii and then even more dramatically over the past three months in which I've been tortured by his ability to scare the living daylights out of me. He says he's just starting my training early. Ha. I think he just likes watching me squirm and scream like a girl.

I did manage to convince him to meet my parents when they came to visit. My father had never seen New England, so we took him to all the hot spots: Shea Stadium, The Meadowlands, Fenway Park and Gillette Stadium where the Patriots play. We went and saw Josh's NFL debut in Buffalo where he kicked three field goals and only one extra point—because the Bills can't do a damn thing in the red zone.

Jack told my father that he was an insurance adjustor and we met when I crashed the Ludlow's BMW. I thought it was mildly amusing until it dawned on me that I never told

Jack about the Ludlow's BMW. Jack knows everything...and I mean *everything* about me. He even knows the size of my underwear and the brand of tampons I buy. He says its part of his job to know these things; I just think he snoops a lot.

He never did tell me what he was doing in Kenya and I finally gave up asking. I guess it will remain a mystery and I should come to accept that it's better for me not to know everything about him. I just have to keep reminding myself it's the price I have to pay for falling in love with a Secret Agent Man.

Charlie Ford Meets Secret Service Man
By
J. D. Tynan

ISBN: 0-9771071-5-8
978-0-9771971-5-6

Price: $22.95
6 X 9 Trade Paperback

Bookseller Name: _____

Address: _____

Phone Number: _____ PO Number: _____

Quantity: _____ Title: _____

Quantity: _____ Title: _____

A Better Be Write Publishing, LLC
1100 Buck St, 1st Fl
Millville, NJ 08332

856-825-6677
856-825-5680 Fax
www.abetterbewrite.com
MM.Stapp@comcast.net

Other Titles By A Better Be Write Publishing, LLC

0-9767732-9-5   Jill 9 - $18.95 (SAME AUTHOR)
0-9767732-0-1 =The Cremator's Revenge $18.95
0-9767732-1-X =Pearls of Wisdom: Surviving Against All Odds- Book One $18.95
0-9767732-2-8 = Cassie's Creepy Candy Store -$15.95
0-9767732-3-6 = The Plight of the Queen Bee – $15.95
0-9767732-4-4 = Deadly Duplicates -$15.95
0-9767732-5-2 = Crest of Eagles $16.95
0-9767732-6-0 = Pearls of Wisdom Book Two –$15.95
0-9767732-7-9 = The Estrogen Underground: Reinvention -$14.95
0-9771971-0-7   The Deviant - $18.95
0-9771971-1-5   Kitty Fantastic - $17.95
0-9771971-2-3   Pearls Of Wisdom: Surviving Against All Odds Book Three - $18.95
0-9771971-3-1   Don't Go Alone! - $18.95
0-9771971-4-X   Queen Bee's Midnight Caper - $17.95
0-9771971-6-6   Rain, Rain, What a Pain! - $17.95
0-9771971-8-2   Caleb's Birthday Wish - $16.95

New Titles- 2007
978-0-9788985-3-3 0-9788985-3-2 The Ant in the Cellar- $19.95
978-0-9771971-9-4 0-9771971-9-0 Thighs of Clay And the Famous Who Have Them- $32.95
978-0-9788985-0-2 0-9788985-0-8 Inside A Haunted Mind - $22.95
978-0-9788985-1-9 0-9788985-1-6 Why Cody Can't Learn - $18.95
978-0-9788985-2-6 0-9788985-2-4 Two Coins -$18.95
978-0-9788985-4-0 0-9788985-4-0 Hidden Among The Petals- $32.95
978-0-9788985-5-7 0-9788985-5-9 Pearls of Wisdom: Surviving Against All Odds Book 4
978-0-9788985-6-4 0-9788985-6-7 Pearls of Wisdom: Surviving Against All Odds Book 5
978-0-9788985-7-1 0-9788985-7-5 Queen Bee's Mystery in the Lilac Tree- $19.95